Two decades
the very best in

HARLEQUIN SUPERROMANCE celebrates

BOOK
1000

To commemorate this special occasion—
and for your summertime reading pleasure—
here are three novellas from three of your favorite authors:

Daddy's Girl by Judith Arnold
Part of Judith's **Daddy School** series

Home, Hearth and Haley by Muriel Jensen
An introduction to Muriel's upcoming
Men of Maple Hill series

Temperature Rising by Bobby Hutchinson
Part of Bobby's **Emergency!** series

Daddy's Girl marks **Judith Arnold**'s tenth anniversary as a Superromance author; her first Superromance novel came out in July, 1991. With more than seventy series romances to her credit, she is looking forward to the publication in August of her first single-title romance for MIRA Books, *Looking for Laura*. And watch for her DADDY SCHOOL single title from Harlequin, *Somebody's Dad*, in February 2002. You can contact her c/o Harlequin Books, 225 Duncan Mill Road, Don Mills, Ontario Canada M3B 3K9.

Muriel Jensen has written nine Superromance books since her first one, *Trust a Hero*, was published in 1990. It is a past, she says, that she is proud of. And she is delighted to be part of Superromance's future, with her upcoming MEN OF MAPLE HILL trilogy. Her heroes in the trilogy will be adept at all sorts of things that, she confesses, she herself will never understand—plumbing, wiring and accounting! You can reach Muriel at P.O. Box 1168, Astoria, Oregon 97103.

Bobby Hutchinson began writing Superromance novels in 1985, and considers Superromance her home at Harlequin. She has a medical series called EMERGENCY!, and *Temperature Rising* fits right in. Her next book will be *Intensive Caring*, which will appear in September 2001. She would love to hear from readers at her e-mail address: bobbyhut@home.com.

$\mathcal{A}$LL SUMMER LONG

Judith Arnold
Muriel Jensen
Bobby Hutchinson

BOOK
1000

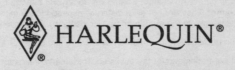

TORONTO • NEW YORK • LONDON
AMSTERDAM • PARIS • SYDNEY • HAMBURG
STOCKHOLM • ATHENS • TOKYO • MILAN • MADRID
PRAGUE • WARSAW • BUDAPEST • AUCKLAND

ISBN 0-373-71000-3

ALL SUMMER LONG

Copyright © 2001 by Harlequin Books S.A.

The publisher acknowledges the copyright holders of the individual works as follows:

DADDY'S GIRL
Copyright © 2001 by Barbara Keiler.

HOME, HEARTH AND HALEY
Copyright © 2001 by Muriel Jensen.

TEMPERATURE RISING
Copyright © 2001 by Bobby Hutchinson.

This edition published by arrangement with Harlequin Books S.A.

® and TM are trademarks of the publisher. Trademarks indicated with ® are registered in the United States Patent and Trademark Office, the Canadian Trade Marks Office and in other countries.

Visit us at www.eHarlequin.com

Printed in U.S.A.

TABLE OF CONTENTS

Daddy's Girl

Judith Arnold

To my wonderful editor, Beverley Sotolov

Dear Reader,

For me, one of the greatest satisfactions of writing fiction is that I can enjoy experiences in my books that I can't enjoy in real life. I have two glorious sons, both teenagers now, but no daughters. Writing *Daddy's Girl* gave me the chance to have a daughter for a while.

I fell in love with Alix. I could see her, hear her voice, smell her sweet baby-powder scent and feel the weight of her in my arms and the silky curls of her hair against my cheek. I had no trouble imagining that a woman like Natalie would find herself instantly attached to Alix—and to Kevin, the kind of man who would devote his life to his young daughter without a moment's hesitation. Just like Natalie, I fell in love with Kevin as I was falling in love with his daughter.

I think you'll fall in love with them, too.

Judith Arnold

CHAPTER ONE

THE HOUSE that Kevin Medina called home was much grander than she'd expected. A two-story brick colonial with Palladian windows and a front porch flanked by pillars, it sat squarely on a generous, meticulously landscaped lot. The grass was uniformly green and velvet smooth, the shrubs neatly pruned, the maple and sycamore trees dense with leaves.

It was a rather imposing residence for a twenty-six-year-old guy who earned his living mowing lawns.

Apparently, it wasn't going to be his residence for long. A For Sale sign stood at the base of the driveway, with a Sale Pending plaque attached.

She strolled up the slate front walk, rang the bell and checked her watch: six-fifteen. She might be interrupting dinner, but that was okay. If she hadn't wanted to interrupt the evening activities of the Medina household, she would have phoned to warn that she was on her way. Interrupting was part of the process for her. She preferred to glimpse people in the midst of their routines, before they had a chance to clean up and present themselves in an artificially favorable light.

Six-fifteen on an early July day found the air warm but not hot, the sky still bright with sunlight. The rhododendron bushes bordering the porch were bright with pink blooms. A bee hovered among the blossoms, its buzz the only sound in this peaceful, affluent neighborhood.

No one answered the door. That was the risk she took when visiting a family unannounced: they might not be home. With a sigh, she shifted her briefcase to her other hand and tried the doorbell once more.

Abruptly, the door swung open to reveal a tall, lean man who was definitely not presenting himself in a favorable light. His brown hair was disheveled, his jaw dark with day-old stubble. He wore grass-stained jeans and a short-sleeved cotton shirt that hung open, revealing a sun-darkened chest contoured in lean slabs of muscle. His feet were bare, and his eyes looked like chips of sharp-edged blue glass. He was frowning.

"Hi," she said with manufactured brightness. "I'm Natalie Baines from Family Services. I'm the court-appointed guardian *ad litem* for your daughter, Alix. You must be Kevin Medina."

His frown intensified as she handed him her business card. He studied it for a moment, then lifted his cool blue gaze to her face. "What are you doing here?"

"I'd like to meet Alix."

He opened his mouth and then glanced away. It didn't take great skill in lipreading to recognize the four-letter word he muttered. Sighing, he turned back to her. "Look, I just got home from work. I was about to take a shower. I had no idea you were coming over."

"I know." She smiled. "That's why I'm here. I like to visit when people aren't putting on a show for me. May I come in?"

He read her card again before tucking it into the breast pocket of his shirt. "I guess so. I'm sorry about—" he gestured at his unkempt clothing "—well, this. My work is dirty, and I usually bring it home with me."

"I'm aware of that, Mr. Medina." She bet he'd clean up very nicely, too. The shadow of beard emphasized his angular jaw and the planes of his cheeks. His scruffy hair was thick and wavy. Dark lashes fringed his eyes, emphasizing their startling color. And what she could see of his chest was quite impressive.

She wondered if he was besieged by swooning, smitten women. He was single, after all. A widower.

And his late-wife's parents were suing to win custody of his baby.

As a social worker, Natalie often worked with tangled families. But custody disputes were the worst. In a sense, they ought to cheer her—certainly it was better for a child to be wanted by everyone than to be wanted by no one. Yet most of the time, the resolution of a custody battle left at least one of the contending parties devastated.

There was only one party she was going to concern herself with in the Medina-Porter battle, and that was Alix. The court had appointed her to represent the child's interests. Whether Alix's father or her grandparents wound up with a broken heart, Natalie's job was to make sure the little girl wound up in the custody of whoever could provide her with the best home and the rosiest prospects for a successful life.

Kevin Medina stepped back and waved her inside. She entered a high-ceilinged, marble-floored foyer. An arching stairway rose to the second floor, and doorways opened on either side. She peeked through one into an elegant living room with pale carpeting and pristine furniture. Through the other doorway she glimpsed a formal dining room, a long mahogany table surrounded by high-backed chairs. Both rooms could have been photographed for some upper-class shelter magazine. In fact, they looked more like photographs than spaces actual people might inhabit.

"Where's Alix?" she asked.

"In her playpen. She can stay safe in there while I'm

showering. If you want to meet her, okay—'' he started down a hall past the stairway ''—but I'm really dying for a shower.''

Natalie followed him into a kitchen that looked blessedly lived in—mail and a newspaper piled on the table, a high chair in one corner, the drying rack stacked with dishes, a package of chopped beef defrosting in the sink. A half-eaten banana sat on a counter, its yellow skin lying limp around it, and a baby bib was draped over the back of a chair. A calendar fastened to the refrigerator door with magnets had nearly every day of the week scribbled in with appointments and reminders.

He continued through the kitchen into a family room, which was even more cluttered and chaotic. One wall was filled with stereo components and a large-screen TV. Opposite it stood a couch. Toys littered the thick green carpeting. The middle of the room was occupied by a mesh-walled playpen.

A toddler stood in the playpen, surrounded by a stuffed koala bear, a few large plastic blocks, a cloth-paged book, a plastic hammer and a colorful xylophone. She wore a yellow T-shirt and a diaper, and her hair was a marvel of tousled blond curls. As soon as Kevin entered the room she started to jump. ''Daddy! Daddy! Out!'' she shrieked, raising her arms high above her head and hopping from foot to foot. ''Out, out!''

Kevin leaned over the padded rim of the playpen and hoisted her up. She flung her arms around his neck and nestled her head against his shoulder. He turned to Natalie. ''She's happy to stay in there unless she sees me,'' he explained. ''Then all she wants is out.''

''Out,'' the little girl said contentedly, cuddling closer to him. Her eyes, as blue as his, settled on Natalie, and she slid her thumb into her mouth.

Natalie studied the two of them, father and sixteen-month-old daughter. They looked good together, natural, comfortable—but she couldn't let their appearance sway her. She was a professional. She had to assess their entire situation, not just their ability to strike a sweet pose when the child was in her daddy's arms.

"You said you just got home?" she asked Kevin.

"About fifteen minutes ago."

"Alix is a pupil at—" she pulled a folder from her brief-case and flipped it open "—the Children's Garden Pre-school. Their pickup time is five-thirty."

"If I'm running late, my sister picks her up," Kevin said. "Then I get her from my sister's house."

"I see." One reason the Porters had initiated a custody fight was that Kevin had enrolled Alix in day care. In the first few months after Madeleine Porter had died, Kevin's mother had provided child care for Alix. But last month, he'd enrolled Alix in the Children's Garden—a highly re-spected facility, arguably the best in town—and his in-laws had decided to request custody of her. If their granddaugh-ter lived with them, they claimed, she would not be raised by strangers. She would be in their home, the sole focus of their attention.

"I've got to put her back in the playpen while I shower," Kevin said. "She's going to scream if I do."

His determination to wash up was admirable, in an odd way. Under the same circumstances, another father might knock himself out trying to charm Natalie and win her to his side. But Kevin Medina seemed prepared to continue his evening the way he began it, and to make no apologies.

"I can hold her if she doesn't want to go back into the playpen," she offered. His dubious gaze prompted her to add, "I'm a social worker. I work with children. And I do need to get to know Alix."

With a reluctant nod, he loosened his grip on Alix, and she tightened hers on him. "No, no! No, Daddy!"

"Just for a few minutes," he murmured to his daughter. "Ms....?" He glanced questioningly at Natalie.

"Baines," she reiterated.

He addressed Alix. "Ms. Baines is going to watch you while I go wash up. Okay?"

"No!"

He peeled Alix's hand from his neck and passed her to Natalie, ignoring her howls and her flailing feet. "She'll calm down in a minute," he predicted. "Sing her a song. She likes songs."

Before Natalie could ask which songs Alix liked, he strode out of the room, his bare feet silent as his long legs carried him away.

"Daddy! Daddy!" Alix pulled away from Natalie, reaching in the direction he'd vanished. "No!"

Natalie took a deep breath and carried the squirming little girl to the couch. Alix had to weigh at least twenty-five pounds, and she was strong. Sitting would enable Natalie to hold Alix on her lap—to pin her to herself.

She was used to dealing with wild children, weepy children, hysterical, distraught children. As a social worker, she'd dealt with far worse than a little girl who didn't want to be left with a stranger, a little girl who might be just as devastated if the courts yanked her out of her father's arms and handed her over to her maternal grandparents.

Sinking into the sofa cushions, Natalie pulled Alix against her chest and stroked her back. "'The wheels on the bus go round and round,'" she sang, her words nearly drowned out by Alix's sobs. "'Round and round, round and round...'"

After a minute, Alix subsided, sniffling and hiccuping and resting her damp head against Natalie's bosom. She

held the child a little closer and crooned more of the song:
"'The wipers on the bus go click-click-click...'"

Alix sighed and sucked her thumb. She was truly a beautiful little girl, her features small and perfect, her cheeks
soft even when they were mottled from crying.

Somewhere in this oversize house her father was showering. He was standing naked under the spray of a shower,
scrubbing the dirt of a day's labor from his skin, lathering
his hair with shampoo, feeling the hot water pound against
the muscles of his shoulders and back.

Natalie hadn't thought about men in a long time. Especially not naked men. Especially not a man with a physique
like Kevin Medina's, with a gaze that could cut through
steel. She didn't *want* to think about Kevin Medina. She
wanted only to figure out what would be best for his daughter.

Alix nestled deeper into her lap, and Natalie continued
to sing about the bus and stroke Alix's curly hair, as she
wondered whether having been assigned to this case was
going to turn out to be a blessing...or a disaster.

KEVIN WAS ALWAYS BEAT when he came home from
work—good beat, a bone-deep exhaustion that made him
feel as if he'd truly accomplished something worthwhile. It
was the kind of exhaustion that could be washed away by
a shower. As the hot water hammered down on his scalp
and shoulders, it dissolved his fatigue along with the dirt.

Ordinarily, he'd emerge from the bathroom feeling re-
freshed. Today, though, all he felt was apprehensive. Why
was that social worker here?

He knew why: to check up on him. To see if he was a
responsible father. To find out if maybe Alix would be
better off with her grandparents.

Just thinking about the custody fight made his stomach clench.

If he'd known Natalie Baines was coming, he would have gotten home from work earlier. He would have put a pair of shorts on Alix after changing her diaper, and made sure he was showered and spiffy. He would have picked up some of the toys and swept the kitchen floor.

Instead, the social worker had seen him and Alix as they usually were at this time of day—a little ragged, a little disorganized. He could just imagine Ms. Baines writing him up in some report: *He abandoned his daughter in her playpen, half undressed and screaming, "Daddy! Daddy!"*

Cripes. He was going to lose Alix.

No. He refused to consider the possibility. He was Alix's father, and he loved her more than anyone else. No one— no matter how rich, how powerful, how married; no matter how clean their fingernails were, how extensive their vocabulary, how expensive their lifestyle...*no one* was going to take his daughter away from him. Not without the biggest fight they'd ever seen.

Especially not the Porters.

He quickly ran a razor over his cheeks and chin, slapped on some aftershave, brushed his hair and dressed in apparel a bit neater than what he usually wore on a weeknight. He even put on a pair of deck shoes. His gaze circled the oversize master bedroom—he'd never felt comfortable in such a plush room, even when Madeleine had shared it with him—and he noticed that the comforter was rumpled. Not that he expected Ms. Baines from Family Services to inspect his bedroom, but you never knew.

She was young and attractive, her chin and cheeks soft, her eyes a gentle hazel and her dark-blond hair pulled into a neat ponytail. Under other circumstances, he might want to think of her in the context of his bedroom.

But she was at his house at the bidding of the court—the court that was considering whether Madeleine's parents deserved to raise Alix. Kevin hated them all: her parents, their lawyer, the judge and Natalie Baines. He hated anyone in a position to take his baby away.

After smoothing out the blanket, he left the bedroom for the stairs. He expected to hear Alix shrieking, but silence met him as he descended to the first floor. Had Ms. Baines absconded with her? Had the social worker decided, after all of a few minutes, that Kevin was an unfit father?

Suppressing his panic, he hurried through the kitchen to the family room. Natalie Baines was seated on the floor, helping Alix construct a tower of blocks. Alix wandered around the room, retrieving scattered blocks—and making the room look a little neater, bless her. As she set each new block onto the tower, she beamed at Ms. Baines and crowed, "Dare!" It was her way of pronouncing *there*.

Kevin felt most of his tension leave him. Not all of it; as long as Ms. Baines was present, she was judging him, and he couldn't relax completely. But at least she hadn't taken off with Alix. And Alix was no longer howling. Things could be worse.

"Hey, Alix," he said softly.

She saw him, broke into an even bigger smile and scampered over to him. "Make a tower!" she boasted, extending her hands to him.

"A very nice tower." He lifted her into his arms. "How about we put some shorts on you?"

"No shorts. No."

He glanced at Ms. Baines, who only smiled. Maybe that meant she didn't think having his daughter prance around in a T-shirt and diaper on a hot evening was a terrible thing. Maybe it meant she'd already made up her mind about him, and dressing his daughter properly wasn't going to change her opinion of his parenting abilities.

"Would you like to eat some supper?" he asked Alix.

"Eat," Alix agreed.

He glanced at Ms. Baines again. Was he supposed to feed her? He hadn't defrosted enough meat for three. And hell, she'd come here uninvited. Besides, if he offered her some food, she might think he was trying to bribe her.

Maybe he'd get lucky and she'd leave.

Trying not to include her in his every thought, he marched into the kitchen with Alix and plopped her on the counter next to the sink. She liked to sit on the counter so she could watch him prepare their food. If Ms. Baines considered it dangerous—damn, there she was, barging into his thoughts again. Anyway, it wasn't dangerous. Alix didn't fidget and squirm. She sat very still, and he kept a close eye on her.

"We're having hamburgers tonight," he told Ms. Baines, feeling a little silly talking to her so carefully. He didn't like having an audience. It made everything feel artificial.

But his audience didn't seem inclined to leave. Holding her briefcase, she leaned against the door frame and smiled encouragingly at him.

He tried to ignore her as he shaped the meat into patties, one for Alix and two for him, and set them in a pan. Usually he served burgers with chips, but Ms. Baines might think that wasn't nutritious. He'd better go with carrot sticks or applesauce or something from the fruits-and-vegetables food group.

Alix sat calmly on the counter, watching him. Her attention didn't bother him. She accepted him, knew he loved her, knew he was her daddy.

Natalie Baines, though... What was going on in her mind

when she watched him? Was she thinking he was nervous? Damn it, he *was* nervous.

Was she thinking that if Alix lived with the Porters she'd be enjoying elaborate gourmet meals every night? She probably would—assuming she didn't screech and say "Yuck" when they presented her with some exotic new cuisine.

He was a hamburger kind of guy. Herbs and sauces didn't mean much to him. If Ms. Baines hadn't shown up, he'd be drinking a beer right now. The day had been a scorcher, and he and his crew had been mowing, edging, pruning and putting the finishing touches on some decorative stone terracing one of the summer people wanted in his backyard. The terracing had been a massive job, and Kevin had been hands-on involved in it for two weeks, from the digging through the concrete pouring to the stone setting. A lot of hard labor went into creating something that pretty. He deserved a beer after work today.

But he'd have to forgo that reward. No way would he give Ms. Baines the opportunity to write a report for the judge that said not only was Kevin dirty, not only was his house messy, not only did he work so late he couldn't pick his own daughter up from the preschool that had triggered the Porters' decision to demand custody of Alix in the first place, not only did he let his daughter run around without any shorts on, but he drank beer while he was taking care of her.

Anger crept up his spine and tapped at his skull. He fought to deny it entrance into his mind. He couldn't afford anger, not tonight. Not in front of Natalie Baines.

"I'd offer you a hamburger," he said, speaking in a pleasantly neutral tone, "but I don't have enough. I wasn't expecting you."

"That's quite all right." Her voice was pleasant, too, as

soft and warm as flannel. He recalled her singing some song about a bus to Alix. Alix must have liked it; she'd calmed down and wound up building a tower. A voice with that kind of power was a treasure.

The most effective tool he had for calming Alix down was to hug her. His singing helped, but he didn't sound anywhere near as sweet as Ms. Baines. Or maybe he just didn't know the right tunes. He'd have to learn that bus song. Not from Ms. Baines, though. If she found out he didn't know the bus song, it would be one more black mark next to his name.

"You're moving," she commented.

Puzzled, he glanced over his shoulder, hoping to read her meaning in her face. Of course he was moving. You couldn't cook hamburgers without moving.

She must have sensed his confusion, because she clarified herself. "I saw the sign outside. You're selling your house?"

Not *his* house. He lived here, he paid the monthly mortgage, but it had never really been *his* house. The Porters had provided the down payment because Madeleine wanted to live in a big, fancy house. Now she was gone, and yes, he was selling the place. He planned to pay the Porters back every damn penny they'd put into it, too. He didn't want to be beholden to them for anything.

"It's too big for Alix and me," he explained, once again managing to keep resentment out of his voice. "This neighborhood isn't really my style. I've signed a contract for a nice ranch house on the south side, but it's on a contingency. As soon as this sale goes through, I can buy that house. I think Alix and I will be happier there." *Alix and I,* he almost repeated. Alix was going to be living with him in the ranch house. She wasn't going to be living with the Porters on their palatial estate, where they could raise her

to be as spoiled and selfish as Madeleine, and where she
would grow up thinking of people like him as the "lawn
boy."

"I'd like to see that house," Ms. Baines said.

"Sure. But you'll have to give me lots of warning for
that. The real estate agent has the key, and I've got to set
it up with her when I want to go inside." No more unannounced visits from Natalie Baines, he thought.

The burgers were done. He flipped his onto two buns,
then slid Alix's onto her Mickey Mouse plate. He cut it
into little pieces and carried it and Alix to the table. "We're
going to eat now," he said. "Do you want to watch us do
that?"

Ms. Baines smiled apologetically. When she smiled,
even with that wistful cast to her eyes, her face was trans-
formed from just plain attractive to extraordinary. "I'm not
your adversary, Mr. Medina," she said gently. "I know,
the legal process is often an adversarial one, but I'm not
taking any sides. My job is to recommend what I think is
best for Alix."

Kevin leveled his gaze at her. She didn't look away,
didn't inch back, didn't try to avoid him. She returned his
stare, cool and steady.

"Let me simplify your job for you," he said quietly.
"*I'm* what's best for Alix."

CHAPTER TWO

"SHE'S A BRIGHT little girl," Molly Saunders-Russo told Natalie. "A bit clingy, but that's no surprise. When a child loses her mother at such a young age, it's normal for her to feel insecure. The first few times her father left her here, she was inconsolable. She still has trouble saying goodbye to him. She'll be moody and withdrawn for a while after he leaves, but once we get her involved in an activity she perks up. And then she's fine for the rest of the day."

Natalie scribbled notes on her pad. She was seated in the office at the entry of the Children's Garden Preschool, interviewing the school's director on the subject of Alix Medina. She'd traveled to the preschool directly from a visit to the home of Alix's grandparents, Vivienne and Carlton Porter.

Vivienne had insisted on giving Natalie a tour of the property. "When Alix comes to live with us, we'll make a play area for her here, with a playhouse and a swing set," Vivienne had said as they'd paced the gardens at the rear of the house. "We have enough land for a horse and barn, if she shows an interest. We could even put up a little tent for her, if she'd like to camp out on the property. We have a pool, so she could take swimming lessons right here in her own backyard. We've also got a tennis court, and a small pond that freezes over in the winter for ice-skating. The point is, living with us would afford her every opportunity to develop her talents, whatever they might be. We can do that for her. Kevin can't.''

Into the house they'd trooped. Natalie was shown the magnificently furnished bedroom where Alix would live, and the adjacent playroom, its broad windows filled with sunlight—''in case she wants to paint. This room has as much natural light as any studio''—and the music room, already equipped with a piano and a barre—''in case she wants to study ballet.''

The tour over, they'd settled in a parlor, where a maid had served lemonade and home-baked cookies. An oil portrait of Alix's mother hung on one wall; on the mantel above the fireplace stood a large framed photo of Madeleine Porter Medina holding an infant Alix in her lap, and several smaller portraits of Alix at various stages from newborn to toddler.

Madeleine had been beautiful, slender and blond, with the sort of polish unlimited funds could buy. Her expression in the painting and the photo contained an interesting blend of elegance and arrogance, but her eyes glinted with mischief.

Natalie noticed that there were no photos of Kevin on display.

''There's simply no way Kevin can give Alix what we can give her,'' Vivienne Porter had confided. ''More important, if she lived with us, we wouldn't be farming her out to some day care center to be raised by strangers.''

If Natalie's observations were anything to go by, the Children's Garden Preschool wasn't just ''some day care center,'' and the children there didn't appear to have been ''farmed out.'' The school was clean and well run, the student-to-adult ratio was unusually low, and so far, Natalie was impressed by the school's director.

But she had to be objective in her evaluation. Was it

better for a vulnerable sixteen-month-old girl who had lost
her mother only a few months ago to spend eight hours a
day in a preschool, or to live with grandparents who could
give her their undivided attention? Was it better for her to
be picked up by her weary, hardworking father—or, as had
happened last night, her father's sister, because her father
wasn't done working at the school's closing time—or to
live in an environment not measured by time clocks?

Of course, the preschool wasn't the only issue Natalie
had to weigh. The Porters were rich. Beyond rich, really.
Their estate in Arlington, Connecticut, was just one of their
homes; they also owned an eight-room apartment on Fifth
Avenue in Manhattan, photos of which Vivienne Porter eagerly supplied to Natalie so she could see the splendid lifestyle Alix would enjoy if her grandparents received custody
of her. In contrast, Alix's father ran a lawn care service.
He'd attended a year of college before dropping out. Fi-
nancially, he couldn't hope to compete with the Porters.

Natalie believed that values and stability and love were
far more important than creature comforts. But as a court-
appointed advocate for the child, she considered it her job
to include all the data in her calculations. And the fact was
that with the Porters, Alix would have the best of everything, at least in material terms.

But would she have the best home? The best family?

An image of Kevin Medina loomed in Natalie's mind:
the way he'd looked when she'd first seen him standing at
the front door yesterday evening, all scruffy and prickly.
He'd been annoyed by her unexpected visit, but his anger
hadn't altered his behavior with Alix. He'd held her and
she'd hugged him tightly. She'd screamed for him, and her
neediness hadn't rattled him at all. Another man might feel
embarrassed about cuddling with his daughter in front of a
stranger. Or he might show off, overdoing the nurturing

act, knocking himself out to prove that he was a perfect father. Or, like Vivienne Porter, he might boast about all the things he could provide for Alix.

Kevin hadn't done any of that. He'd exhibited an uncommon ease with his daughter, holding her, cooking for her, advising Natalie to sing to her. Being Alix's father was apparently as organic to him as breathing.

The truth was, ever since Natalie had met Kevin, she'd had trouble putting him out of her mind. Not just because of his relaxed relationship with his daughter, not just because of his barely disguised resentment of Natalie and the custody battle she represented, but because of his riveting blue eyes and his sturdy shoulders, because of his sleek chest, his labor-honed body and the graceful strength of his arms as they held Alix. Just as his wife's painting in her parents' home had explained why Kevin would have fallen in love with her, a few minutes in his presence had made it clear to Natalie why Madeleine Porter might have fallen in love with him.

"Kevin does have a little trouble getting here by five-thirty," Molly was saying. "But he's made arrangements with his sister to pick up Alix on days when he's unable to get here on time. Of course, the summer is his busy season. By mid-October, his workload will taper off. I understand he does some winter contracting—tree clearance, snowplowing, and freelance work at Murray's Greenhouse Center. I don't think the pickup time will be a problem for him then."

"Tell me more about Alix," Natalie said, reminding herself that her focus was the child, not the father. "You mentioned she was clingy—"

"Normal behavior for a child who's just lost a parent, especially a child as young as Alix. Other than that, she seems like a healthy, well-adjusted girl. Her verbal skills

are above average for her age, and she seems to enjoy the
other children in her group. Her play is age appropriate.
She shares well, she doesn't hit or bite, she gets cranky
before naptime but wakes up in a good mood. Again, everything is in the normal to above-average range.''

"How about her grooming?'' Natalie asked. "Does she
ever come to school dirty or poorly dressed?''

"No. On a couple of occasions, Kevin forgot to pack
spare diapers for her. But that's also normal during the first
few weeks a child is enrolled here. It's a whole new routine,
and parents need to adjust to it as much as children do.''
The cheerful, dark-haired woman tapped a pencil against
her fingertips, as if she were ticking off items. "She always
has her towel and a change of clothes, so she can participate
in water play outside. He packs healthy lunches for her—
in fact, I think he sends her with too much food, and she
rarely finishes everything, but that's better than sending her
with too little. She's clean and alert. She talks about her
daddy a fair amount.''

"Does she talk about her mother?''

"Rarely.'' Molly lowered her pencil and leaned forward.
"With some children, that kind of avoidance is because of
grief, because they don't want to mention the dead parent.
But I don't think that's the case here.''

"What do you think it is?''

Molly shook her head slightly. "I may be wrong, but I
have the feeling Kevin has always been Alix's primary
caregiver, even when her mother was alive.''

Natalie flipped through her notes. "Her mother didn't
have an outside job.''

"No, but—'' Molly sighed. "I don't want to be a party
to gossip, and that's really all it is.''

"Anything you can tell me that might shed some light
on Alix's situation would be useful,'' Natalie reminded her.

Molly seemed to struggle with herself. She sighed again. "I'd suggest that you look into the circumstances surrounding the accident that killed Alix's mother. As I've said, all I've heard are rumors. They could be completely wrong. It would be better if you investigated it yourself."

Natalie appreciated Molly's tact almost as much as she appreciated the heads-up. She had to remember that Alix's mother was not involved in the custody challenge. Her mother's parents were, though, and if there had been problems between their daughter and Kevin, those problems might spill over into the decision.

"Anything else you think I should know about Alix?" she asked.

Before Molly could answer, the front door swung open and Kevin Medina entered the school.

He'd clearly come straight from work; he had on a navy-blue T-shirt and jeans, and like yesterday, he wore a slight stubble of beard. Also like yesterday, his eyes were shocking in their intensity, and his physique was an advertisement for the benefits of strenuous physical labor.

As his gaze intersected with hers, she rose to her feet. Molly glanced behind her, saw him and grinned. "Hi, Kevin. You're here early today."

Natalie glanced at the wall clock above the desk—quarter to five. Was he picking his daughter up early to compensate for yesterday? Was he trying to win points with the court, proving he was willing to work shorter hours so he could take Alix home on time?

"Yeah, we finished up a little early," he said pleasantly. Natalie could feel his gaze on her, and she met it with a nod. "What are you doing here?" he asked her.

"Asking Molly about how Alix is doing in school."

Kevin turned to Molly, a hint of worry flickering in his eyes. "How is Alix doing in school?"

"Fine," Molly reassured him, giving his arm a gentle pat that made Natalie oddly jealous. She wished she could give Kevin a gentle pat, so he'd know she was on his side.

But she *wasn't* on his side. She was on Alix's side.

And if she longed to touch his arm, that urge was far more complicated than simply wanting to indicate whose side she was on. His forearms were tanned and sinewy, his wrists bony, his fingers thick and strong. She'd seen those hands hold his young daughter tenderly, and the thought of such manly hands exercising such gentleness made her breath catch in her throat.

"Ms. Baines is just doing her job," Molly continued. "And she's doing it well. Don't get paranoid, Kevin."

"Yeah, right." A halfhearted smile twisted his lips.

"Why don't you go on back and get Alix? I want to finish up with Ms. Baines, and then we'll talk."

Kevin nodded and sauntered down the hall, past the offices to the main playroom. Natalie wondered what Molly was going to talk to him about. More reassurances? Advice on how to impress the social worker? Suggestions on how to dupe her?

Natalie didn't think so. She believed Molly was doing her job well, too—a job that entailed not just taking care of her students but also catering to their parents.

A frazzled-looking mother carrying a newborn in a Snugli pouch strapped across her belly entered the school. "Pickup time must be busy for you," Natalie said, sliding her folder into her briefcase. "I won't take up any more of your time, Ms. Saunders-Russo."

"Call me Molly," Molly insisted.

Natalie smiled. "Call me Natalie." She handed Molly a card. "If you can think of anything else I need to know about Alix—or her father—give me a call, okay?"

"Sure." Molly wedged the card into the leather frame

of her blotter and shook Natalie's hand. She was petite, but her grip was solid. "Kevin's a good man," she said. "And a good father."

"I appreciate your input." Natalie nodded and headed for the door, feeling another unwelcome twinge of envy that Molly was free to ally herself with Kevin.

Natalie wished she could, too. But she couldn't. She couldn't touch him, couldn't think about him in any but the most impartial terms, couldn't spend another night like the one she'd just spent, her mind filling with visions of him every time she closed her eyes. As long as she was Alix's guardian *ad litem,* she couldn't allow herself any personal feelings for him at all.

KEVIN WAITED in the entry hall until Molly was done chatting with a mother. She'd said she wanted to talk to him, and if it wasn't for the fact that he'd seen her conferring with Natalie Baines, he would have been fine with that. Molly often liked to talk to parents when they picked up their kids; she'd tell them how the day went, remind them if they'd forgotten something, update them on the kid's nap or appetite.

But with Ms. Baines in the picture, Kevin couldn't quell his anxiety. They'd been discussing him, he knew—him and Alix. The court-appointed social worker had probably been pumping Molly for information. And now Molly wanted to tell him how bad it was, how many hoops of fire he should be prepared to jump through in order to keep his daughter.

Alix had wrapped herself around his shin. She was impatient to leave, but he had to hear Molly out.

At last the mother left, and Molly turned to him. Her smile made him feel only marginally less nervous.

"Am I in trouble?" he asked, trying to ignore the weight

of Alix as she sat on his instep and tugged at the laces of his work boot.

"With Ms. Baines?" Molly's smile widened, and she shook her head. "I didn't have to stretch the truth to tell her you're a terrific father. But custody battles can be awful. I've witnessed more than a few."

Kevin supposed she would have a first-row seat at any such battles that involved her students.

"It's probably none of my business," she went on, "except that Alix's well-being *is* my business. I was wondering if you've got a good attorney."

"I have a lawyer," he said to her. The lawyer who had helped him incorporate his business and was currently over-seeing his house transactions had also counseled him on his legal battle against the Porters.

Molly shook her head again, this time without smiling. "You need a *good* lawyer, Kevin. Your in-laws can afford the best lawyers in Connecticut, if not the world. You need someone good enough to fight on their level."

He wished he could afford what the Porters could afford when it came to legal representation. The fact was, he earned a decent living, enough to support Alix and himself comfortably. But a top-of-the-heap lawyer was probably out of his price range.

"My brother-in-law is an attorney," Molly said. "So's my sister, but she works as a public defender. My brother-in-law is high-powered—and he's *good*."

"And he charges, what? A thousand bucks an hour?"

"If you want, I could talk to him. His fees are on a sliding scale. He might be willing to work out something with you. I just think…" She sighed and glanced down at Alix, who had managed to untie Kevin's shoelaces and seemed awfully proud of herself. "I think you need the best there is. In this kind of case, my brother-in-law is the best.''

''Okay.'' He hated being indebted to people, but Molly was right. He needed the best. If her brother-in-law won him full, permanent custody of Alix, he would find a way to pay him back.

''One other thing,'' Molly added. ''You might want to take some Daddy School classes.''

''What?''

''Daddy School. It's a program I run with a friend. We give classes and workshops on how to improve your fathering skills.''

''You just said I was a good father,'' he argued.

Her smile returned. ''You are. But you're facing a lot right now—you've been facing a lot for quite a while— and you might find the classes helpful. If you have any doubts, any questions about what you ought to be doing for Alix, the classes could answer them. And they're fun. Try our Saturday-morning class—it's right here at the school, and the fathers all bring their children with them. The children get to play, while we have our workshop. Alix will enjoy it.''

''Okay.'' He sighed. Molly was right; he was facing a lot. And although he hated to be indebted to anyone, he'd be a fool not to accept help when he needed it. ''Thanks.''

He wiggled his foot free of Alix, gathered up her tote bag and lunch box, took her hand and walked out of the building with her. The early-evening sun hung high and bright, roasting the asphalt of the parking lot.

Natalie Baines was loitering near his truck.

Why was it that every time he saw the woman he wanted to curse? It couldn't be only that she represented the entire court process he despised. After all, she might ultimately argue for him in the custody case.

No, the reflexive anger he experienced when he saw her had to do with other things. Her glossy hair, the color of weathered beach sand, and her skin glowing with honey undertones. Her soft lips and feminine curves and the small gold beads that adorned her delicate earlobes. All of that—combined with the knowledge that an unbreachable wall stood between them—made him want to put some distance between her and himself.

Of all the women in Arlington, Natalie Baines was *not* the one whose soft lips and feminine curves he ought to be noticing. She was more off-limits than a preacher's daughter or a boss's wife. She had more power over him than any other person, with the possible exception of the judge. She was the one whose report could determine whether he would keep his baby. If he ever let himself acknowledge her beauty, if he ever acted on his attraction...

Well, no wonder the sight of her made him want to curse.

Of course, he had something of a history when it came to inappropriate women and inconvenient desire. In her own way, Madeleine had been even more off-limits than Ms. Baines. But that hadn't stopped him from going after her.

No, he hadn't gone after her. She'd gone after him—and there had been no legal quagmire, no custody fight, nothing to prevent him from letting her snag him. There were *plenty* of things preventing him from experiencing even the tiniest bit of interest in Natalie Baines.

He wondered what she thought of his truck. Would he lose points in the competition with the Porters because he drove his daughter home from preschool in a hardworking pickup, with Medina Lawn Service painted on both doors? He had a child seat set up for her, and the truck's interior was clean and safe, but his truck couldn't compare with the Porters' fancy vehicles.

As he neared the truck, the social worker hunkered down, apparently not minding that the hem of her skirt was brushing against the ground. "Hi, Alix," she said, giving his daughter a big eye-level smile.

Alix sucked her thumb and stared at Ms. Baines. Kevin wondered if she remembered her from yesterday—the lady who sang the bus song and built a tower of blocks with her.

"Did you have a good day at school?" Ms. Baines asked.

Alix nodded.

Kevin appreciated her effort. Most people lacked the patience to converse with toddlers—and they lacked the sensitivity to squat so the kid didn't have to feel she was talking to a giant.

At last she straightened up and turned to Kevin. "I'd like to meet with you alone, if possible," she said. "I've seen you with Alix, but we need to talk, just the two of us."

"Okay." He might be able to present himself in a better light if he did a one-on-one with her. "We can't meet during the day, though. I don't even take a lunch break most days. I work straight through, or grab a bite between jobs."

"I understand. Could we get together some evening?"

"Sure. I've got to line up a sitter, but... Sure. We could meet for dinner."

She smiled. "I'll pay for the meal. If you feed me, it could be construed as a bribe."

He shrugged. "I'm not going to argue if a lady wants to treat me to dinner."

"Hire a baby-sitter and give me a call," she said. "You've got my number, right? I gave you my card."

"I've got it." Was she testing him, trying to find out if

he'd lost her business card? He wasn't careless, especially not with an object of such vital importance.

"Great." She was still smiling, as if trying to coax an answering smile from him. He didn't want to smile. He didn't want to glimpse her even white teeth, her faint dimple, the glitters of light in her eyes.

But it would take a stronger man than he was to resist smiling back at a woman as attractive as Natalie Baines.

CHAPTER THREE

MOISE'S FISH HOUSE was his kind of place—good food, unpretentious decor, waiters who delivered dinner without a fuss and didn't refer to themselves as "waitrons" or "servers." He was glad Natalie Baines had chosen this place to meet him.

Hell, he was glad she'd chosen to meet him at all—and he shouldn't be. He should view this Thursday-night dinner as an opportunity to convince her that Alix belonged with him. He'd showered, dressed in khakis and a polo shirt, dropped Alix off with his sister and swung by the real estate agent's office to grab the key for his new house. He'd cajoled her into letting him borrow the key long enough to show the place to Ms. Baines, if she wanted to see it. She might not like it. She might think it was too small compared with the house he and Alix were living in now. But he wanted to be helpful and agreeable, to prove to her that he had nothing to hide.

He hadn't had dinner with a woman he wasn't related to since Madeleine died. Even before she died, they rarely went out for dinner. Well, *she* went out, but not with him. He used to come home tired from work and eager to spend time with his daughter. "I've been with her all day," Madeleine would complain. "Maybe you want to sit around at home all night. Not me. I need a life."

Some life she'd found for herself, he thought with a pang of bitterness. He shook it off and entered the restaurant.

Natalie Baines was already there. She wore a sleeveless sundress that looked a little too soft and flowery to be work clothes. Had she rushed home from her office and showered, too? Had she fixed herself up for him?

Why would she? She wasn't the one who had to make a good impression.

She smiled from the table where she was sitting. He pointed her out to the hostess who had greeted him at the door, then wove among the tables and took his seat across from her. "You look good," he said automatically, because it was true and it was the sort of thing he'd say to any woman who looked as terrific as she did. But it was a boneheaded remark in this context, and he wanted to kick himself for having blurted it out.

Her smile deepened. "Thank you."

All right. Maybe his compliment hadn't screwed things up too badly. God, but he hated being so on edge, so anxious to get every last detail and gesture right. He'd never felt this way around women before.

He kept himself from making any other misguided comments by burying himself in the menu for a few minutes. He ordered a bowl of chowder, a salmon steak and a ginger ale instead of the beer he would have liked. She asked for some shrimp thing and an iced tea, which told him he'd been right to skip the beer.

Around them, other diners seemed to be having a grand time. They chatted, bickered, murmured, laughed. He just sat like a job applicant, stiff and hopeful, his hands clenching against his knees where she couldn't see them.

She managed to avoid looking directly at him until their drinks arrived. She took a sip, her lips pursed around the straw, and then gave him another smile. "You're nervous," she guessed.

"Not really," he said, then decided lying wasn't going

to help his case. "Yeah, I'm nervous. There's a lot at stake."

"Does it make you feel any better to know that I care about Alix and I want what's best for her? You want what's best for her, too. We both want the same thing."

"But we might not agree on what the best thing for her is," he pointed out.

She smiled hesitantly. "Trust me, Kevin. I'm not going to recommend anything that would harm your daughter. Can I call you Kevin?"

"Sure—if I can call you Natalie."

"By all means, call me Natalie." She acted as if she thought this meant they were friends. But as long as she had the power to persuade the court to take away his daughter from him, they could never be friends.

His soup arrived, along with a basket of fresh-baked bread. Natalie helped herself to a slice and a pat of butter, while he tasted his soup. Normally, eating the clam chowder at Moise's was an experience on a par with great sex or watching the Red Sox beat the Yankees. But tonight, he was so tense he could barely taste it.

"Alix seems like a healthy, well-adjusted child," Natalie said. "That's going to work in your favor. The courts don't like to remove a child from a situation where she's thriving. They also don't like to remove a child from a birth parent unless they have to."

"So—that means it's looking good for me?" he dared to ask.

"I still need some information," she said, deftly avoiding his question. "First, a little more background on you. You didn't finish college, right?"

"My father died," he explained. "There were money considerations. I left school and came home so I could help my mother out."

"And you took a job mowing lawns?"

"It was what I'd done in high school. The guy I worked for in high school hired me to do landscaping work. He was still paying me high school wages, though, so after a year I set up my own company. There's lots of building going on in Arlington, lots of new construction. The region offers plenty of work for landscape outfits. I've done fine. I have two full-time people working for me, and ten part-timers, students working summer jobs and the like. If you need to see my financials—"

"That may not be necessary," she said. "I don't think I'm betraying any confidences when I say your in-laws are extremely wealthy. But my only concern is that you have enough to support yourself and your daughter in a stable, solvent manner."

"I do." He ate some soup. "I'm willing to have my accountant show you the books, if you want."

"I'll let you know if I need that information." She spread a dab of butter on a chunk of bread and daintily consumed it. "I expect this question may be painful for you, but how is Alix coping with the death of her mother? When a child is a little older, I can ask the child herself. But Alix's verbal skills are pretty limited, so I have to ask you."

Stirring his spoon through the creamy broth, he contemplated his reply. He recalled that line from the Miranda warning he'd heard a million times on TV cop shows: *anything you say can and will be used against you in a court of law.* He had to choose his words very carefully, to not speak negatively of Madeleine, to not imply that she'd fallen way short as a mother.

"I'm sure Alix misses her mother," he finally said. "She doesn't talk about it much."

"Does she have nightmares or obvious mood swings?"

"Not really, no. I mean, her moods are right out there. If she's tired, she gets crabby. If there's a chocolate chip cookie in the vicinity, she gets happy. She's not a real complex kid." Bad answer. It might make him seem as if he wasn't tuned in to his own daughter, as if he didn't care enough about her to analyze the nuances of her temperament. "She gets sad, sure. She needs cuddling a lot. I don't mind that. I'm her father. If my girl is upset, I want to be there for her."

"Of course." Did she think he was laying it on too thick, coming across fake? She glanced at him, her expression cautious, her smile hesitant. "Have you and your in-laws ever considered the sort of arrangement where, for instance, you might leave Alix with them during the day, instead of at the Children's Garden Preschool, and then you could pick up Alix up from your in-laws at the end of the day?"

"That wouldn't work," he said quickly but firmly. It wouldn't, because he didn't want Alix spending her days with those stuck-up creeps, the parents who'd spoiled their own daughter, catered to all her whims and treated the father of their grandchild with undisguised contempt. They might speak respectfully of him to Natalie, but they'd never treated him with respect to his face. They thought he was trash, and they hadn't wanted Madeleine to marry him and have his child. They didn't deserve Alix, not even for a few hours a day.

"Why wouldn't it work?" Natalie asked.

He had to come up with a better reason than the fact that his in-laws turned his stomach. "I think the Children's Garden is an excellent program," he said. "I think it's important for Alix to spend time with other children her own age. Since I work, I can't organize play dates for her the way stay-at-home parents can. And frankly, I don't see the Porters organizing play dates for her, either. They aren't

friendly with other young parents, and all they seem interested in is protecting Alix, sheltering her at their estate. I
think she's better off learning how to play with other kids.
She's got to develop her social skills." *There.* He was a
good parent. He knew about socialization, about the importance of peer-group play.

Natalie nodded. "I hate having to ask you about all these
things, Kevin, but it's my job."

"I understand."

"I'm sure some of these questions must bother you."

"It's okay."

She drew in her breath, a warning to him that her next
question was going to bother him. "When your wife died
in that car accident," she said, "she wasn't alone."

It wasn't even phrased as a question. The fact was, Madeleine had been with another man. And Natalie knew it.
She must have done some research—and if she did, she
knew what kind of a woman Madeleine was. Kevin didn't
have to protect her reputation.

But he wasn't going to speak ill of Madeleine. He never
had when she was alive, even though she'd been bitchy and
disloyal. Any criticism of his wife implied a criticism of
the man who'd married her. Her bad behavior reflected on
him.

He decided to keep his comments as brief as possible.
"That's right," he said laconically.

The waiter arrived to clear away his soup bowl and de-
liver their main courses. For a minute, Kevin let the presentation of the fish and vegetables and fresh silverware
distract him.

But as soon as the waiter was gone, Natalie pressed
ahead. "Did you know the man who was driving the car
when it crashed?"

"No."

"He was a friend of your wife's?"

Yeah, and I was—what's the word? A cuckold. Except that he wasn't. He'd known about her affairs. He'd even talked to his lawyer about a divorce. His lawyer had advised against it: *If you leave her, she'll get the kid. Especially when a child is as young as your daughter. No judge is ever going to give the father custody when a kid is that young.* So Kevin had discarded the idea, except to hope that Madeleine would choose to leave him and Alix.

She'd left, but in a terrible, tragic way.

"I know this is difficult," Natalie said gently. "It's important for me to get a complete sense of the family dynamics. Anything you can tell me would help."

He sighed. "Madeleine wasn't happy as a wife and mother," he conceded. "I'm sorry about that. I had hoped she would be happy, but she wasn't."

"How did you meet her?"

"I was doing landscape work on her parents' house. She was there, and we just…clicked." More than clicked. Madeleine had devoured him like a shipwreck survivor stumbling upon a banquet. And like a normal man, he'd responded. She'd been gorgeous, she'd been hot, and they'd had a grand time—until they'd had some sort of contraceptive failure. Madeleine had talked about getting an abortion, but he'd convinced her not to. He would marry her, he promised, and then they could have even grander times, not having to sneak around and hide from her parents.

He'd been surprised, but greatly relieved, when she'd said yes. Part of it was rebellion, he knew; she'd wanted to shock her parents, and they'd followed her script and been shocked. But their princess was pregnant, so they'd pinched their noses and accepted the "lawn boy" who'd insisted on making an honest woman out of her.

By the time Alix arrived, Madeleine had already grown

sick of being married. Kevin had done what he could. He'd let her parents sink their own money into a house he hated, just because Madeleine had wanted to live there. He'd taken on the bulk of the baby chores, seeing to the night feedings, changing diapers. Occasionally he'd demanded that Madeleine stop acting like a selfish brat and shoulder some of the responsibilities, but he hadn't pushed her. He'd already pushed her into marrying him and having the baby. Her unhappiness was partly his fault.

Her affairs, though, had been hard to take—the nights she hadn't come home until two, the evenings he'd arrived home to find Alix neglected in her playpen while Madeleine was giggling on the phone with this or that mysterious caller...Jack or Robby or Edward. Edward had been driving his Porsche the night she'd died. He'd died with her. It had sure been an exciting little car, a lot classier than Kevin's truck.

He dragged his thoughts back to the present, to this table at this restaurant and the woman sitting across from him. She studied him, her eyes hinting at a sympathy he didn't want. "Look," he said gruffly. "Madeleine's dead. She died too young, and it was a terrible accident, but my little girl is still alive and that's the most important thing to me."

"The Porters spent a lot of time telling me about everything they could provide for Alix that you can't. Why don't you tell me about what you can provide for her that *they* can't?"

He ate, buying time to put together a persuasive answer. "They can provide a lot of material stuff," he said. "They've got money. But they can't provide her with a father. I'm the only father she's got, and I don't care how rich they are, the Porters can't go out and buy her a new one."

"That's true enough."

He tried to restrain himself, but resentment started to boil up inside him. Madeleine might have been spoiled, but her parents had been the ones to spoil her. If only they'd backed off and stayed out of Madeleine and Kevin's relationship, the marriage might have had a chance. But the instant Kevin would say he couldn't buy Madeleine something she wanted—not just her ostentatious dream house but a big diamond solitaire to go with the plain gold wedding band he'd given her, or a three-hundred dollar pair of shoes—she'd pitch a fit and storm off to Mother and Dad, who would buy her whatever she asked for and assure her that Kevin was useless.

"I can give Alix a sense of security, an understanding that money doesn't buy love," he continued, struggling to keep his voice from revealing his anger. "I can give her my values, my work ethic. I can teach her how to make plants grow, how pruning a tree can make it healthier, how earthworms aerate the soil. I can give her her own true daddy." He clamped his mouth shut against adding that despite all their millions of dollars, the Porters could never give her any of those things.

Natalie was watching him, her eyes intent, her teeth working her lower lip. "You feel very passionate about this, don't you."

"Damn right I do," he retorted softly, not caring that his use of the word *damn* might count against him.

"How do you visualize Alix in five years?" she asked.

The question was creative enough to defuse his anger. He chewed it over as he chewed some food. "She'd be in first grade. Smartest kid in her class. Her favorite book would be *Charlotte's Web*. I'd have to read it to her, though. She'd be smart, but that's a hard book for a first grader."

"Why *Charlotte's Web?*" Natalie asked with a smile.

"It was my favorite book when I was a kid," he explained.

She was still smiling. "How about yourself? How do you picture yourself in five years?"

"Working hard. The business would have expanded some. I'd like to set up a nursery like Murray's. I've worked there, and I think Murray lacks the energy to do the job right. If he was thinking of retiring, I'd buy him out."

"So you'd be working at a desk?"

"I'd still be doing some of the heavy lifting," he said. "A desk job would make me crazy if I had to do it full time. But I'd have more people working under me, and steadier hours."

Natalie nodded. "Would you be dating a lot?"

Ordinarily, he'd accept the question on its face. It was valid; she wanted to know if he was going to have hot-and-cold-running women in the house where his daughter was growing up, if he was going to get involved with potential stepmothers for his daughter and then break up with them, causing Alix unnecessary pain.

But the question had its own special resonance coming from Natalie. Maybe because she was the sort of woman he'd like to be dating—someone smart and pretty, someone who had Alix's best interests at heart. Someone with the silkiest-looking hair he'd ever seen.

"I'm not a run-around guy," he said. "I'd like to meet the woman of my dreams and settle down, give Alix a mother and myself a good wife."

"Alix's mother wasn't the woman of your dreams?"

"No." He shouldn't have answered; it wasn't Natalie's business—but he couldn't help himself. He'd never before admitted out loud what his hope was for his future, but Natalie—the woman he was supposed to think of as his opponent, his possible nemesis in court—had unlocked something inside him. She'd gotten him to give voice to a dream he hadn't dared to confront before.

He risked a glance at her. Her smile was compassionate but utterly lacking in pity. He prayed she wouldn't use what he'd just said against him. He'd never felt so vulnerable.

"I hope that happens for you, Kevin," she murmured. "I hope your dreams come true."

CHAPTER FOUR

As THEY LEFT the restaurant, he mentioned his new house. "I got the key from the real estate broker, in case you want to look at the place."

She did. Professionally, she wanted to see the kind of home he hoped to make for his daughter, and personally...

Damn it, she shouldn't want anything personally. But when he'd confessed his dream to her, about settling down with a good wife—her personal feelings had kicked in mightily, wickedly. She was overflowing with personal feelings for Kevin Medina.

"I can drive you over there," he offered. "It'll just take a minute to get Alix's car seat out of the way."

"Maybe it would be easier if I followed you in my car," she said. The thought of climbing into that snug cab with him unnerved her. Over the course of their dinner, she had gone from thinking he was an amazingly handsome man to realizing he had a deep, sensitive soul. How could the Porters not want their beloved granddaughter to grow up in the shelter of Kevin's love?

Natalie had lost all objectivity, obviously. It would be wise for her to drive in her own car, alone, using the opportunity to collect herself.

As she steered out of the parking lot behind his truck, she pushed the button to open the window at her side. Mild evening air washed over her face, scented with the summer fragrances of mowed grass and warm asphalt. His truck rumbled slightly as he shifted gears and headed down the road. If she were a little girl, she'd think riding in a truck was much cooler than riding in a pathetically ordinary car like her Camry.

Her thoughts wandered from the truck to its driver. The men she dated tended to be, like her, college-educated professionals. She met them through work or at parties, and they generally resembled her, at least on the surface: literate, articulate, earnest. Most of the working-class people she encountered were clients, seeking her assistance.

Kevin was too complicated to fit any sort of label, working class or otherwise. He'd had a year of college, and he was clearly ambitious when it came to his business. Yet he took pride in the hard labor he performed, in his uncluttered values. He was a man who made a career of keeping plants alive and healthy.

What a fine role model for a daughter.

She was racing way ahead of herself. Although she'd entered this case already predisposed toward the father—the courts, as she'd told Kevin, generally didn't take children away from their parents unless there was a compelling reason to do so—nothing the Porters had said or done had been *bad*. They loved Alix. They believed they could make a wonderful life for her. Their motivation seemed partly financial, but Natalie was good at reading between the lines, and she suspected they were afraid of losing contact with their granddaughter. It sometimes happened in such situations: the surviving parent went on to make a new life, and the grandparents got left behind.

Perhaps the court could suggest visitation rights for the grandparents to protect them from that possibility.

Kevin had led her into a cozy residential neighborhood at the south end of town. The houses lining the streets were small, but tidy and well maintained. The sidewalks teemed with children playing in the waning summer light, some on bicycles, some on scooters. A small cluster of middle-school kids engaged in a rowdy game of street hockey that took up an entire cul-de-sac and another cluster of younger children raced through a sprinkler, shrieking giddily as the silvery water hit them. Natalie noticed swing sets in back-yards, basketball hoops jutting out above garage doors, pastel chalk drawings marking a driveway. Through her open window she smelled the smoky aroma of someone barbecuing dinner on an outdoor grill.

This was a neighborhood where Alix would find friends right on her block. It might not be as elegant as the street on which she and Kevin currently resided, but she'd be a part of a community here.

The truck turned the corner and Natalie turned, as well. Maples and oaks lined the street, spreading shadows across the pavement. Kevin steered up onto a driveway and shut off his engine. Natalie parked behind him and climbed out of her car.

The ranch house was dark, but the sky held enough light for her to see that it was as neat as the houses on either side of it. The yellow shingles and black shutters had been recently painted, the lawn recently mowed, the shrubs pruned. A bird feeder strung between two trees was over-flowing with seeds; Natalie wondered whether the agent kept it filled or whether Kevin had been stopping by to fill it. She'd bet on Kevin.

As evening settled around the property, she heard the rhythmic chirping of crickets and the distant hum of a ci-cada. The place felt peaceful, soothing and safe.

Kevin gazed at her in the waning twilight, as if searching her face for approval. It bothered her to realize that he wanted her approval for his custody case and not because of *her,* not because he wanted *her* to care about the home he'd chosen for his daughter.

She had no right to be bothered, and she shrugged to shake off the sentiment. "It looks lovely," she said.

"It's a lot smaller than where we're living now," he warned as he headed up the front walk.

"It looks big enough," she assured him.

"Madeleine would have thought—" He cut himself off.

She joined him on the front porch, watching as he busied himself with the key. "What would Madeleine have thought?"

"That it was a dive," he finished, a tinge of bitterness coloring his words. "Of course, she grew up in much more elegant homes."

"There doesn't seem to be anything dive-like about this house."

The lock gave, and he pushed open the front door. He blocked her entry with his body for a moment as he groped along an inner wall for a light switch. Once he'd found it and turned it on, he let her enter.

The interior smelled of fresh paint and carpet shampoo. The rooms were indeed small compared with the rooms in the massive house he and Alix were currently occupying— except that they were occupying only part of it. She recalled the immaculate living and dining rooms in that house. To her mind, a house where rooms went unused was more like a museum than a home.

She imagined that with fewer rooms and less space, Kevin and Alix would use every square inch of this house. The place was empty of furniture and lamps, which meant that only the rooms and halls with ceiling fixtures could be illuminated. But light from the entry and kitchen spilled through the open doorways, making everything visible. The living room looked out over the front lawn, the dining room was big enough to accommodate a table for eight and a sideboard, and the kitchen opened onto a screened back porch. She could picture Alix playing on that back porch, pedaling a tricycle in circles while Kevin kept an eye on her from the kitchen.

"It's lovely," she murmured.

"It's built solid," he said, "and it's got central air, which is important." He grinned and spread his arms as if to display the sultry heat in rooms that had not been cooled for a while. "The roof is only three years old, the furnace only eight. I'm not sure I like all this carpeting—there's hardwood flooring underneath it—but my mother told me carpets are good when you've got a young kid. If Alix falls, she isn't going to get hurt. Maybe when she's older, I'll tear all the carpeting up and refinish the floors."

Natalie had the feeling he wasn't speaking only of decorating ideas. He would personally tear the carpeting up and refinish the floors. He was strong and capable, not afraid of hard work.

He swung open a door off the kitchen. "Downstairs there's a finished rec room big enough for all Alix's toys. Big enough for a pool table, too," he added, then flashed her a grin.

It was the first time she could recall him joking like that, admitting to a personal desire without her having to interrogate him first. "Do you play pool?"

"Like nobody's business. And I'm going to teach Alix, too. I can tell just by looking at her—she's got the eye for it."

Natalie wished she could watch him play pool. She wished she could play it with him. Not that she was at all skilled, but she wanted to see him laugh and show off. Most of the time, he was terribly cautious around her, and she didn't blame him—he was undoubtedly afraid that a single slip might jeopardize his custody case. But just this once, he hadn't measured his words before speaking. He hadn't paused to analyze whether admitting he was a master at pool might hurt his chances in court.

"You know," she said, weighing her own words to make sure she didn't cross any ethical lines, "you're in good shape, Kevin. In terms of Alix, I mean. The burden of proof lies with the Porters. If they can't prove you're unfit to raise Alix, the court's not going to take her away."

His grin faded as he peered into her eyes. He was searching for something—a guarantee that the case would go his way, perhaps, or a promise that she'd speak on his behalf before the court. She couldn't make promises or offer guarantees. All she could do was write up her report, send copies to his lawyer, the Porters' attorney and the judge and hope the right decision was made.

But she wished... She wished she could tell him what he so desperately wanted to hear. Just to make him smile again. Just to make his face light up the way it had when he'd talked about teaching his daughter to play pool. Just to let him know she was not his enemy.

They stared at each other for a moment in the uneven light. The warm air wrapped around them, still and silent. They might have been the only two people in the world, and they had things they wanted to say to each other, things they wanted to ask—but they couldn't. The only sound between them was their quiet breathing and the muted, distant chirping of the crickets' summer song.

He broke away first, turning his head slowly, clearing his throat. "You want to see the bedrooms?" he asked, then seemed to cringe.

She knew the rooms would be empty. There was nothing embarrassing or suggestive about looking at them. "Sure," she said, because she wasn't yet ready to leave.

He cleared his throat again and led her down a dark hall, patting the wall until he found a light switch. The hall lamp was dim and dingy. "I've got to put in a new light fixture here," he muttered as a vague apology.

"It's okay, I can see."

"This is going to be Alix's bedroom," he said, nudging open a door. The room was square, maybe twelve by twelve, with a broad window opening onto the backyard. The inadequate light from the hallway made it hard to determine the color of the carpeting, but she thought it looked tan, or maybe mauve. "By the time we move in, she'll be ready for a bed. She hates her crib, anyway. She's always trying to figure out how to climb out. I'd just as soon put a mattress on the floor for her. When she's ready, we can put in a bed frame."

Natalie nodded. She loved the pride that filtered through his voice as he talked about his daughter.

"Her bookcase will go there—" he gestured toward one wall "—and her dresser there. The closet's pretty big, so when she's a teenager and has to have a different outfit for every day of the year, she'll have the space for her wardrobe."

He backed out of the room, pushed open another door and said, "This will be a combined den and guest room. I've got one of those convertible sofas, and we'll stick in the old TV." He continued down the hall, pointing out a bathroom on the way, and then opened the door at the end. "This will be…"

His bedroom. She knew it was empty, knew it was nothing but a large expanse of carpet and walls and windows. Yet she hesitated before entering, just as he had hesitated to name the room. Her being there with him carried no meaning, of course, no dangerous implications. It was just a vacant room. Not yet his.

But when he stood in it, lit more by the glow of a summer moon slanting through the window than by the murky light from the hall, it *was* his. His aura filled the room, his silhouette dominated it and a strange sensation fluttered in her throat and lower, in her abdomen, when she contemplated him actually living in this room, sleeping in it…making love in it.

It was Kevin's bedroom, and knowing she was inside it threw off her equilibrium. The room's lack of furniture only emphasized that she and he were all alone here, filling the space with themselves and each other and the pale moonlight. It was more intimate this way than it would have been with a bed. Just the two of them, a man and a woman with nothing between them, nothing in their way.

Except reality, she reminded herself, turning abruptly from him and stalking down the hall, trying to escape the strange pull of the room, of the man.

She didn't stop until she was back outside on the front porch. She heard him behind her, switching off the lights as he came. When he joined her on the porch, he spent a little time locking the door and double-checking it.

The sky had darkened to a rich royal blue, and the crickets were singing their hearts out. No more yells and laughter drifted through the air; all the children must have been called home by their parents as night descended upon the neighborhood. The breeze that caressed Natalie's bare arms was surprisingly cool.

Without looking at Kevin, she pictured his motions from the sounds he made: the jiggle of the door handle, the *click* of the key, the whisper of his hand descending into the pocket of his trousers. She felt like a fool, fleeing from him when all he'd done was show off the house he hoped to live in. For God's sake, how could she have been so rattled standing with him in a dark, unfurnished room?

She lifted her face to look at Kevin. He was staring at her, and his eyes were so crystalline that she could see right through them to the confusion that lurked within. He'd been rattled, too. Whatever had happened in that bedroom hadn't happened to her alone.

"Are you okay?" he asked, his voice scarcely louder than a whisper.

"Yes." She forced a smile. "I should be getting home, though. I appreciate your spending this time with me." She sounded like a bureaucrat—a lobotomized one, at that—but she didn't dare to say anything more personal.

Kevin was the daring one. He raised his hand and traced her lower lip with the callused edge of his thumb. Her mouth tingled, and she had to clamp her teeth together to keep from sighing. Whatever electricity had passed between them in the bedroom was still alive. One brush of his thumb against her lip, and she felt sparks firing throughout her body.

Without a word, she hurried down the path to her car, flung herself into the driver's seat and drove away.

HE CURSED.

Natalie Baines was a real menace to his vocabulary. More to the point, she was a real menace to his sanity.

Why the hell had he touched her? What kind of moron was he? That one touch could cost him his daughter.

He followed the path she'd raced down just a minute ago, reached his truck and rested his forehead against the cold chrome of the door frame. And cursed again.

Had she known what he'd been thinking when he brought her to his bedroom? Had she realized how beautiful she'd looked with the moonlight bathing her face? Had she been aware of how aroused he'd gotten, just gazing at her?

He had to be crazy. Natalie Baines held in her hands his

future, his heart, his life. She could write a report that would steal his daughter from him. *Why had he touched her?*

He couldn't help himself; that was why. He couldn't stop himself. Just one time, one touch. One tiny lapse.

He could only hope she'd accept it for what it was—not as the reckless advance of some smooth operator but simply the instinctual gesture of a man who was deeply, dangerously attracted to her. He knew his touch had been out of line. He knew it wouldn't happen again. But it didn't make him a bad father. He was just a normal, healthy guy.

He braced himself for another restless night. Like last night, like the night before. Like every night since Natalie Baines had entered his life. His sleeplessness was mostly caused by worry that this whole custody situation was going to go badly for him. But it was also caused by his awareness of her. After his marriage had started falling apart, he'd lost his natural affection for women. After her death, he hadn't had time even to think about women.

But he was thinking about a woman now. And he'd touched her.

And the worst part was, even if that touch might lead to a catastrophe in the custody ruling, one small part of him didn't regret reaching out, connecting with her, imagining himself fitting into her life in a way that had nothing to do with Alix and the Porters and the legal system. One small, extremely male part of him wished he'd had the guts to kiss her.

CHAPTER FIVE

NATALIE STARED at the words marching across her monitor. She'd typed her report, and she didn't know whether to save it, print it out or delete the whole thing.

Objectivity. How had she lost it? How was she ever going to get it back?

She'd arrived at her office early Friday morning and typed the report into her computer, heeding her brain and ignoring her heart. Her hope was to get her thoughts on Alix Medina's custody decision articulated before her emotions could break loose and influence her.

She was pretty certain that, even if Kevin hadn't stroked his thumb across her mouth last night, even if he hadn't looked as if he'd had to call upon every last ounce of willpower he possessed to keep from kissing her, even if she hadn't desperately wanted his kiss, she would have advised the court to leave Alix in Kevin's custody. He was a competent father and his daughter was doing well under difficult circumstances. If the Porters truly loved Alix, they wouldn't want to tear her from her father's arms.

On the desk next to her keyboard sat her folder of notes, and between the lines of those notes lurked her impressions and suspicions. Her interviews and research painted the story clearly enough: Kevin had been working as a landscape services contractor for the Porters when he and Madeleine Porter became involved. The Porters had been less than thrilled with their daughter's marriage to Kevin.

They'd no doubt expected her to marry someone from their own social class—a wealthy, polished gentleman. Not the gardener.

Natalie had to wonder whether they'd launched their custody bid as a way to punish Kevin for not being the son-in-law they'd wished for.

No. She would not ascribe motives to the Porters for which she lacked evidence. The court wanted her unbiased opinion, not conjecture. The Porters were Alix's grandparents, and they loved her. Natalie's feelings for Kevin couldn't alter that truth.

Through the open doorway of her office drifted the voices of her colleagues. She had a typically busy day ahead of her; counseling sessions and a department meeting crowded her calendar. If she could just get this report written and filed... If she could just convince herself that her report was completely impartial...

If she couldn't convince herself, her only option would be to tell the judge that her objectivity had been compromised and that she had to withdraw as Alix's guardian *ad litem*. But she knew the judge would be furious if she did that. Everyone was overscheduled and overworked. Who could possibly take this case over from Natalie and get a report written in time?

She *was* being objective. She objectively believed Kevin Medina was a wonderful father—

The phone beside her elbow rang. Sighing, she turned from her computer and answered. "Good morning, Natalie Baines speaking."

"Natalie? It's Molly Saunders-Russo from the Children's Garden Preschool."

Picturing the forthright, dark-haired preschool director, Natalie smiled. "Hi, Molly."

"I'm not sure if you've filed your report on Alix Medina

yet, but if you haven't, I wanted to discuss something with you."

Natalie glared at her monitor. No, she hadn't filed the report yet. She only hoped that whatever Molly wished to discuss wouldn't complicate her assessment of Kevin even more. "Sure," she said.

"I believe Alix ought to stay with her father. I wasn't sure if I was clear on that when we spoke earlier this week."

"You were," Natalie assured her.

"Well, I wanted to add something to what I said back then. I thought you ought to know that Kevin intends to take some Daddy School classes."

"Daddy School?"

"It's a program I run with a friend of mine. We give classes to fathers on how to improve their parenting skills. This morning he told me he plans to start attending."

"Do you think he needs classes in how to be a father?" Natalie asked, bewildered. How could this be helpful to Kevin's case? It sounded as if Kevin felt so insecure about his abilities as a father, he wanted to go back to school to learn how to raise Alix.

"I'm not saying he *needs* classes," Molly clarified, "but I think he'll enjoy them and benefit from them. The other fathers who attend Daddy School get a lot from it. We meet Saturday mornings at the Children's Garden, and the fathers bring their children with them. The children get to play, while the class discusses issues relevant to fatherhood. We might talk about discipline, or bedtime, or teaching children the value of money, or teaching them how to share. The fathers exchange ideas, and I offer suggestions from the perspective of a preschool professional."

Natalie opened her folder of notes and jotted *Daddy School* on the top page. It sounded like a useful program, but still… Wasn't Kevin a good enough father without having to take lessons?

Molly must have guessed what Natalie was thinking. "The thing about the Daddy School is, the fathers who sign up for the classes are the kind of men who want to go the extra mile for their children. They work all week long, and then on Saturday, instead of flopping down in front of the tube or hitting the golf course, they spend their mornings learning to be more effective parents. To me, that's an indication of their priorities. When Kevin Medina told me this morning that he planned to come to tomorrow's Daddy School class, I saw it as a really positive thing."

When Molly put it that way, Natalie saw it as a positive thing, too.

"Maybe," Molly added, "the real question is, do you think Alix's grandparents would take classes to make them better parents? Would they do that for Alix?"

Natalie tried to imagine it, and she couldn't. Molly was right: Kevin's willingness to take these classes tipped the scale even more in his favor. "Thank you for sharing this information," she said.

"We all want what's best for Alix," Molly reminded her. "Personally, I think what's best for her is to stay with her father."

"I appreciate the input," Natalie said, meaning it. If Molly had offered information that placed Kevin in a less favorable light, Natalie would have appreciated that, too—but perhaps not as much.

After thanking Molly again and saying goodbye, Natalie let out a long breath. Her gaze veered back to the monitor, and a deep worry gnawed at her gut. She ought to have been thrilled to receive more proof that Kevin was the better parent for Alix. She *was* thrilled. And that was the problem. Her being thrilled meant she'd lost her objectivity.

Thinking about it some more, she acknowledged that, in fact, she wasn't supposed to be objective. She was supposed to be completely biased toward Alix.

As far as she was concerned, the best thing for that darling little girl was to remain with her father, a man so devoted to his daughter that he was going to spend his Saturday mornings taking classes to become a better daddy. Biased or not, objective or not, that was what she was going to put in her report.

HE WASN'T SURE about this Daddy School stuff—but he'd be the first to admit he didn't know everything there was to know about being a father. His own father had been a great guy, yet he'd only had to be a father, not a mother, as well. And although Kevin didn't remember his own infancy, he'd be willing to bet his father had never changed a diaper in his life. He'd been more of the traditional-type dad, happy to throw a football around with Kevin, eager to teach him how to repair a window fan or change the oil in a car, but avoiding the touchy-feely stuff a hands-on father had to know.

And Kevin wasn't just a hands-on father; he was the hands-on father of a girl. His own father had doted on Kevin's sister, but he hadn't really known how to talk to her. When Kevin was fifteen, the old man had managed to mumble something to him about condoms, but he'd never even gotten that far with Kevin's sister. Their mother had taught her what she needed to know about her own body, and Kevin had taught her what she needed to know about boys.

The thought of having to sit down with Alix ten or twelve years from now and explain menstruation and birth control to her boggled Kevin's mind. Maybe by then his dream would have come true and he'd have found a good wife who could be a mother to Alix, someone who could help him teach his daughter the facts of life. Someone soft-spoken and fair-minded, someone willing to sing silly songs to her and build towers out of blocks with her…

In the meantime, he figured it wouldn't hurt to take some Daddy School classes.

The morning was misty with drizzle, and Alix wanted to stomp in all the puddles between their parking space and the front door of the Children's Garden. Kevin hustled her along, and she started to protest—until they got inside the building and she realized where they were. "Cool!" she bellowed, which Kevin understood to mean *school*. She sometimes dropped her *s*'s.

The children were all escorted upstairs to a spacious play area overseen by one of the preschool teachers, while Molly Saunders-Russo shepherded the eight fathers into a smaller area on the first floor. They had to sit on the carpet—the chairs were designed for toddlers, not full-grown men— and Molly embarked on a discussion about finding a balance between the inner child and the outer adult.

Kevin listened, more interested than he'd expected to be. He used to have an inner child—he recalled times as recently as two years ago when he'd believed a list of the top ten reasons for living would have to include softball and beer with buddies, midnight drives to the beaches along Connecticut's south shore, Jackie Chan movie marathons, eating ice cream directly from the container and good sex with a woman who was looking for nothing more than good sex with him. All those gloriously immature pleasures had left his life when Madeleine had told him she was pregnant. He'd instantly become a total adult, both inner and outer. And he'd been so busy loading up on responsibilities, he hadn't even stopped to think whether he missed the child who'd died inside him the moment his daughter had been conceived.

Until Molly had uttered the words *inner child* in this Daddy School class, he hadn't even thought about it.

"I'm not talking about selfishness," she explained to the eight fathers in the class. "Sometimes people act out in immature or selfish ways and justify their behavior by saying they're simply obeying their inner child. It doesn't work that way. The inner child is the part of you that experiences life in the playful, uninhibited way your children experience life. And when you listen to your inner child, it can help you to understand your children. They haven't internalized their 'inner child' yet. It's simply the way they relate to the world. When you tune into that sensibility, it can help you understand why your kid doesn't just want to make a big structure with blocks but also wants to knock the structure down. Why your child doesn't only want to paint a picture, but also wants to splash paint all over the table. Why your son wants to bang his fork in the mashed potatoes. Mashed potatoes are gooey and gloppy and fun to play with. How many of you remember the joy of splashing paint and playing with mashed potatoes? Any of you?"

A few brave souls raised their hands. Kevin tried to remember. He didn't think he had ever painted as a kid. He did like splashing water around, though. He used to splash so much water out of the tub during his baths that the kitchen ceiling directly below the bathroom had sprouted a water stain.

He listened, as Molly explained the importance not of indulging the inner child but of tuning in to him, listening to him, letting him guide the fathers in their attempts to understand their children. What she said made sense. He was doing a decent job of raising Alix, making sure she ate right and was clean and properly dressed, getting her to school and home on time, reading to her, singing to her when she was in a snit—but he'd never given much thought to how well he understood her. As she got older, he would want to understand more, and better. He didn't want her ever to think he wasn't the go-to guy with her problems. He didn't want her calling Grandma Porter if she needed to be understood.

The two hours of the class sped by. Despite the discomfort of sitting on the floor, he easily could have stayed another hour, absorbing Molly's words of wisdom. But the children trooped down the stairs, and the men all stood and stretched the cricks out of their necks and backs. Alix charged straight toward him, nearly knocking over a boy who had a good three inches and fifteen pounds on her, and leaped into Kevin's arms. "We play!" she reported. "We play games!"

"You played games upstairs?"

"Games!"

"That's great. Now it's time to go home."

"Home!"

Since she was already in his arms, he carried her down the hall to the front door, figuring that if he didn't put her down, they could avoid the puddle stomping on the way back to the car. Of course, if he tuned in to his inner child, he'd probably remember the joys of puddle stomping, too. But his inner child didn't have to run the laundry when Alix got muddy water all over her clothes. Laundry was just one more chore in his outer adult's overheated schedule.

In the parking lot, he spotted Natalie.

She was standing by his truck, just as she had the other day after she'd met with Molly. She hadn't met with Molly today, though. The preschool wasn't officially open, and Molly had been teaching Daddy School.

Natalie had come to see him.

He didn't know how he knew that—and in fact he could be completely wrong. It was just a whimsical thought, a hope. A groundless wish that Natalie Baines would have driven to Alix's preschool on a Saturday morning just to see him, not to evaluate or interrogate him but to give him a shy, hesitant smile like the one she was giving him now.

"Hi," he said as he approached her. Alix didn't suck her finger this time. She studied Natalie openly. Maybe she recognized her.

"Molly mentioned you would be attending this special class she gives," Natalie said. "She said it met here on Saturday mornings."

Then, she *had* come to check up on him, to do the evaluation and interrogation thing. He felt something deflate inside him, something that should never have inflated in the first place.

"Yeah, well…" He hoisted Alix a little higher in his arms. The drizzle glittered in her hair and dampened her cheeks, but the air was so warm that he didn't worry about her getting a chill. "It was interesting."

"I submitted my report yesterday," Natalie said. Her hair glistened, too, as if someone had woven diamonds through the strands. "The judge has it, the Porters' attorney—and the court informed me you've got new legal representation."

"Yeah. Molly's brother-in-law, actually."

"Dennis Murphy. I asked around. He's got an excellent reputation."

"Good." So Natalie had turned in her report. That meant she wasn't here to evaluate him. Maybe she'd stopped by because she and Molly had gotten to be friends or something. Maybe she'd been curious to see what a Daddy School class was like. Maybe—

"So unless I have to testify in court, which is unlikely, my work as Alix's guardian *ad litem* is complete."

Had she tracked him down here to tell him that? If so, was she going to tell him what the report recommended? He studied her face, as if he could read an answer in her radiant eyes and that tentative smile. The only answer he read was the first one he'd come up with: she'd come here to see him.

"You want to go someplace and get lunch?" he asked.

Alix erupted enthusiastically. "Lunch! Get lunch!"

Natalie grinned. "I'm with her. Let's get lunch."

TEN MINUTES LATER, she found herself seated across a table from Kevin and Alix at a local sandwich joint. Alix was strapped into a high chair, and Kevin had given her a collection of sugar and jam packets to play with. As long as she didn't open any of them, they'd be fine.

Natalie shouldn't be with them, but it was too late. She'd reread her report a dozen times yesterday, decided it was exactly what she would have written even if Kevin didn't have such stunning blue eyes, such broad shoulders, such a stubborn chin and such work-toughened fingers. He was a good father. There was no legitimate reason to remove his child from the home. The overwhelming wealth of his in-laws didn't justify their becoming Alix's guardians. However, in the report she recommended that Kevin allow the Porters to remain in their granddaughter's life. They had already lost a daughter. They shouldn't have to lose contact with their granddaughter, too.

But it was done. The report was filed. It was no longer an issue between her and Kevin.

The waitress served them quickly, no doubt aware of how profoundly a bored toddler could disrupt a restaurant. The peanut butter sandwich she brought for Alix was cut into small wedges, and the cup of milk had a lid on it, with a straw poking through.

After she presented Kevin and Natalie with their adult sandwiches—roast beef on rye for him, a turkey wrap for her—he thanked the waitress and sent her away. "Can I pay for this, or would I be charged with bribery if I did?"

"I think we're okay on that." She smiled.

He smiled back, obviously recognizing that they were operating under new rules now. The court and its rules no longer applied to them. These new rules were the rules of Thursday night, the rules of a man and a woman gazing at each other and feeling a pull as strong and fluid as the ocean's tide.

"You know a lot more about me than I know about you," he commented, after shooting a glance at Alix to make sure she was eating her sandwich. She was, more or less, although a significant portion of her peanut butter remained on her lips rather than in her mouth.

Natalie's amusement at Alix's messy face faded as she turned back to Kevin. She knew a lot more about him because she'd had to investigate him. Did he resent that? She couldn't tell from his voice.

The only way to address the imbalance was to share some of herself with him. "I'm a social worker," she said. "I grew up outside Hartford, went to college in Boston, got an MSW and landed a job here in Arlington."

"MSW?"

"A master's degree in social work." Did he mind that she had a postgraduate degree and he'd dropped out of college? *She* didn't mind. If she hadn't had a master's degree, she wouldn't have been named Alix's advocate and they never would have met.

"I've got two sisters, both older than me. I've got two

nephews and a niece, all under the age of three, which is how come I know songs like 'The Wheels on the Bus.'''

"Maybe you can teach me that song," he requested. "Alix sure likes it."

"Bus!" she chimed in, then sang, "Go up-n-down!"

"She's a great kid," Natalie said, smiling at Alix again, and then—because all that sticky goo smearing her lips looked uncomfortable—reaching across the table with her napkin and dabbing at Alix's mouth.

"Are you seeing anyone?" Kevin asked abruptly.

She almost dropped her napkin. The question so...blunt. It clarified for her that she hadn't misunderstood him when he'd brushed his fingers against her mouth, that he'd wanted to kiss her as much as she'd wanted to be kissed.

"No," she said quietly. "I'm not seeing anyone."

He smiled. A dazzling smile, shimmering with promise, with hope, with healthy male sexuality. He was a single parent, he was a Daddy School student, he was a business owner who worked damn hard. And he was...Kevin.

The smile he gave her was the smile of a man who knew what he wanted and had every intention of going after it.

CHAPTER SIX

AFTER LUNCH, Kevin suggested that they take a short walk to "burn Alix out," as he put it. The peanut butter sandwich and the special clown-shaped cookie the waitress had brought her had fueled her, and she squirmed and bounced with an excess of energy. Even though the air was still muggy enough to feel like a weight on her skin, Natalie had no objection to taking a stroll.

As they neared the corner, Kevin pointed out a small warehouse-shaped building across the street. It had three steel garage doors on its front facade. "That's my headquarters," Kevin told her.

"Where you work?"

He motioned with his head that she should follow him across the street. When they reached the building, he dug a key ring from the pocket of his jeans and inserted a key into a lock beside one of the garage doors. A motor hummed as the door slid open.

"It's not really where I work," he corrected her. "I work at people's houses. This is where I store our gear and take care of the paperwork."

She peered inside the dimly lit garage. The bays held a pickup truck and two flatbed trailers laden with industrial-size lawn mowers. Shovels, hoes and other gardening equipment lined the perimeter of the concrete floor and filled the rows of shelves on the walls.

"There's an office in back," he continued. "I've got an

office manager who works a few hours a day, returning phone messages, setting up appointments, overseeing the billing and accounts and stuff. Some lawn services operate out of the owner's house. I thought this would be more professional.''

Natalie understood that he wasn't showing off his business in the hope of persuading her to tilt her report toward him. It was too late for her to alter the report, and he knew it. He was sharing his place of business with her for a more personal reason—because he was justifiably proud of what he'd accomplished in a few short years.

Alix tugged at her father's hand and let out a whine. "Go home!"

"How about a *please?*" he hinted.

"Go home peeze!" she demanded, the courteous word undercut by her petulant tone.

"It's naptime," he informed Natalie as he bent down and scooped Alix into his arms. He straightened up and his gaze collided with Natalie's. "If you want..." he began, then hesitated.

Gazing into his eyes, she could think of plenty of things she wanted. "Yes?"

"You could follow us home. Once I get Alix down, maybe we could, I don't know, watch a video or something."

"I'd like that." She liked more than it. She liked his diffidence, and his confidence. She liked his straightforward approach.

Kevin didn't play games. He was frank. If she went to his house and he asked for something beyond watching a video, something she wasn't prepared to agree to, she would be just as frank. She had the feeling she could say no to Kevin without inflicting major damage on either of them.

And for the time being, she was happy she could say yes.

HE CHANGED Alix's diaper in the bathroom, chatting about the potty while he did so. Madeleine had bought the potty when Alix was a year old—way too soon to even consider training her, but Madeleine had hated changing diapers and wanted to push the process along. It had been pointless then, and it was still too soon now, according to Kevin's mother. But he saw no harm in keeping the potty in the bathroom and talking to Alix about it. Maybe one of these days, she'd express more than a passing interest in it.

Today wasn't the day. She was cranky and fretting, both tired and overstimulated by her morning at the preschool and her lunch at the diner. She tugged on her ear, whimpered, "No nap!" when she wasn't whimpering, "No potty!" and clung to his neck when he picked her up from the counter. Her face was warm and wet with tears, as he walked down the hall to her bedroom.

It was a horrible room, all pink and gilt. Madeleine had chosen the decor, and it reminded Kevin of a book he'd once read about Marie Antoinette. More to the point, it didn't seem to reflect Alix's taste. When he let her pick out her own outfits, she never went for the frilly stuff. She liked bright colors, simple styles.

Once they moved to the new house, he'd be buying her a bed and putting the crib in storage. He supposed that for the time being she could keep using the dresser Madeleine had picked out for her—glossy white with scrolly gold trim—and the lacy floral curtains. He'd keep his eye open for yard sales, though. Sometimes you could find a real bargain, especially with children's furniture. He'd buy Alix a good, classic, solidly built dresser and desk, pieces he could sand down and refinish for her.

She was still fussing when he lowered her into her crib. "No, no, no!" she wailed, struggling to hang on to him as he straightened up and pulled free of her grip. "No, Daddy! No nap!"

He handed her a teddy bear and massaged her little shoulders. That sometimes calmed her down. If he knew Natalie's song about the bus, he'd sing it for Alix. Instead, he sang an old Bruce Springsteen tune, "Atlantic City" because it was quiet and gentle and he knew most of the words.

Less than a minute after her last "no nap!" howl, she was sound asleep.

He tiptoed out of her bedroom, leaving the door cracked open. Inhaling deeply, he closed his eyes and pictured Natalie downstairs, waiting for him.

A ripple of anticipation slid down his spine. He felt sure of himself when it came to his daughter, but not when it came to Natalie. What was he supposed to do with her? She'd seemed interested in watching a video, but which one? His video collection tilted heavily toward Disney animated films. And while they watched, should he offer her a drink? A soft drink or something alcoholic? Should he sit next to her on the couch, or keep his distance?

He strode back down the hall to the bathroom to wash Alix's tears off his neck—and maybe run a comb through his hair and brush his teeth. He wasn't used to experiencing uncertainty around women. When Madeleine had started flirting with him two years ago, he hadn't stopped to consider that she was obscenely rich and about as pretty as the average fashion model. The attraction had been strong and mutual, and he'd responded without introspection or doubt. He'd always gotten along well with women, all kinds of women. If he was interested, he acted on that interest. If the woman was interested, too, great. If she wasn't, no hard feelings.

Natalie was interested. He might not have been socially active in the past couple of years, but he hadn't lost his ability to recognize a particular look, a particular body language. Natalie was as interested as he was—and he was as nervous as a schoolboy on his first date.

He wondered why. They'd been able to talk to each other just fine at lunch. She wasn't sitting in judgment of him, not anymore. She'd come to his house because she wanted to be here.

He left the bathroom and headed for the stairs. Whatever happened, happened. He would come out of it all right. So would she.

He found her standing in the family room, her back to him as she studied his CD collection. Dressed in crisp white shorts and short-sleeved blue sweater, she looked cool and comfortable despite the sweltering air outside. The shorts were knee length, but they offered a nice view of her calves and her rear end, round and inviting, emphasizing the narrow width of her waist.

Damn. He wanted her, wanted her in a much more adult way than any schoolboy on his first date.

"Hey," he said softly.

She spun around and smiled, and he wanted her even more. He wanted to plunge his fingers into her soft, pale hair and cover her mouth with his. It no longer mattered that she'd once been an agent of the court, invading his life to check up on his daughter. She wasn't that person now. She was just Natalie, with the most open, genuine smile he'd ever seen, the most intelligent eyes, and arms that could comfort a child or embrace a man.

"I see you like Diana Krall," she said, gesturing toward his CD rack. "So do I."

"She's got a real sexy voice," he said, then cringed inwardly. What he'd said was the truth, but he shouldn't have used the word *sexy,* not when he was standing alone in this room with a woman he desired so much.

Natalie's smile abandoned her mouth and moved upward, into her eyes. "I never thought about it that way, but I guess she does. Is Alix asleep?"

"Dead to the world." He crossed the room to stand beside her. "Would you like me to put on some music?"

"Sure."

He picked one of his Diana Krall CDs and inserted it into the player. After a moment, Krall's sultry voice filled the room.

He was standing close enough to Natalie that he could gather her into his arms if he dared. Close enough that he could pull her against him and dance through the room with her, avoiding Alix's scattered toys if he was careful.

But she was a social worker. Someone whose job it had been to evaluate him, to analyze him and write him up. Someone who might, in fact, have written to the court that he was not a good enough father to be allowed to keep his daughter. After all, how good a father could he be if he was thinking about seducing a woman in his family room while his daughter napped upstairs?

The hell with it. Natalie's report was already submitted. It was too late for him to worry about it now.

He lifted a hand to her hair and ran his fingers through it. It was softer and silkier than he'd imagined.

"Kevin—"

"I know," he murmured, not sure *what* he knew.

"It's just that…"

"I know." If she told him to back off, he'd do it in an instant. But she simply stood before him, gazing up at him, angling her head slightly into the curve of his palm. "One

kiss,'' he promised, setting a limit for himself, letting her
know he wasn't about to forget that daughter upstairs, let
alone the fact that he'd known Natalie only a week.

Her nod was so slight that it was almost imperceptible.
But if he didn't exactly see it, he felt it against his hand,
and that was all he needed.

He bowed his head and brushed her lips with his. Like
her hair, her lips were softer than he'd imagined. They
moved with his, against his, gently, shyly.

He recalled that evening a few days ago, in the bedroom
of his new house. That was where he wanted to be with
her, not here in this pretentious palace. It had always been
Madeleine's home, not his. It fit him as badly as a borrowed
suit.

He wanted to make love to Natalie in a world that belonged to him.

He couldn't stop kissing her, couldn't keep himself from
cupping his hand against her cheek and circling his other
arm around her waist, covering her mouth with his, tasting
her, nipping and licking and taking. She opened to him,
lifting her hands to his shoulders and allowing him to draw
her close. When he'd whispered that he knew, *this* was
what he'd been talking about. He knew that this kiss was
meant to be, this moment inevitable. He knew that there
were probably a few good reasons he and Natalie ought to
cool it, ought to be careful and take it easy—and he knew
that all those good reasons had been rendered meaningless
the instant his lips had touched hers.

He'd never enjoyed a kiss so much. He'd never felt so
moved. Not physically moved—sure, he'd love to run his
hands all over the beautiful curves of her body, he'd love
to fling her down on the couch and strip her naked and sink
into her—but moved on some deeper, more personal level.
Moved to believe he needed to touch not just her body but

her soul. Moved to believe he needed to tear himself open and let her see who he truly was.

It was the way he'd felt that first evening when she'd stopped by, taken his screeching daughter from him and sung the bus song. As wary of her as he'd been, he'd accepted her. He'd recognized a connection, something that made her fit into his world so easily, so naturally, he couldn't imagine her ever leaving it.

The intensity of the feeling frightened him. He'd never felt it before, not even with Madeleine. Not even when he'd stood in an overly ornate room at her parents' country club and let the Porters' dear friend, a Superior Court judge, pronounce him and Madeleine husband and wife.

He hadn't felt it then, but he felt it now with Natalie Baines.

Somewhere, far in the distance, he heard a sound. His telephone.

He inched back from her and watched as her eyes fluttered open. The phone rang again, and he suddenly remembered that if he didn't answer it quickly, the ringing would wake up Alix. Swallowing a curse—at having to stop kissing Natalie and at the possibility of Alix's nap being ruined—he hurried into the kitchen to answer.

It was his real estate broker. She'd called to update him on how the mortgage application of the couple who wanted to buy his house was coming along. He ought to care. He wanted to get out of this house and into the other house.

But more than that, he wanted to get out of this phone call and back into Natalie's arms.

After ten minutes, the broker wore herself out and said goodbye. He hung up the phone and turned to find Natalie in the doorway. Just the sight of her sent heat surging through his body. He'd promised her one kiss, and he was wondering how to go about breaking that promise.

"This isn't anything I expected," she said, a faint rasp in her voice.

He drew in a breath and braced himself. "What do you want to do about it?"

"Go a little slower, maybe?"

"Okay." At least she wasn't storming out and slamming the door behind her. A little slower he could handle.

"I mean... Your life is in a state of flux right now. You're about to move. You've got to resolve the custody dispute. Your wife died only a few months ago."

"My marriage died a long time before she did," he said quietly, then shut his mouth before any more words slipped out. He'd made a vow to himself not to speak ill of Madeleine. No matter how lousy their marriage had been, she was the mother of his daughter. He would never have wished on her the fate she'd met. "We'll go slower," he promised, then forced a smile because he really didn't want to go slower at all. "Are you still interested in watching a video?"

THEY VIEWED the first half of *Men In Black,* which Kevin predicted would be Alix's favorite movie in about eight years, when he would finally allow her to watch it. Then the child woke up with a shouted demand to be rescued from her crib. They spent the rest of the drizzly afternoon playing with Alix—tossing a Nerf ball around the room, building elaborate structures with her blocks, acting out assorted scenarios with her cast of stuffed animals.

Natalie found the activities exhausting but fun. Even more fun was watching Kevin play with his daughter. He gave the stuffed animals goofy falsetto voices and had them crack silly jokes. He tried to teach Alix how to throw the Nerf ball overhand. "You throw like a girl," he teased her.

"A girl!" she crowed. "Daddy girl!"

"You're Daddy's girl?" he translated. "I'll buy that."
He tossed her the ball again, then said to Natalie, "That
Daddy School class I went to today? It was all about tapping into your inner child so you can communicate better
with your kid." When Alix threw the ball back to him, in
a reasonable imitation of his overhand motion, he let out a
cheer. "Way to go, Alix!"

"You seem to have a very active inner child," Natalie
remarked.

"A loud one, you mean?"

"An enthusiastic one." And she adored him for it.

As the afternoon blurred into evening, he abandoned her
and Alix so he could rustle up some dinner. "You'll stay,
won't you," he half asked. The casualness of his invitation
made it more precious to Natalie. He was treating her as if
she belonged here, as if it were a foregone conclusion that
she would stay.

So she stayed. He prepared spaghetti and meat sauce and
a simple salad, and he opened a bottle of Italian table wine.
The three of them ate, two of them actually consuming their
food and the third alternately devouring a few strands of
pasta and then relocating a few strands to an inappropriate
place: the floor, the tray of her high chair, the top of her
head. When they weren't laughing at Alix, scolding her or
cleaning up her messes, they managed to talk—about Natalie's caseload of struggling families, about the sense of
satisfaction she felt at even the smallest signs of a client's
progress.

"Why did you choose that career?" he asked. "It must
get depressing sometimes."

"Human nature fascinates me," she explained. "I'm not
a saint, Kevin. I didn't go into the field to save the world.
Alix—stop that!" she interrupted herself as Alix draped a
limp piece of spaghetti across her nose.

Kevin plucked the spaghetti from Alix's sauce-covered fingers and chuckled. "So, you're not a saint?"

"Not by a long shot. Don't get me wrong—I love helping people. But success in a job like mine is measured incrementally. In the meantime, I get to study human beings up close, learn what makes them tick, figure out where their buttons are and how to push them. And then, when there *is* a success…it's the most exciting, gratifying thing."

He smiled. It was a friendly smile, a comprehending smile—and yet something in it, a dark, seductive shimmer, reminded her that perhaps there were other equally exciting, gratifying experiences awaiting her. Experiences with Kevin.

Damn, but she didn't want to slow down with him. She'd been attracted to him from the moment she'd first seen him, and that attraction had expanded, broadening and deepening with each breath she took. Maybe it was crazy—but what in this life wasn't crazy? It was crazy for a pair of wealthy in-laws to think they could win custody of his daughter. It was crazy for her to spend so much of her life seeking glimmers of hope in hopeless situations, and to work so hard for such a pathetically small income. It was crazy for Alix to be wearing a splotch of spaghetti sauce on her dimpled knee.

It was crazy for her to help Kevin clear the table and stack the plates in the dishwasher, crazy for her to offer to help him with Alix's bath, crazy for her still to be in his house once he'd settled his daughter down for the night. Crazy for her to be standing in the hallway, as he turned on Alix's night-light, closed the bedroom door and stopped beside her.

"This was good," he murmured, his eyes a soft, summery blue as he gazed down into her upturned face. "Today, I mean. Everything about it. It was one of the best days of my life."

"Mine, too," she admitted. Crazy, but true.

"I hate to say this..." He brushed a knuckle along the edge of her jaw, so lightly that she was amazed at the fierce flush of warmth his touch sent through her. "But I think you should probably leave."

She frowned in surprise. Hadn't he just said this was one of the best days of his life? Why did he want it to end?

"Because if you don't," he explained, leaning down to graze her forehead with a kiss, "I'm not going to be able to go slower."

She understood, then. She understood that he was giving her a choice.

She *did* think they should slow things down. She wasn't impulsive, foolish, careless with her emotions. It would be crazy for her to stay.

Yet when she thought about it, staying seemed like the only sane thing to do.

She rose up on tiptoe, cupped her hands around his cheeks and pulled his mouth down to hers.

CHAPTER SEVEN

THE SUN WAS BRIGHT Monday morning and the ground had dried after its weekend soaking, as Kevin and his crew made their rounds through a north side neighborhood. He watched one of the college kids he'd hired for the summer riding the back of a mower like a chariot driver, his body erect as he steered the broad blades across a half acre of front lawn. The kid had stripped off his shirt. Kevin used to work shirtless sometimes, too. Perhaps if he'd kept his shirt on, Madeleine wouldn't have sidled up to him one fateful June day, offered him a glass of iced tea and stroked her fingertips across his chest in a deliberate tease.

These days, he kept his shirt on.

Leaning into the cab of his truck, he reached for the cell phone and punched in his office number to collect messages. One was from a persnickety customer who found one or two grass clippings on her driveway every week and made a big deal out of this horrendous lapse. Another was from a sales rep for an advertising circular, wanting to know if Kevin was planning to continue running his ads into August. The third was from his new lawyer, Dennis Murphy, asking him to call back.

He climbed into the truck and shut the door so he wouldn't have to compete with the raucous drone of the mower engine. Then he pulled Murphy's business card from his wallet and punched in the number. He had to talk his way past two secretaries before he reached the man. No wonder the guy charged so much—all those support-staff salaries he had to pay.

"Hi, Kevin," Murphy greeted him. "I wanted to let you know that we received a copy of the report from the guardian *ad litem.*"

Natalie. Kevin closed his eyes for a minute and let a heated memory sweep through him. A memory of the Saturday night he'd spent with her, of her smooth, soft, honey-toned skin, her breasts so sensitive to every caress, every kiss, the way her body had arched, the way she'd taken him so deep inside her, the way she'd clutched his shoulders and bit her lip and moaned when she'd come, and all he'd been able to think of was making her come again.

He'd gone a long time without sex. Months before Madeleine had died, their bed had become unfriendly territory. They'd been great together before Alix was born, but then resentment had turned Madeleine from him. She'd decided, belatedly, that she hadn't wanted to marry him, that she couldn't bear to spend her life as the wife of a man who refused to spend money he didn't have on her expensive whims. She was used to getting everything she wanted, and Kevin hadn't been willing to play that game with her. So she'd slammed the door on him.

But it wasn't the fact that he'd been celibate so long that made sex with Natalie spectacular. It was that she was Natalie, a woman who cared about him, who meshed with him, who appreciated his fierce devotion to his daughter, who understood and respected him.

"Are you still there?" Murphy's voice threaded through the phone.

"Yeah," Kevin said, shaking his head clear. Her report. That was why Murphy had called.

Kevin almost didn't want to hear about it. He just wanted

to think of Natalie as Natalie, a woman, a lover. Not a legal advocate for Alix.

"It's just what we need," Murphy said. "I think it's going to get rid of this custody case for us without our even going to court."

Kevin's shoulders slumped as a tension he hadn't acknowledged drained from his body. "Great," he said, suffering a twinge of guilt that his relief was based on more than the custody situation. If Natalie had loved him personally but written negatively about him in her report, he wasn't sure how he would have handled it.

"When you've got a free moment, you might want to stop by and give the report a look. I've got meetings today until about three in the afternoon, but after that I'll be in my office."

"Okay. I'll be there sometime after three." He said goodbye, turned off the cell phone and sank back against the seat, grinning. Natalie had written a report proclaiming that in her professional judgment he was the best parent for Alix. Thank God. Thank Natalie.

His smile faded slightly as he entertained the possibility that maybe she didn't think he was the best parent. Maybe she'd only supported him in the report because she liked him, or because she was attracted to him. Maybe she'd written it as a personal favor to him, and her professional judgment had nothing to do with it.

It didn't matter why she'd written what she had, he told himself. All that mattered was that he was going to keep Alix, and the Porters were going to take their money and their condescension and butt out of his life.

He inhaled, let his breath out slowly and shoved open the door. He had lawns to mow and edge, trees to prune and weed killer to spread. He could obsess about the report later.

He wasn't going to stop obsessing about Natalie, though. He knew she'd be with him all day, hijacking his memory, haunting his mind. The heat of the sun sliding over his back reminded him of her hands, warming his skin with their touch. The scent of summer flowers and warm, damp earth reminded him of her fragrance, sweet and earthy. The brilliant light reminded him of the way her eyes glowed when she smiled.

Somehow, he made it through the day without his crew realizing how distracted he was. By three-fifteen, only one house was left on the schedule. Kevin told the guys to take care of it, and he drove back to headquarters to unhitch his trailer and wash up. Once he was presentable, he cruised through town to Murphy's upscale office.

The receptionist buzzed Murphy to announce Kevin's arrival, then led Kevin down a hall. His work boots left elaborate tread marks in the plush carpeting. He imagined that most of the clients who trod this hallway wore leather-soled loafers, the sort of expensive footwear favored by people who could afford what Murphy usually charged for his services. Kevin wasn't a charity case, but he knew Murphy was giving him a price break. *I live with Molly's sister,* he'd explained with a grin. *If those powerhouse Saunders women tell me to charge you a discount rate, I'm sure not going to fight with them about it.*

Murphy was lounging on the large leather sofa in his office, his feet kicked up on the coffee table, when Kevin was ushered in. He put down the stack of papers he'd been perusing, rose from the couch and shook Kevin's hand. "Here we go," he said, crossing to his desk and lifting a document. "Give it a look and tell me what you think."

Kevin settled into a chair and began reading. The report went on for several pages, describing Kevin's lifestyle, his work situation, the hours he kept and his child care arrange-

ments. It evaluated the quality of the Children's Garden
Preschool. It mentioned the Porters' affluence, their grief
over the loss of their daughter and their love for their granddaughter. But the next paragraphs floored him.

There is no question that the Porters could offer Alix
more in terms of material benefits. However, the
courts are not in the business of awarding custody to
the adults who can supply the most toys. The real issue
is that Kevin Medina is a diligent, disciplined, deeply
affectionate father who has been providing his daughter with superb parenting since infancy. Alix is a well-
adjusted child who is obviously strongly attached to
her father. To separate them would be a travesty, and
I strongly urge the court to let Alix remain with her
father.

I would also urge the father to facilitate a relationship between the Porters and Alix. They are her grandparents, her familial connection to her deceased
mother, and as such they should maintain a central
place in her life.

He nearly crumpled the paper. A central place in Alix's
life? The Porters viewed him as trash! They'd requested
custody of Alix only because they despised him so much.

And he was supposed to "facilitate" their relationship
with Alix?

Like hell.

"What's the matter?" Murphy asked.

Kevin set the paper down on Murphy's desk, barely controlling his yearning to toss it to the floor and grind his heel
into it. "I don't want the Porters to be central in Alix's
life."

Murphy nodded sympathetically. "That's just the guardian's recommendation. The court isn't likely to enforce it."

"They aren't going to grant—what's it called? Visitation rights?"

"Doubtful that they'll bother with anything enforceable. But if we get as far as standing before a judge, he'll probably recommend something along the lines of regular visitation. Once you've got custody, it'll be your call how often your daughter gets to see her grandparents."

"I don't want her seeing them at all," Kevin muttered. "They're malicious. The fact that they even started this whole custody thing proves they have no respect for me, no trust in me. They've hated me from the start, tried to break Madeleine and me up—and pretty well succeeded."

"On the other hand, they're your daughter's grandparents," Murphy observed. "Grandparents' rights is a movement these days. If you keep them from having any access to Alix, they could haul you back into court. They might not win, but it's an expensive, exhausting process. You know that. You don't want to drag this thing out."

"They wanted Madeleine to have an abortion." Rage welled up inside Kevin as he remembered. "They didn't even want Alix to be born. And now they want to take her away from me. And I'm supposed to be nice and let them visit her?"

"They're her grandparents," Murphy repeated, his voice quiet but forceful. "They're her mother's parents. There's a connection there. Do you want to deny your daughter that connection? How would you explain it to her, years from now, when she asks how come you never let her get to know her grandparents? 'They hated me, so I kept you from them'? That won't cut it, Kevin. Not for her."

What Murphy said made sense. Kevin resented the words, but he couldn't deny the truth in them. He'd have no qualms about denying the Porters access to their grand-daughter. But denying Alix access to her grandparents wasn't fair.

Perhaps he could find it in himself to be bigger than the Porters, kinder, more generous. If he had to, he could arrange to let Alix visit with them—only, he'd stick around for the duration of the visit so they couldn't undermine him behind his back. He'd dealt with worse in his life; he could deal with this.

His anger shifted, taking on a new form, and a new target. He realized the Porters weren't the ones twisting his innards with rage. Natalie was.

How could she have forced the Porters down his throat? How could she say they were in any way deserving of time with his precious daughter? How could she have taken their side, even if only on this issue?

How could she have betrayed him?

NATALIE HAD JUST CONCLUDED an hour-long counseling session with one of her clients, a single mother of two who'd recently left the welfare rolls but was still a little shaky about her ability to hold her small family together. Natalie had reviewed her client's budget for the week, given her a pep talk and sent her on her way. Her phone rang as she finished writing up her notes on the session.

"There's someone here to see you," Sandy out at the front desk reported. "He doesn't have an appointment. He says his name is Kevin Medina."

A lovesick grin spread across Natalie's face at the mere sound of his name. *Kevin.* Oh, God. She had it bad.

"Send him in," she said, not caring that a mountain of paperwork remained on her desk awaiting her attention. Kevin had come to see her. Maybe he couldn't wait until after work hours. Maybe he had it as bad as she did.

She closed the folder in front of her, clicked her pen shut and glanced up as Kevin swung through her open door. Her smile froze, then splintered as she read the fury contorting his handsome features.

"Kevin?" She wasn't sure whether to rise, circle her desk and embrace him. Something awful must have happened, and she wanted to comfort him. But not when he appeared poised to lash out at anyone who got too close. She hadn't realized he had a temper; she'd never seen any evidence of one until now.

"Your report," he growled. "That custody report—how could you write that?"

Her report? She fell back in her chair, utterly confused. Her report was so strongly favorable toward him, she'd been afraid the court might view it as too subjective. Why on earth was he steaming about it?

"The report supports your custody claim, Kevin. I'm not sure what's got you so upset—"

"You said the Porters should be allowed to visit Alix."

All right. He was angry with the Porters, not with her. And why shouldn't he be angry with them, since they'd hired an expensive lawyer with the aim of convincing the court to take his child away from him?

But they were Alix's grandparents. Natalie had mentioned them in the report only so Kevin wouldn't allow his justifiable anger to block a relationship between Alix and the Porters.

"I think they *should* be allowed to visit her," she said as placidly as she could. If she could get him to cool off, surely she'd be able to explain her reasoning.

"They're nasty," he retorted. "They're greedy. They're horrible. They think they can control people with their money. They're bigots. They think I'm beneath them because I'm not rich. They've always treated me like a ser-

vant. They tried to steal my daughter from me because they
think I'm worthless.''

"You're not worthless, Kevin. Surely you know that.''

"*I* know it. They don't.''

"Well, once the court assigns you permanent full custody of Alix, they'll figure it out.''

"Natalie.'' He stormed to her desk and leaned across it,
his fists planted on the paper-strewn surface. "They call
me the 'lawn boy.' They always have. To my face. Even
after I married their daughter. *The lawn boy.*''

She checked the impulse to answer him logically, to
point out, yet again, that a young girl who lost her mother
should not lose her mother's parents, too; that although
grandparents didn't have legal rights, they had certain social and moral rights, which Natalie had chosen to acknowledge in her report; that ultimately it would be better for
Kevin if he allowed his daughter to maintain some ties with
her mother's family. If he didn't, if he cut her off from the
Porters, she might lose more than he would gain. And if
she lost, he would lose, as well.

She could see that he didn't want to hear what she had
to say. The rage burning in his eyes flared with pain. His
in-laws had belittled him, debased him. All the logic in the
world couldn't undo the disrespect they'd shown him and
the hurt they'd caused him.

"They're a part of your daughter's life,'' she said gently.

"I don't want them to be.''

"But they are. You can't change that, Kevin. By hon-
oring it, you become a better father to Alix.''

"That,'' he said, his jaw so tense he could barely form
the words, "is a load of crap. I trusted you, Natalie. I
thought you knew what kind of man I am. I didn't think
you'd get suckered in by all their wealth and their fancy
manners.''

"I didn't get suckered in by anything, Kevin! I expressed what I believe to be Alix's best interests. That was my job, and that's what I did." She wanted to cover his fist with her hand, to stroke the violence out of it. She wanted to remind him of the love they'd shared over the weekend, the closeness, the understanding. She'd never responded so strongly to a man before, so totally. *She* respected him.

In fact, she respected him so much that it had never occurred to her that he wouldn't be able to get past his own resentment and act in Alix's best interests. If he had Alix's best interests at heart the way Natalie did, he'd recognize what a mistake it would be to cut the child off from her grandparents.

"When you calm down, Kevin, I think you'll realize I'm right about this," she said.

He pushed away from the desk and started toward the door. "I don't think I'll ever calm down," he said, then stalked out the door, out of Natalie's sight, out of her life.

CHAPTER EIGHT

NATALIE RESISTED the urge to cry. She'd confronted many difficult cases in the three years she'd been a social worker, and she'd learned not to dissolve into tears over them. It wasn't that she'd developed a hard heart; it was that she'd learned she couldn't be effective if she fell apart.

But this was different. Kevin's case was going to turn out well. He was going to get what he wanted: full, uncontested custody of his daughter. Natalie had contributed to that positive outcome. She'd done what she could to make it happen.

Yet she wanted to weep for a perfectly selfish reason. Thanks to her report, Kevin hated her.

She hadn't known the Porters had treated him with such disdain. But even if she had—well, maybe she would have phrased that passage of her report a little differently, or counseled the Porters on the importance of building a better relationship with their son-in-law. She still would have advocated that Kevin allow them access to Alix, because Natalie's job was to represent Alix, and it would be best for Alix to have a relationship with her maternal grandparents.

But now Kevin hated Natalie. He thought she'd somehow allied herself with the Porters. His reaction wasn't logical, but it was real.

She couldn't change her report for him. Even if she could, she wouldn't. She'd struggled to maintain her objectivity, and the report she'd written reflected that objectivity. If Kevin had the tiniest shred of objectivity, he would acknowledge that her report was correct.

Tears threatened. She sighed deeply several times, and blinked her eyes dry. She told herself she couldn't possibly love him. Just because he was strong and resolute, just because he was profoundly devoted to his daughter, just because he refused to speak ill of his late wife even though their marriage had obviously been a disaster... Just because he could be both funny and serious, both modest and proud, both forceful and tender... Just because making love with him had felt like coming home, becoming whole, discovering some essential truth about herself and the world and the power of love....

Damn it, she *did* love him. And the only way she could think of to win his love was to do something she simply refused to do: change her report.

A fresh supply of tears filled her eyes, and all the deep breathing in the world couldn't keep them from falling.

HE WAS IN A SOUR MOOD when he delivered Alix to the Children's Garden the following morning.

He should have been ecstatic. His lawyer, Dennis Murphy, had telephoned him at home the previous evening to say that after reading Natalie's report, the Porters' lawyer had contacted him to say they were withdrawing their custody bid. They wanted to meet to work out a visitation plan, but Murphy assured Kevin that there was no great rush to set up a schedule. "Right now, break open the champagne. You can work out the details when you're done celebrating. I'll be in touch once all the paperwork is filed with the court."

Kevin hadn't broken open the champagne. He'd sat in the den, nursing a beer and watching Alix play with her blocks. Every now and then she'd burst into a verse of the bus song: "Up-n-down!" she'd sing, and, "Wee dondy bus go roun-roun-roun!"

He wished he'd never heard that song. He wished Natalie had never taken his fussy baby from his arms and sung to her. He wished she'd never entered his house, entered his life, written her goddamn report.

The report that had won him full custody of his daughter.

He knew he wasn't being rational. But the Porters…how could he be rational about them? They were despicable. And Natalie had written that they should maintain a "central place" in Alix's life.

He had another beer after he put Alix to bed. Two beers weren't enough to get him drunk, but he awakened the next morning with a throbbing headache. He hadn't slept well. Lying in bed alone made him remember what lying in bed with Natalie had been like.

Natalie, who had betrayed him, who had taken their side.

"What's wrong?" Molly Saunders-Russo asked, as he slid Alix's lunch box onto the shelf of her cubby.

"Nothing. I've got to go now, Alix—"

"No go, Daddy," Alix said without much conviction. She was already drifting down the hall to join her classmates. Instead of clinging to him, she abandoned him.

"No separation anxiety. I think she's finally adjusting to school," Molly said, smiling in approval.

Either Alix had adjusted or she was tired of her father's gloomy company. He'd barely talked during breakfast, and his sullenness had darkened the atmosphere in the truck cab on the drive over to the school. He couldn't blame his baby for wanting to get away from him.

"So, what's wrong?" Molly asked again.

"Nothing."

"A problem with your court case?"

"As a matter of fact, no. We won without going to court."

"I told you Murphy was your man," she said, beaming at the supposed prowess of her brother-in-law.

But Murphy really hadn't done much. What had decided the case was Natalie's report.

"You ought to be happy," Molly chided.

"You're right. I ought to be. It's just that they're saying—Murphy and Natalie both—they're saying I've got to keep the Porters in Alix's life."

"Of course," Molly said, as plainly as if she were agreeing with a claim that water was wet.

"You think the Porters should be in her life?" he asked.

"They're her grandparents."

"They're jerks."

"They want to give Alix their love," Molly pointed out. "A child can never get too much love, Kevin."

"Yeah, but…" He let out a long breath. Standing in the building's entry in his faded jeans and scuffed work boots, he felt like what he was: a blue-collar laborer. Simple, unglamorous, no dash, no flash. The exact opposite of the Porters. "What if they tell Alix I'm a working-class nothing?"

Molly peered up at him, her eyes round with astonishment. "You're her father. You'd tell her they were wrong."

"What if she didn't believe me? What if she believed them?"

"*You're* her father. *You're* the one who gets to teach her values. We talk a lot about teaching values in the Daddy School, because daddies are so important when it comes to giving their children strong moral underpinnings. That's your job, Kevin, and as far as I can see, you're doing fine. Why would you ever think your in-laws could undermine all the wonderful values you've been teaching your daughter?''

He hadn't considered it that way before. And when he did, he stumbled onto an answer he didn't like: he was insecure. He believed, in some dark corner of his mind, that the Porters' wealth might be enough to turn his daughter against him.

"Have a little faith in yourself, Kevin," Molly advised. "If Natalie Baines said she thought the Porters should remain in Alix's life, it must be because she knows the Porters pose no threat to your relationship with Alix. She knows that nothing can come between you and your daughter. Not even the Porters and all their money."

"Maybe," he murmured, nodding his thanks and heading out the door. He didn't break stride until he reached his truck. Gripping the door handle, he paused.

Have a little faith in yourself, Molly had said.

She was right. Natalie had more faith in him than he had in himself. She knew just how tightly bound he and Alix were—too tightly bound for a couple of arrogant rich folks to get between them. Natalie knew that letting Alix spend some time with her grandparents every now and then couldn't possibly undercut her love for her father.

She had that much faith in him.

He yanked open the door and climbed in behind the wheel. Revving the engine, he reached for his cell phone and punched in the office number. "I'm going to be a little late," he said to his office manager. "We've got the Garden Street neighborhood on the schedule this morning. I'll meet the crew there as soon as I can." He disconnected and steered out of the parking lot.

Natalie's office was less than ten minutes from the preschool, even with morning rush-hour traffic clogging the roads. He found a parking space and searched the employee lot until he spotted her car. Drawing in a deep breath for courage, he squared his shoulders and sauntered into the building.

"Is Natalie Baines in?" he asked the receptionist.

The woman must have recognized him from yesterday. She smiled inquisitively. "I doubt she's in her office. She usually makes the first pot of coffee in the lounge. If you want to wait a minute—"

"I don't," Kevin said, pushing past the reception desk in search of a lounge with a coffeemaker. He easily found the room, a short walk down the hall from the entry. The room held a few chairs with patched and taped upholstery, a sagging couch, a round Formica table surrounded by molded plastic chairs, a wall of bookshelves, a refrigerator, a sink and a coffeemaker.

And Natalie.

Her back was to him. She'd pulled her hair into a loose ponytail that fell in soft waves below the collar of her dress. Her legs were strong and tanned, and he remembered the way they'd felt wrapped around him, the way her arms had felt, the way her body had felt. Longing overwhelmed him.

Her hands moved with deft precision, scooping ground coffee into the basket. She filled the decanter with water, emptied it into the well of the coffee machine and punched a button. Then she turned around, saw him and let out a gasp.

"I'm sorry," he said.

"That's all right—you didn't scare me," she murmured. Her cheeks were the pink of new roses, her lips pursed in surprise. Her eyes shimmered with uncertainty.

"I'm apologizing for yesterday," he said. Some men had trouble apologizing, but Kevin didn't. When he did something wrong, he admitted it. He'd done something seriously wrong yesterday: he'd doubted her. He'd accused her of

siding with the Porters over him, when all she'd ever done
was side with Alix.

She drew in a tight breath and let it out. "All right."

But it wasn't all right. Her eyes didn't change. They still
looked skeptical, hesitant, a little teary.

"You were right about the Porters. They are Alix's
grandparents. Nothing's going to change that."

A little of the skepticism faded from her face.

"And I—I was reading my own situation with them into
it. It's not just about me and them. It's about Alix and them,
and Alix and me. She's at the heart of it."

"Yes."

"And so...I'm sorry."

"I'm sorry, too," she said.

He stepped into the lounge. The freshly brewed coffee
smelled enticing, but he wanted to smell her—that sweet,
womanly fragrance he'd fallen in love with. "You don't
have anything to be sorry for," he said.

"Yes, I do. I didn't know the Porters had treated you so
shabbily. I'd like to discuss that with them before visitation
arrangements are made. They need to know that they
shouldn't put you down. Not to your face, not behind your
back—and definitely not to Alix."

"It's okay. I can handle it."

"I'm a social worker, Kevin. I work with families. Let
me help smooth the way. I wish you had told me how bad
things were between you and the Porters. I could have es-
tablished some ground rules before writing my report."

"I didn't want to bad-mouth them," he said. "I thought
it would make me look spiteful."

"I would never describe you as spiteful."

He moved closer to her, close enough that if he lifted
his hand he could touch her. "I was scared of losing my
daughter," he confessed. "I guess that's a fear all parents

have. But I have a little less of it, thanks to you.'' He found the nerve to gather one of her hands in both of his. He ran his fingers over the soft, silky skin. Her hands were so graceful, so slender, so unlike his. ''Can you forgive me for acting like an ass yesterday?''

''Oh, I think I can manage that.''

He heard the hint of humor in her voice. Lifting his gaze from her hand to her face, he saw laughter in her eyes, and love. ''I need you to keep me from being scared.''

''I can do that, too,'' she said, her face serious now. Her words were a solemn promise.

He pulled her into his arms and kissed her. Her kiss gave him the faith he needed, the fearlessness, the strength to confront all the challenges that might rise before him.

Love meant risk, he realized. Because he loved his daughter, he would risk letting her know her grandparents. And because he loved Natalie, he would risk letting her see his fear.

''You are the bravest man I've ever known,'' she whispered.

''No,'' he said. ''But I love you, and that makes me braver.''

''Then just keep loving me.'' She smiled and kissed him again. And he understood that loving her was the wisest thing to do.

Home, Hearth and Haley
Muriel Jensen

To Ben and Jerry,
who enhance my victories and soften my defeats

Dear Reader,

I love Massachusetts. I spent the first ten years of my life in New Bedford on the southern coast, where most of my family still live. My younger sister, though, lives in Agawam, in western Massachusetts, the setting for the fictitious Maple Hill.

I'm honored that *Home, Hearth and Haley* is helping to celebrate Superromance's 1000th book. When I was a young woman with a full-time job and all the demands of being a wife and mother, reading romance got me through the rough spots.

Now that my life is more wonderful than anyone deserves, I hope my books help maintain all the wives and mothers out there who do the biggest job of all—love!

This novella launches the beginning of my MEN OF MAPLE HILL series. Imagine a Colonial town square, church spires, maple leaves…apples and woodsmoke on the wind. Then think about strong men and wonderful women on a collision course with destiny—and romance!

See you in Maple Hill.

Muriel

CHAPTER ONE

"THE THINGS I DO," Bart Megrath muttered as he drove into Maple Hill, Massachusetts, a place he'd never been, to help people he'd never met. A wide rustic sign carved in the shape of a tall maple in full red and gold fall dress welcomed him to Maple Hill, Population 4,012. Founded 1702.

The little valley town in western Massachusetts looked as though three hundred years hadn't touched it. As the sun went down on the hot and windy August day, he passed colonial homes set back on green lawns, a picturesque old barn that housed an antiques shop, an inn that, judging by its name, the Old Post Road Inn, had once been a stop on the old post road. A horse and buggy stood in the parking lot next to a Mercedes.

Downtown, the road narrowed and the houses were closer to the street. Lantern streetlights enhanced the colonial atmosphere, as did the flower wreaths on the doors and the candles in the windows.

He winced a little, thinking that the place was a little over-the-top cozy, then pulled up to a stop sign at the end of the street. He found himself facing a genuine old town square, complete with a bronze statue of a minuteman and a woman in eighteenth-century dress in the middle of the green.

A low stone wall surrounded the common, and all the shops on the streets that faced the square probably dated back to the early 1700s, or had been built to appear as though they did. A fifty-star American flag and an old colonial flag with thirteen stars in a circle flew from a pole.

Bart sat and stared for a moment, certain he could hear a fife and drum.

Then the driver behind him honked his horn, and Bart came back to reality. He turned right according to the directions given to him, and looked for the Maple Hill Police Station.

He was here for Hank Whitcomb, a client of his. Because Hank was also a friend, Bart had flown more than fifteen hundred miles from his home in Cocoa Beach, Florida, detoured inland to avoid the hurricane pounding the Florida coast, then driven to Maple Hill from the airport in Albany, New York. And he'd done all this to rescue Hank's sister.

"I *want* to go myself," Hank had told Bart worriedly just that morning, "but we've got seven astronauts on their way home, trying to deal with a mechanical problem that's only temporarily fixed. And now we've got a hurricane happening and I have to divert the shuttle to Southern California! It's not like I can just walk away from that—even for my family."

Hank was the project director for the NASA mission and Bart knew his friend had barely slept in fifty-six hours. For the past three days, the shuttle's mechanical problem had dominated the news. Getting the astronauts home safely was paramount.

"I'll take care of the family emergency for you," Bart had reassured him. They were standing in a hallway outside Mission Control. "I've already booked the flight, and I called your mom just as you asked, to tell her I was coming. I just need a little more information. Why was your sister arrested?"

"For assaulting the mayor." Hank closed his eyes and

shook his head. "It happened during a demonstration in front of City Hall."

"*Did* she assault him?"

"He wasn't assaulted—he tripped. And my mother says it wasn't Haley's fault. Unfortunately, the mayor broke his nose.

"Haley publishes the newspaper, and she's on City Hall's case all the time. She suspects the mayor is crooked but so far hasn't been able to prove it. She's caused him enough grief, though, that everyone else was freed after the demonstration but her, and she's been charged with assault."

"Who was demonstrating and why?"

Hank sighed again and ran a hand over his face. "The Revolutionary Dames, a group my mother belongs to, and a few other concerned citizens. Apparently, Maple Hill got federal money to build a shelter for the homeless, but it's been months and so far nothing's happened. The mayor says they're waiting for the go-ahead from an architectural review board, but Haley thinks something else is going on."

Bart groaned silently. In his experience as a criminal lawyer, activists were always trouble. They were idealists in a world that refused to accommodate them. And those who tried to defend them usually lost.

But Hank was his friend. Had sat with him for days after Bart's wife, Marianne, and their unborn twin boys had died in the crash of a light plane taking her to visit her sister in Texas. He'd propped Bart up at the funeral and wept with him, then three weeks later, dragged him out of the house for a cup of coffee, when all Bart had wanted was to be alone and die himself.

Hank had kept on him day after day, meeting him for lunch, inviting him for dinner, sending him clients so that he was forced to realize he still had a life to live. Somehow, Bart had gotten through.

Now he spotted the police station at the far end of the green. It was a square brick building, with columns in front topped by globe lights. He pulled into a parking spot behind a black-and-white, right in front of the station.

The desk sergeant was pleasant and cooperative, but Haley Whitcomb's bail was excessively high for her "crime." Vengeance was probably at work here.

Bart knew, however, that this was no time to take a stand for justice. To ease Hank's mind, he'd promised to do the expedient thing and simply get her out.

He started to write a check.

"That alone won't do it, Mr. Megrath," the sergeant said with a regretful shake of his head.

Bart looked up from his checkbook. "What will, Sergeant?"

"One of the conditions of her release," the man said, "is that she apologize to the mayor."

Bart glanced at the clock. It was just before nine p.m. "Can we call him at this hour?"

The sergeant shrugged. "Wouldn't do much good. Haley's refused to apologize."

Bart would see about that. "If I can convince her that she should," he asked, "can we find the mayor?"

"He's at a town hall meeting." The sergeant reached for the phone. "But I'll see what I can do. Brody?" He beckoned to another officer, who sat at a small table bearing a coffeepot and a box of pastries. "This is Bart Megrath, Haley's attorney. Mr. Megrath, Officer Brody. Would you take him to see her?"

"Sure." Brody grinned at Bart over his shoulder as they were buzzed through a door. "Wearing your Kevlar, Mr. Megrath? Had your shots?"

Bart smiled politely at the attempt at humor and followed the officer intrepidly to a cell at the far end of a dimly lit corridor.

"Your attorney's here, Haley," Brody said, then unlocked the door and stepped aside to let Bart in. "Shout if you need me," the officer said quietly to Bart. "Her last attorney left on a stretcher."

A young woman in jeans and a pale-blue cotton shirt several sizes too large for her stood in the middle of the room, her arms folded, dark hair caught in a braid that fell to her shoulder blades. Her eyes were the color of strong coffee. Her pink-cheeked face appeared surprisingly serene, considering her circumstances.

"I don't have an attorney," she said, maintaining her stance in the middle of the cell.

"Hank sent me," he said, offering his hand. "I'm Bart Megrath."

Her defiance softened instantly. "How is he?" she asked as she shook his hand. "Mom called him, didn't she? I asked her not to because I heard about the astronauts. He must be so frantic."

"Actually, they're on their way home, but because of the weather, they're being diverted to Southern California." He sat on a bunk and she took the one opposite. He saw glimpses of Hank in the directness of her gaze and the honesty of her smile. Hank, though, was high energy, whereas she behaved almost as if she were at prayer. "But I'm here to talk about you."

She looked him over critically and seemed to find him disappointing. He couldn't help being annoyed.

"Thank you," she said with regal control, "but there's nothing you can do for me. My bail is very high, and the conditions of my release are impossible."

He swallowed his annoyance, happy to argue with her

assessment of the situation. "Your bail's been paid," he countered, "and I wouldn't call a simple apology 'impossible.'"

She frowned. "Who paid my bail?"

"I did."

"But it was…"

"High. Yes. Look, I came fifteen hundred miles as a favor to Hank because he was worried about you and can't afford to be distracted right now. You can pay me back."

She blinked several times, apparently surprised. He imagined she wasn't surprised very often.

"I will not apologize to the mayor," she said finally. "So, I appreciate that you made the trip, Mr. Megrath, but I'm afraid you've made it for nothing."

He leaned toward her, his elbows on his knees. "I didn't come here for nothing, Haley," he said in the same quiet tone she'd used but with an edge he'd learned in the courtroom. "I came here for Hank. And I'm not going to let you refuse my help and continue to worry him because your pride is getting in the way of an expedient solution to your problem."

He saw a flash of temper in her eyes, then the swallow and the slowly indrawn breath that banked it. "It isn't pride, Mr. Megrath. It's principle. The mayor…"

"Is crooked," he said more quietly. "Hank told me about your suspicions. But how do you intend to prove that from a jail cell?"

HALEY DIDN'T KNOW what to make of Bart Megrath. He was tall, big and handsome in a pin-striped gray suit. The fashionable, button-down attire lent a certain refinement to short brown-blond hair, roughly sculpted cheekbones and chin and gray-blue eyes that conveyed the playfulness of an adventurer rather than the seriousness of a lawyer.

He held her gaze and she looked deeper, puzzled by the sadness under the playfulness.

He got to his feet and paced the cell in about three strides. "The way I see it," he said, "you'll never prove your suspicions in here. I understand the mayor's fall wasn't your fault, but if an apology can get you out of here, give it to him. That way, Hank and your mother won't have to worry about you, and you can continue your investigation."

Easy for him to say, Haley thought, folding her feet up under her. Men always took the simple way out, and there was no reason to believe Bart was any different just because Hank had sent him.

But he had a valid point, and she'd been coming to it on her own the past day-and-a-half. She'd happily sit here until her sixtieth birthday if it would prove the mayor was a criminal—but now that the passion of the moment was gone, she knew it wouldn't prove anything, except that she was stubborn.

"I'll do it for Hank," she said finally.

Bart went to the door and shouted for Brody. The officer appeared at the small window. "You need reinforcements?" he asked.

"I need the mayor," Bart replied.

Brody's mouth fell open.

"As soon as possible, please," Bart added.

Brody's footsteps could be heard as he ran down the hall. "He did it, Sarge!" His voice floated back to the cell through the small, grated window in the door. "The Florida fellow made Hellfire Haley change her mind!"

CHAPTER TWO

MAYOR JOHN WALTHAM didn't look crooked, Bart thought. In fact, his stature and military bearing captured attention. The only imperfection in his appearance was a bandage over his nose that didn't quite cover all the purple bruising.

But he'd brought along Haley's sole reporter to photograph Haley's shaking his hand and apologizing. He was apparently smaller of stature than his height suggested.

The reporter was a coltish little blonde about Haley's age, who looked miserable with her task.

Half expecting Haley to change her mind and close the door on her cell, Bart was pleasantly surprised when she apologized graciously, then extended her hand toward the mayor and smiled for the photograph.

"Haley, I..." the reporter began, ignoring the camera she was holding.

"Focus, Deb," Haley said, maintaining her pose. "We need a three-by-three for the front page."

"What?"

The mayor smiled magnanimously for the camera. But when he glanced at Haley, his expression was cold. "Tell her to do it," he whispered.

"Go ahead, Deb," Haley said to her reporter. "I know what I'm doing."

The reporter reluctantly focused, then took several shots.

The mayor straightened the lapels of his white linen jacket and smiled at Brody and the sergeant, who stood in the doorway. "Get her her clothes," he said. "She's free to leave." He turned to Haley, his expression darkening subtly. "You might remember from now on who you're dealing with."

Haley smiled at him. "With your picture on the front page, Mr. Mayor," she replied, "everyone will remember who we're dealing with."

The mayor was halfway to the door, but he stopped to do a double take in her direction, looking suddenly unsure that his gloating photo op was a good idea. Yet he clearly couldn't suggest she not use the photo. He pulled Bart's check from a pocket, tore it into two and said with obvious reluctance, "I'm dropping the charges."

Brody brought Haley her clothes, and Bart stepped out of the cell so that she could change. He found himself in the middle of a whispered altercation between Deb and a young man in evening clothes who was trying to pull away from her.

"...Don't have time for this," the young man was saying. "Off-duty personnel and volunteers have been called in because that Florida hurricane may get up here. I have to—"

"She spent a day-and-a-half in jail and was just humiliated because of you, Will Hamilton!" Deb accused, holding on to the young man's jacket as he tried to pull away. "You're a rat!"

"She shouldn't harass the mayor all the time," he said defensively, removing her hand from his sleeve.

"It's her job to watch him!" Deb snapped. "And you know the mayor fell over *your* feet, not hers."

"I've got to go."

"Don't call me again! Ever!"

After that interesting exchange, Bart would have liked a

word with Deb, but she ran past him in tears, headed for the door.

Haley emerged from her cell in a pair of khaki shorts and a red T-shirt with Maple Hill Mirror emblazoned on the front. She'd freed her hair from its confining braid and brushed it out, and it rippled down her back, red highlights gleaming under the fluorescents overhead.

He experienced an odd hitch in his chest.

She glanced at him in surprise. "I thought you'd be on your way back to Florida by now," she said.

He cleared his throat, having to look away from her hair to get his lungs working again. "I'll take you home."

"Thank you, but I'm not going home." She strode past him toward the door. "I'm going to the office, and that's only two blocks away."

He caught her arm at the door. "I promised your mother I'd take you home."

She frowned at him, annoyance in those dark eyes again. "I'll call her from the office," she vowed.

He checked his watch. "It's almost ten, and you've just spent thirty-six hours in jail. Your mother would be very relieved to see you."

She huffed impatiently. "Maybe attorneys get to keep nine-to-five hours, but newspaper people often work around the clock, particularly on small-town weeklies."

He reached beyond her to push the door open, then drew her with him into the hot, windy night air. "I'm an attorney," he said, taking her arm once more as they walked down the steps to the sidewalk. "And you'll notice that I just stopped working five minutes ago."

The air was heavy, the wind was hot, and the strange electric atmosphere not only surrounded him but seemed to invade his person, as well. It took effort to drag air into his lungs, then expel it. He felt as languid as the night.

Haley sighed and turned to him, her expression apologetic. "I'm sorry," she said. "I didn't mean to sound ungrateful. I appreciate that you came all this way to get me out of jail, but your work is finished…Mr.…Megrath."

She was staring at him, her voice fading with her whisper of his name. The wind stirred her hair, but she didn't seem to notice. The same charged tension he felt looked out at him from her eyes.

She lifted a hand to touch him, then changed her mind with a groan.

"Finished," she said, as if she hadn't heard herself the first time. "You're finished here."

He stared into her upturned face and knew his work wasn't finished at all. Nothing about this trip was *finished*. Suddenly, he felt as though everything in his world was different, and he needed time to analyze why.

Meanwhile, he'd just been responsible for her humiliation at the hands of the mayor, and he sensed he had to do something about that. Just what, he wasn't sure, but something.

He led her toward his car. "Sorry. When I called your mom on my cell phone on the way in from the airport, I promised her I'd have you home by ten. We're almost going to be on time."

WHAT WAS HAPPENING to her? She'd just felt a sort of stutter in time—everything stopped for a full twenty seconds while she'd gazed into Bart's eyes and seen…what? A harbor? Safety? It was as though a light had appeared at the end of a dark tunnel and beckoned her.

But that made no sense. Safety and security were things she now knew she had to provide herself.

So, why had she been entranced?

Because she'd seen him react to her, that was why. That moment of awareness had snared him as well as her.

But it had to be the threat of the hurricane sharpening the air that she'd mistaken for something internal, something…emotional.

She couldn't quite believe she was letting him put her in the car. "You know, you're almost as bad as Hank," she said, as he climbed in behind the wheel.

She realized he probably only had her best interests at heart, but she didn't like losing her autonomy. At the moment, though, she wasn't sure what to do about it.

He put the key in the ignition and laughed away any hope that she'd offended him.

"Hank and I have a lot in common. Which way home?"

She pointed west. "We live on the lake."

Her mother was beside herself with relief that Haley was home. Why, Haley couldn't imagine. Dangerous activities had never been an issue. They'd taken karate lessons together, her mother had cheered her on every year during the Massachusetts Ten Mile Marathon and she'd given her rappelling gear for Christmas.

Haley patted her mother's arm consolingly as Adeline Whitcomb dabbed at her nose with a tissue. "Good heavens, Mom. What did you think would happen to me? I'm fine."

Then she saw the reason in her mother's eyes. *I didn't think anything would happen to you five years ago when you left on a simple dinner date with Paul. Then I had to pick you up at the emergency room and take you to a psychiatrist for six months afterward.*

But all her mother said was "Mothers worry. It's what we do. And God knows, you've given me sufficient cause."

"I'm fine, Mom," she said again.

Humoring her daughter, Adeline nodded and turned her attention elsewhere.

"Bart?" she asked with a smile.

"Yes, ma'am. I have something for you from Hank." He leaned down to wrap her in a hug.

She hugged him firmly in return. "I can't thank you enough for coming to our rescue. I was frantic about Haley, and I realized she'd never give an inch. I hated to bother Hank with such a thing right now, but I knew he'd have a solution. You must be a good friend to have come all this way."

"No trouble," he said, with a warning glance in Haley's direction. "He's been a good friend to me. I was happy to help."

"How is he?" she asked anxiously. "Is he going to get that shuttle home?"

Megrath nodded. "It's looking good now. They just have to divert the shuttle to the West Coast because of the hurricane."

"Speaking of that," she said, pointing toward the kitchen, "you may as well let me fix you something to eat and plan to spend the night, because Lulu is bearing down on Massachusetts, and airports are closed all over the state."

Megrath took that news with suspicious equanimity—not what you would expect of a busy lawyer faced with a delay in getting home.

"Thank you, but you're sure that won't inconvenience you?" he asked.

Haley was certain he was pretending a concern he didn't feel. He was happy to have an excuse to stay. What was he up to?

"Not at all," her mother interrupted. "You can sleep in

Hank's old room. Haley, will you show him upstairs so he can freshen up?''

"Sure." Haley led the way with hurt feelings. *I'm the one who stood up to the mayor,* she thought. *I'm the one who was unjustly imprisoned. I'm the one Mom was supposed to be so worried about. But by all means, let's show Bart upstairs so he can freshen up.*

She ushered him into the large blue-and-beige room at the end of the hall. It had once been decorated with everything aeronautical, but now had a quilted bedspread and drapes that her mother had made and an old trunk and a bookcase Haley had found at the Red Barn Antiques.

"Okay, Megrath, what's your game?" she asked, filling the doorway with her presence, feet apart, arms at her sides. She looked him in the eye, knowing how to make herself appear formidable.

He turned to her, pulling off his jacket. "Ah…golf, I'd say. I'm a scratch golfer with about a two handicap. Though I'm not bad at basketball, eith—''

"Megrath," she interrupted him wearily.

"Yes?" he asked innocently.

She didn't buy that pose for a minute. "You know what I mean.''

"Ah.'' He dropped his jacket on the foot of the bed and came back to where she stood, leaning a shoulder against the wall and smiling down into her eyes. "I think I do. You mean what is my ulterior motive?''

"Yes," she said without returning his smile. "I do.''

He folded his arms and appeared to consider. "Let's see. A beautiful woman, a heartless villain, a small-town intrigue—''

"Come, now," she cut in. "Men find me scary. Everyone knows that. And I'm sure that before you even left Florida Hank warned you I was difficult. So, what is it really? Why this persistence? The Whitcombs are an old family. Are you thinking there might be some money or prestige here for you that might make your 'favor to Hank' worth your while?''

He was on to her now. Her demeanor of invincibility was a clear case of—to quote Shakespeare—"she doth protest too much.'' She wasn't big and tough at all; sometimes she felt very small. He could see fear in her eyes.

Dealing with that first would have been more satisfying, but undercutting her arguments would be more effective.

''Money,'' he said, repeating the word with the same scorn for it she'd used. ''Have you ever heard of the Megson computer?''

''Of course. Who hasn't? Most reliable PC and best laptop available.''

He nodded. ''From a line of computers developed by Greg Megrath and Hal Bronson, my father and my uncle. My trust fund is probably bigger than the state's budget. I don't need your money.''

She looked astonished, then horrified, then momentarily at a loss. He took advantage of the moment.

''Ever hear of Julia Porter Bartholomew?'' he asked.

She probably knew she was about to be ambushed, but she squared her shoulders and held his gaze. ''Well-known blueblood philanthropist from Philadelphia. Built a music center and a hospital for children.''

''Very good. She's my grandmother. She's dined at the White House and at Buckingham Palace and did a benefit for Italian orphans with the Three Tenors.'' He let that sink in for a moment.

''So, it's the small-town intrigue, then,'' she concluded. ''You want to know what the mayor is up to?''

He couldn't help but stare at her. She *was* obtuse. But agreeing with her could end this interrogation and pave the way for getting to know this emotional porcupine without the risk of getting pricked himself.

"I made you apologize to him," he said, "then I saw what a jerk he was. I owe you some help proving that he's up to something."

She shifted her weight and studied him suspiciously. "I'd already come to the conclusion that I'd have to apologize."

"Really. What were you waiting for?"

"The right moment."

"And that was going to come...?"

"When I was good and ready."

"Well. I'm glad I was there to witness it."

"You didn't *make* me do anything."

"I never claimed to."

"And you don't *owe* me anything."

"I know."

They stood face to face, neither willing nor able to speak the truth aloud.

"There's an attraction here we have to explore."

Her mother called up from downstairs that she had coffee and a snack ready. Haley turned on her heel, and he followed her out, watching her straight back and letting his eyes slip to the seductive sway of her tight little backside.

He wished she owed him something. He knew precisely what he'd ask for.

CHAPTER THREE

HALEY TRIED to get out of the house before Bart or her mother woke up. She'd been listening to the radio news and had learned that Hurricane Lulu would arrive shortly.

But Haley had forgotten that her mother's life work was to thwart her daughter's every scheme.

"You're not going to the office today?" Adeline demanded, standing in the kitchen doorway, as Haley dropped an apple and a jar of peanut butter into her backpack. She pointed to the madly waving tree branches beyond the kitchen window. "The wind's already up, Haley. The radio—"

"I heard it, Mom. I'm a newspaper publisher. A hurricane is news."

"Will Deb be there with you?"

"Deb has a baby. I told her to stay home." Haley shouldered her pack. "I'll be fine. I have to board up my windows and set the vital statistics before the power goes. I'll call you on my cell phone."

Adeline folded her arms. "You can't get out of the driveway," she said, looking smug. "Bart's car is parked behind yours and he's still asleep."

Haley drew a breath and headed for the back stairs. "I'm going to wake him up."

"You're not!"

Haley couldn't believe she was doing this, either, as she ran lightly up the stairs and toward the room Bart Megrath occupied. Not only was it rude to wake a houseguest, but in his case she was sure it was somehow dangerous. She liked him much better asleep.

He was very much awake, though, when she reached his room. He stood there in brown slacks and a three-button beige cotton sweater, looking fresh and vital, exuding energy and intelligence.

She stared, feeling curiously off balance for a woman who always knew what was what. She also felt challenged, and she didn't like that. She was usually the one who backed people into a corner and made them uncomfortable.

"Good morning," he said, smiling. "I'll drive you."

"I just need you to move your car," she said, finally finding her voice.

He pushed her gently aside and headed for the stairs. "I'll drive you. If you're going to board windows, you'll need help."

"How do you...?"

He hurried down the stairs. "I heard you arguing with your mother. And I've been listening to the radio, too."

She rushed in his wake, resenting the fact that she was forced to chase him in her own home.

"It's rude to eavesdrop!"

"I apologize," he said, turning to face her at the bottom of the stairs. "But the heating vent in the bathroom is right over the kitchen." He offered a hand to help her down the last few steps.

She was so surprised by that chivalrous gesture that she took his hand. It was warm and strong. She finally had to pull her own hand away to sidestep its seduction.

"Bart!" her mother said. "I'm so sorry Haley insists on doing this. Can I make you bacon and eggs?"

"That's a good idea." Haley pulled out a kitchen chair at the small farm table in the middle of the room, eager to divert him from his purpose. "Why don't you move your car, then come back and sit down—Mom will make you a good breakfast."

Her mother was already pouring him a cup of coffee.

He accepted it gratefully, and just as Haley began to think he was going to cooperate, he smiled at Adeline.

"Can I take it with me? I think I'd better help Haley with her windows."

Her mother agreed with a "so there!" glance in Haley's direction.

"Look," Haley said, when they stood outside near the driver's side door of his car. "I wish you would stop thinking of me as some personal obligation. Hank sent you to get me out of jail, and you did that. But that doesn't make you responsible for me in any way, or mean that I should be permanently indebted to you. Now, I know you can't leave because of the weather, but please just move your car and let me get on with my life."

The wind whipped around them. Leaves and pine needles flew, and she had to hold down her hair.

"Pardon me," he said calmly, sipping from the cup her mother had given him, "but what makes you think that what you want out of a situation is all that matters?"

She was startled again. Her habit of plain speaking usually *did* get her what she wanted.

"This is *my* town." She spoke clearly and looked right into his eyes. "My home, my newspaper."

"And your...what?" He studied her as though seeing something in her eyes that concerned him. "Your hiding place? Your prison? And I don't mean the one I got you out of. I mean the one that's made up of whatever it is that frightens you."

She hated being surprised all the time. And she really

hated that he'd seen that in her, when she'd been so careful to keep it to herself, to hide it way down.

"Hank told you," she accused, certain that was the only way he could know.

"Told me what?"

But as she gazed at him, she knew Hank hadn't told him anything. He had a reporter's ability to see beneath the surface. Or maybe that was a skill attorneys honed, too.

She turned away from him, went to her truck and let herself in. He climbed into his car, inched it neatly out of the driveway, then parked it on the edge of the lawn.

She backed out, intending to race toward town without him, but something prevented her. She didn't know what it was and she didn't want to try to figure it out. It was probably no more complicated than that boarding windows was much easier with one person holding and another hammering.

That was all.

She waited at the foot of the driveway, the truck's motor idling. Bart climbed into the passenger seat and wisely said nothing as she spewed gravel, headed for town.

THE *Maple Hill Mirror* was located in a small, eighteenth-century storefront with four-on-four paned windows. The shop was painted taupe and gray, with dark red trim, and stood shoulder-to-shoulder with shops of similar construction—a bakery, a dress shop, a drugstore, a gift shop and a stationery store.

The newspaper's office was off-white with blue-and-white checked café curtains at the windows. It had three desks located behind a counter that separated them from the front of the shop.

"I have nails and tools in the back," Haley said, dropping her backpack on the last desk and opening a door that led into a pitch-black room.

Bart put his coffee mug on her desk and followed her. They'd taken only a few steps when he heard a breath of movement somewhere ahead of her, then her startled scream.

Bart shoved her aside. As he reached blindly in the direction of the noise, he connected with what felt like an arm—albeit a scrawny one. He gripped it, determined that it wouldn't escape.

Glaring, overhead fluorescents went on, and Bart found that he held a boy of about fourteen, who blinked against the brightness. He wore a navy-blue sweatshirt and jeans, neither of which seemed to have been washed in a while. His dark hair was mussed, as though he'd just awakened.

That suspicion proved founded when Bart noticed a simple cot set up in the midst of a veritable warehouse of old printing equipment, outmoded by the up-to-the-minute computers in the front office.

Several rough blankets had been shoved to the foot of the cot, and a pillow covered in a pink-and-green flowered case showed the indentation of a head.

"Mike!" Haley gasped as she came toward them. "Did you sleep here again?"

The boy nodded, then squinted into Bart's face. "You're denting my humerus, man," he said.

When Bart raised an eyebrow at the curious choice of words, Haley smiled and tugged at Bart's arm. "They're studying the human skeleton in biology. Let him go, Bart. He works for me."

Bart freed the boy, then made a point of straightening out the sweatshirt he'd half pulled off the boy's arm. "I'm sorry," he said. "I thought you were an intruder."

The young man shrugged off the apology. "I am, sort of. I didn't ask if I could spend the night. I just did."

"You know you can stay here anytime." Haley dug in her purse and handed him several bills. "Go buy some breakfast at the bakery. And get juice, not soda, okay?"

"Okay." He ran a hand through his thick hair in a vain attempt to smooth it. "You want an apricot star?"

"Please." Haley turned to Bart. "How about you? You haven't eaten. A maple bar? Apple fritter? Raspberry danish?"

"Yes to all three," he said with a grin, and handed the boy another bill. "Juice for me, too."

The boy smiled and offered his hand to Bart. "Mike McGee," he said.

"Bart Megrath." Mike's hand was thin, but his grip was strong. Bart wondered what his story was.

Mike loped off, and Haley went to a long plank table against the wall. It was littered with tools and things he couldn't even begin to identify. Her movements were quick and angry as she sorted through to find a hammer and a jam jar filled with long nails. For the first time that morning, he sensed that her anger wasn't directed at him.

"Doesn't Mike have a family?" he asked.

She gave him a dark glance as she pushed past him to where an ancient eight-foot wooden ladder rested against the wall. "Not in the true sense of the word, no. He has a mother, but she's a 'working girl,' if you know what I mean—and when she has a...guest, Mike's not allowed to come home."

She grabbed the ladder and pulled it away from the wall.

Bart reached over her head and placed his hands on hers to stop her. "I'll carry it," he said. "Nobody's reported her to Children's and Family Services?"

"I have several times, and so has a neighbor." Haley

stepped out from under his arm. "It's very heavy," she warned.

He shooed her out of the way, swung the ladder onto its side and carried it one-handed toward the door, just to show her that he could. It *was* heavy.

She didn't seem to notice or appreciate his muscle.

"Nothing's ever done about her, so I just do what I can to take up the slack without hurting Mike's pride. Unlike a lot of kids in his position, he goes to school, does his best to keep this job and is a pretty nice kid, if a little offended by accepting help from a woman."

She ran around Bart to open the door for him, then flattened herself against the door frame so that he had room to go through. He shamelessly enjoyed the touch of her breast against his upper arm when he squeezed by, the grasp of her fingers on his shoulder as she guided him around a low-hanging light fixture in front of the door.

He propped the ladder up in front of the first window, then went to Haley's truck to get the boards he'd noticed she'd put there. The wind was a little stiffer already. Up and down the street, shopkeepers were boarding their windows, bringing in flowerpots and other outside decorations.

"I can do this," he said, as she helped him carry a board to the ladder. "Is there anything else you have to do?"

"I'll do it when we're finished."

"Do it now," he told her, climbing the ladder and taking the board from her. "It'll save time."

She looked up at him, hands on her hips. "Pardon me," she said with an innocent smile, "but what makes you think that what you want out of a situation is all that matters?"

He had to laugh despite his exasperation. "Where are the hammer and the nails?"

She handed them up. Then she held the bottom of the board, while he hammered the top into the window frame.

As he nailed the bottom into place, Haley went to the truck for another board. Mike appeared with two bags of doughnuts and a paper tray with a covered paper coffee cup and two bottles of juice.

Bart and Haley moved with him into the shelter of the storefront, where he distributed the drinks. "I was just in time!" he said, handing Bart his juice. "They're getting ready to close."

"Smart people." Bart took several sips of juice, then handed the bottle to Haley. "You want to help me with the other board," he asked Mike, "while Haley gets some work done inside, so we can leave quickly? You can have breakfast right after."

"Sure." Mike eagerly handed everything he held to Haley, who sputtered a protest. She was forced to go inside when Bart closed the door on her and urged her to hurry up.

Bart climbed the ladder, and Mike held up the board, having to steady it with one hand while he flexed his left arm.

"Sorry I grabbed you so hard." Bart hammered in nails. "I didn't know you were a friend. You all right?"

"Sure," Mike replied, no evidence of anger in his manner or his voice. "It's nice to know somebody's looking out for Haley. She's usually the one taking care of everybody else."

"You like your job?"

"Yeah. I get to type if there's time—I'm not very fast yet. But usually I just clean up. And I go to a meeting now and then for her if she doesn't have time, and just tape it for her. Usually piddly stuff, like the garden club or the quilting ladies."

The top of the board hammered in, Bart climbed down the ladder. Mike helped him move it out of the way.

"Haley's the best. That guy should have been beaten up by somebody," Mike said, handing Bart a nail as he crouched to secure the bottom of the board.

"What guy?"

"The one who ran off when she was attacked."

When she was attacked. Bart heard those words with complete surprise, followed quickly by cold rage. He stopped hammering and looked up at the boy. "Attacked by whom? When?"

Mike shrugged. "I'm not sure. Five years ago, I think. Everybody knows about it. She and this guy were gonna get married. They went out one night, and these three guys jumped 'em. Her boyfriend ran away and left her."

Bart didn't want to ask what had happened next, but had to know.

Mike shook his head, saving him from having to pose the question. "They didn't...you know." Another shrug stood in for the offending thought. "But they were dragging her into their car. An off-duty cop was driving by, called in the assault and ran out to help her. The guys shoved her out onto the sidewalk, jumped into their car and ran away."

Bart instantly recalled the fear he'd seen in her eyes. No wonder she was so prickly, mistrusted men and tried to keep people far enough away that they couldn't hurt her.

He wished he'd been there the night of the incident. He'd have chased the car down, then he'd have found the boyfriend and treated them all to back-alley justice.

That kind of assault on anyone was reprehensible, but on Haley, whom he knew stood up for justice and for neglected children, it made his blood boil. The knowledge that a man who claimed to love her had abandoned her to her fate made him want to kill.

He drove in three more nails.

"Hey," Mike said. "The board's supposed to protect the glass. You keep hitting it like that, you'll break it. Here. This narrow one goes on the door."

Bart nailed it in place, taking care to keep his temper out of the hammer.

"Don't tell her I told you," Mike said quietly. "She's touchy about it. That's why she takes karate and does all that stuff to make her strong. So nobody can ever scare her like that again."

"Don't worry." Bart handed Mike the hammer and the jar of nails, then tipped the ladder onto its side. "You want to get the door?"

Haley was on a computer, a star-shaped pastry sticking out of her mouth as her fingers flew over the keys. She'd turned on all the lights. With the windows covered, he felt as though he was inside a vault. She didn't seem to notice Mike or him, as they walked through to put away the ladder and the hammer and nails.

"I hear you got her out of jail," Mike said.

"Yeah. I'm a lawyer and a friend of her brother's."

"In Florida?"

"Yeah."

"And you came all this way?"

"Yeah."

"You in love with her, or something?"

Bart stopped cold. "I just met her yesterday. And I don't think she likes me."

Mike grinned. "She treats all guys like that. Except me. Usually they just walk away. But you stay and fight with her."

Bart's relationship with Marianne had been based on friendship and having many things in common. They'd gotten along very well and had loved being together. He couldn't imagine what it would take to reach that point with Haley. Complete surrender on his part, probably.

"Arguing with people's a habit because of my job," he said. "And I kind of owe her some help. It's a long story."

Mike nodded. "Because the mayor made her apologize and made Deb take a picture."

When Bart looked surprised that Mike knew that, the youth explained. "I was here last night when Deb came back to work on her film. You're going to help Haley get the mayor?"

"Yes."

"After that, she needs to get some happiness."

Bart put a hand to the boy's shoulder, mystified that in all Mike needed himself, he was thinking about Haley.

Mike seemed to understand the thought and shrugged. "She gave me the little bit I have. At first I used to think that when I grew up, I could marry her and protect her and make her happy. But it's not realistic. I'm only fourteen. She'd have to wait four or five years before I could do it, and she needs somebody who can take care of her now."

Bart smiled. "She doesn't want anyone to take care of her."

With a knowing smile that was filled with as much sadness as mirth, Mike nodded. "That's what she says. That's what I always say. But I like it when she asks me if I've eaten or not, if I'm warm enough, if I'm doing my homework. I'd like to have a father who was around, and a mother who thought I was as important as her tricks. I'm sure Haley would like it if some guy stood by her, instead of running off like the boyfriend did."

Bart couldn't believe this kid. How did that kind of sensitivity develop in such a young person? Clearly, his potential far exceeded his circumstances.

"I could see about getting you into a foster home that could provide those things," Bart suggested cautiously.

Mike frowned. "They'd take me out of the county," he said. "They never leave you in the same county where your real family is. Then, who'd help Haley, since you're probably not staying?"

Bart didn't know how to answer that. "Just something to think about," he said. "Come on. I could really use something to eat."

Bart and Mike talked baseball stats while they had breakfast. When Mike scarfed his oversize maple bar in a matter of minutes, Bart shared his apple fritter.

Haley continued to work, her danish down to one large bite still protruding from between her teeth while she typed. She hit a function key, bit the piece in half, chewed while she entered another command, then popped the last bite into her mouth and saved onto a disk.

She had an expressive mouth, he noticed. It smiled, pursed, twisted. And while she thought, it puckered. It was the puckering that made him wonder what it would be like to kiss her.

She appeared to be all efficiency as she watched the screen, and Mike had told him that she was caring and considerate, but was there a passionate side? Or was it buried so deep that it couldn't be retrieved?

No. Nothing was irretrievable. If he could be brought back to life, anyone could— And he'd felt her reaction to him. She had passion. She just didn't want to acknowledge it.

He was snapped out of his thoughts when something outside bumped and banged its way down the street.

"What's that?" Mike asked worriedly.

"Probably just a trash can," Bart guessed. The wind was getting stronger by the moment. "How're you coming with that?'' he asked Haley as he gathered up the empty paper bags and used napkins.

"I'm finished," she said, sipping at her coffee without moving her eyes from the screen. "I'm just making sure my layout looks good."

"Then, speed would be appreciated. It's getting bad out there."

Her eyes still on the screen, she replied, "You go on ahead. Take Mike with you. I'm going to stick around and watch for front-page pictures, for—"

"We're all going home." He spoke firmly, certain it was a waste of breath, but compelled, anyway. "I'll drive you around for photos when the worst is over."

"News is immediate," she said, "not after the fact."

He looked heavenward in supplication. "I appreciate that, but how 'immediate' can you be in a weekly newspaper? This is Monday and your paper doesn't come out until Thursday." He pointed to the special-event front pages tacked to the wall behind her—all with Thursday dates.

"My readers will know the difference between a photo taken at the height of the storm and one taken when it's over."

"If you risk your safety at the height of the storm, there might not be a photo at all. Maybe not even a paper. And then who's going to take down the mayor?"

She ignored him for a moment while she studied the screen, then she shut the computer and covered it.

"My job," she said with strained patience, "is to be here."

"Your job is to stay alive to keep reporting. We're going home." He handed her her backpack. "You don't want your neighbors to see me carry you out to the truck, do you?"

She looked him up and down with deliberate challenge. "You think you could? Mike can verify that I'm a brown belt in karate. I also work out with free weights every—"

Moving quickly, he put his shoulder to her waist and lifted her off the floor. Anchoring her legs to his chest, he ignored her strangled gasp of surprise.

Mike ran to open the door.

Bart strode out the door to the truck, feeling fortunate that she'd left it unlocked.

"You'll pay for this," she said with such malevolence that he'd have worried if he hadn't been accustomed to dealing with criminals who also threatened him on a regular basis.

He had to give her credit, though. He had her in a grip she couldn't have escaped whatever her skills, so she didn't struggle.

"Relax," he said, tipping her onto her feet and pushing her backward into the truck before she could consider retribution. "Make room for Mike."

The boy crowded in beside her, and Bart ran around the truck and got in behind the wheel.

Her cheeks were red, her eyes explosive. "Just wait!" she whispered harshly.

He simply smiled as he turned the key in the ignition and headed for the lake. Considering what form her vengeance might take was more intriguing than alarming.

He himself was a black belt. Fourth degree.

CHAPTER FOUR

HALEY COULDN'T REMEMBER ever being this angry; she felt as though she could have pedaled the truck home. But Bart was doing such a good job of driving it, dodging falling branches, sailing shingles and other debris that littered the road.

Her mother met them at the door. She held it open and gestured them to hurry inside. A hard, driving rain was falling, pummeling the flowers and bushes, throttling the trees.

"We've lost power," she said, shooing them toward the bathroom. "Hi, Mike. Dry yourselves off. I've got a fresh pot of coffee in the big thermos, and sandwiches. The fridge will stay cool for a while. I thought we'd picnic in the living room."

Haley was still so angry that she was surprised she wasn't steaming. The three of them crowded into the small bathroom off the kitchen. She handed Mike a fat blue towel and slapped one at Bart's middle.

"Thank you," he said, giving an exaggerated gasp that made Mike laugh.

At a glare from Haley, he scrubbed at his wet hair, then hung the towel on the side of the tub and excused himself.

She tossed her own towel aside, prepared to follow him, when Bart caught her arm and quietly pushed the bathroom door closed.

"Maybe we should have this out," he said.

She instantly felt as if her lungs had collapsed. The space was small, the air gone, the walls pressing in on her. It wasn't fear, precisely, but a sort of tension she thought she understood but couldn't quite believe. She could not be interested in any man. This one in particular.

He stood squarely in the middle of the room, relegating her to the small space between him and the door, between the tub and the sink and counter that ran along one wall.

He made her feel small and fragile. And again there was that sense of being challenged.

Her usual approach in such circumstances was to attack.

"How dare you use physical force to make me do what you want me to!" she barked at him, taking a step forward to prove to him that she wasn't intimidated.

He frowned at her in concern. "How dare you put so little stock in your own safety?"

He knew. She didn't know why she was so sure, but she was. Her mother could have told him. Or Mike had. He hadn't known this morning, but he knew now.

She folded her arms. "I've made myself tough enough to handle anything. And my job—"

"You've made your body tough," he disputed, "and certainly your attitude. But the person inside you is afraid of everything."

She wasn't sure whether to be hurt by that, considering the five years' effort she'd put into toughening up, or to simply be angry that he'd say such things to a woman he didn't even know.

She ignored the random thought that he didn't feel at all like a stranger, despite the fact that she'd met him only yesterday. They'd made some immediate connection she couldn't explain.

"Living despite the fear," she said, her throat tightening, "is what life is all about."

"Living despite the fear is courageous," he agreed. "But *trust* is what life is all about. Trust eventually dissolves the fear."

She swallowed, very close to tears. And she didn't know why. She hadn't cried about It since It had happened. "You've heard the story."

His eyes softened; his voice quieted. "Yes," he replied. Mercifully, there was no pity in his eyes.

"I couldn't trust Paul Abbott, and I was engaged to marry him. Who can I trust after that?"

"He's only one man in the thousands of people who cross your path. I'm sure there's someone else you can trust."

"It's easier to not take the chance."

He nodded. "I used to feel that way. But your brother taught me differently."

She didn't want to continue this conversation, but that remark intrigued her. She jabbed a finger at one of his well-rounded biceps. "Now, what would you have to fear with all that muscle?"

He turned to lean back against the counter, as though finding what he was about to reveal difficult to bear without support. "The heart's a muscle, too, and mine was broken."

Instinctively, she took a step toward him, feeling a sudden, tenuous empathy. Most people thought brokenhearted was just an expression, but there was a physical pain in the chest when emotional pain was great. She remembered that very clearly.

"What happened?" she heard herself whisper.

"My wife was killed in a plane crash a year-and-a-half ago," he said, drawing a deep breath after he'd said the words, as though he needed the oxygen. "She was visiting her sister, who'd just had a baby, and they were going to 'talk shop.' She was excited about…''

Haley put a hand to her chest, feeling that pain—for him.

''She was five months along with twins. Of course they died. I died, but my body kept on.'' He drew another breath, which seemed to have a cleansing effect. His voice grew lighter; he raised his eyes from the floor. ''I burrowed into the darkness, completely shut off from anything that would require me to do anything with anyone that didn't involve my work. I couldn't trust a life that would give me so much with one hand, then kill it with the other.''

She found it hard to imagine that he'd endured such a loss. He'd seemed so sure of himself, so in charge, yet so at ease in his life.

''Your brother brought me back,'' he said with a small smile. ''He'd nag me until I'd meet him for a beer, pester me to come for dinner. He kept after me, until I finally realized that life is less painful if you live it than it is if you try to pretend you're not a part of it and let it bang you around.''

She had to treat such an honest revelation delicately. ''I'm so sorry for your loss. It must have been horrific. And I'm glad Hank's been a good friend to you. I think he's very special, too.'' Now she had to be honest, as well. ''But please don't think you're going to pay him back by saving his little sister, because you're not. I like the way I've structured my life.''

''Really,'' he said skeptically. ''With all those walls and no doors that open?''

She angled her chin. ''I'm safe.''

''You're alone,'' he corrected.

''It's the way I want it.''

He said nothing for a moment, then straightened away from the counter. ''Are you sure?'' he asked conversationally. "I mean, have you been with anyone since that night?"

She wouldn't dodge the question. "Made love with anyone, you mean?"

"Not necessarily. I mean, have you let anyone close enough to share your fears, or do you just push everyone away with your verbal karate?"

"I don't need anyone," she replied calmly. "I'm strong enough now to stand on my own."

"No one's that strong. You may be strong enough to defend yourself, but how do you deal with joy, with excitement, with dreams? They can be pretty puny things when there's no one to share them."

She opened her mouth to dispute that, then came to the shocking realization that in the past five years she couldn't remember having felt joy or excitement. And she had no dreams, really. She just worked hard every day to see that people knew the truth. But her own truth was pretty bleak.

Suddenly she was overwhelmed with grief for all she'd lost that night.

Tears sprang to her eyes without warning, then fell before she could even prepare to stop them. She had a desperate need to run.

She yanked the bathroom door open and did just that.

CHAPTER FIVE

MIKE LEANED toward Bart, showing him the spray of playing cards in his hand, and pointed to the Joker. "What's that guy worth again?" he whispered.

Adeline had gone into the kitchen to prepare dessert, and Haley puzzled over the cards in her hand. She, Bart and Mike sat on the living room floor around a blue-and-white checked tablecloth that earlier had held their lunch. Outside, the hurricane raged, and they occupied their time by keeping low and away from the windows.

"Fifteen points, I think," Bart replied quietly. "Or you can pair them up with anything because they're wild."

"I thought the twos were wild."

"Deuces," Bart corrected. "They're wild, too. This kind of rummy is a girl's game. They give themselves all kinds of easy advantages."

Haley looked up from her cards at that, a curious softening in her since their exchange in the bathroom. He'd expected her to be angry that he'd pushed her like that, but she'd been no more hostile than usual this afternoon. In fact, there was a vulnerability about her as she relished the card game, which he found charming.

Maybe he was getting to her. He hoped so; she was certainly getting to him.

"Deuces *and* jokers wild," she said, "is a perfectly acceptable form of the game."

"It's your turn," Bart reminded her.

"I'm thinking."

"Could you think a little faster? Mike and I are getting old here."

She cast him an amused glance. "Well, *you* are, anyway. Be patient. There's a certain strategy involved."

"You lose your turn after five minutes, you know."

She glanced up in doubtful surprise. "You do not!"

"Yes, you do," he insisted. "Whenever you play deuces and jokers both wild, there's a five-minute limit placed on your turn to make a play."

"I never heard that rule."

He refolded his legs with a groan. "It's right in the *Florida Family Amusements Rule Book,* Hurricane Edition. Ask anybody."

She broke into a broad smile that finally turned to laughter. "You're crazy!"

"So I've been told. You've got thirty seconds left."

"Don't need it," she said in sudden triumph. She rearranged the cards in her hand, separated them into two bunches, then set them down on the tablecloth in two elaborate sprays. "Da-dum!" she trumpeted. "Rummy!"

Mike looked from all the cards in his hands to Bart, who also held a considerable number. "What just happened?" he asked.

"She won," Bart said succinctly. "We lost."

"Again?"

"'Fraid so."

Mike, who also seemed relaxed this afternoon despite the weather, grinned at Haley. "I think you have cards up your sleeve."

She pulled up both sleeves to prove that she didn't. "I have *talent* up my sleeve," she teased Mike.

"Good." Adeline placed a tray with half a three-layer chocolate cake on the tablecloth in front of Haley. The tray also held plates and a knife and forks. "Put that sharp talent to work cutting cake. I'll be right back with the coffee."

Bart cleared away the cards.

"I've never been on a picnic," Mike said as he smoothed the tablecloth. "Even an inside one. This is cool."

Bart imagined there'd been lots of experiences Mike had missed that everyone else took for granted. He remembered almost guiltily his own privileged childhood with loving parents able to give him everything. He had to talk to Haley about doing something for Mike.

He put the cards aside, the storm making it almost too dark to see any longer, anyway. The wind raged beyond the windows in whining gusts, and Haley looked up from the cake to cast a worried eye at the windows.

"I hate it when it does that," Mike said, following her gaze.

"Yeah," she agreed quietly.

Bart suspected that an enemy she couldn't overpower with her carefully maintained physical strength was really a worrisome threat.

"It's out there," Bart said, "and we're in here. And I imagine this house has stood for a long time."

"Since the twenties." Adeline had returned with a coffeepot and four cups. "It was built by a couple from Boston who liked to summer here. Mike, would you rather have cocoa or milk?"

"No, thank you." He took one of the cups looped on her fingers. "I drink coffee at the *Mirror* office all the time. But I need lots of cream and sugar."

"Help yourself." Adeline put the sugar and creamer in front of him and distributed the rest of the cups.

"No ice cream for the cake?" Haley asked.

Adeline, who'd just laboriously resumed her place on the floor, groaned.

"I'll get it." Bart got lightly to his feet at the same moment that Haley sprang to hers.

She made a staying gesture. "I'll get it. Mocha chocolate chip or raspberry ripple?"

"Bring them both," Adeline said. "We'll only lose them if we don't get power back tonight."

While Haley dug into the freezer, Bart opened utensil drawers in the kitchen until he found an ice cream scoop.

"Why don't we scoop ice cream into a bowl," she suggested, putting the cartons down on the counter. "Then I can put the cartons right back in the freezer to help keep everything else cold for as long as possible." She reached into a cupboard for a bowl, then took the scoop from him and moved to the sink to run it under hot water.

Both looked up as a powerful gust twisted the branches of the old ash tree beyond the window. The gust increased in intensity instead of dying down, leaves flew, branches twisted, and a loud *crack* split the air.

HALEY SAW THE LIMB break as though in slow motion. The wood that carpenters used to make sturdy tables and chairs simply snapped like a twig.

She watched in terrified fascination as the driving gust blew the branch toward the window where she stood. *It's going to kill me,* she thought with curious calm, *and I'll be through with this desperate need to be stronger than every—*

Before she could complete the thought, there was a steely arm around her and a hand over her face. She was going down, driven not by the tree limb but by Bart's weight. They landed hard as glass exploded and the branch thundered into the room.

Bart's body was wrapped all around hers. She heard his

grunt of pain as something struck them, jarring him but leaving her unharmed.

She lay still, waiting for the noise to stop, but now that the window was broken, the sound of the hurricane filled the kitchen.

"Oh, my God!" She heard her mother's anxious voice, and saw Mike's feet appear near her head.

"Bart's bleeding really bad!" Mike said. "Haley? Are you okay?"

Haley untangled an arm to reach above her to Bart's head. "Bart, are you all right?" she demanded. "Bart?"

"Yeah." He uttered a small gasp, then pushed himself off her.

He kept a hand on her when she tried to get up. "Stay there a minute," he said. "Let me lift you up. There's glass everywhere."

"I can—" she began, but he'd already plucked her off the floor by the waist. He carried her to the doorway of the bathroom, then put her down.

She turned in concern and saw large pieces of glass all over his shoulders, blood in his hair. Her mother was already peeling off his shirt, easing it away from a six-inch gash across his back.

"Oh, Bart!" Haley gasped at the sight. She took the shirt from her mother, rolled it into a ball to keep the glass inside and placed it in the bathroom trash.

Her mother shoved him farther into the bathroom, while rain and debris caught by the wind blew into the kitchen.

"Let me find a board for that window," Bart said, pushing against Adeline's mothering hands.

"After I fix this cut," she insisted. "I think one of the smaller branches got you. Sit down on the edge of the tub and be quiet."

"But I—"

"Quiet!"

Bart sent a smiling glance at Haley as he obeyed. "Now I see where you get it."

"Just shut up and let her fix you," Haley snapped at him, wondering at the rush of anger inside her and perplexed by a softness she hadn't felt in years. "What did you think you were doing, anyway?"

"Shielding you from the tree," he replied quietly, then winced as her mother applied antiseptic. "Why? Did you intend to fend it off with a karate move?"

"No, but I didn't expect you to risk—"

"I didn't risk anything. I knew I could get you out of the way in time."

"But not yourself," she returned.

"At the moment," he said with unnerving seriousness, "that didn't matter."

Everything inside her shook. Bart had just protected her, jeopardizing himself to do it. His action threw into question everything she'd come to believe in the past five years. A man might love a woman, but that didn't really mean anything in the crunch of life or death. Self-preservation still prevailed there.

"Well…don't do that again!" she yelled at him, her anxiety working its way out.

"Did I upset your conviction that all men are like your old boyfriend?"

She opened her mouth to reply, but no words would come. Her entire world was on its ear.

Her mother cast her a worried glance as she worked on Bart's back. "Haley, I think you'd better sit down," she said.

She ignored her mother, pacing the tiny room. "I've learned to take care of myself!" That was a shout for the world in general.

"Yeah, well, a half-ton tree limb might have been more than even you could handle. Relax. It's no big deal. It just means you're wrong about men, that's all. Me, in particular. You can still be as tough as you want."

She stopped pacing to peer over his shoulder.

"How deep is the gash?" she asked her mother.

"Not deep enough for stitches, I don't think," Adeline replied. "The head bump is superficial, too. You aren't seeing double, are you, Bart?"

When he didn't reply, Haley looked down and found him grinning. The way she stood to check the wound on his back, her breasts were a mere inch from his face. He seemed amused by the "seeing double" question.

She gave him a scolding glance and took a step back.

"I'm fine, Adeline," he said to her mother. "Just slap a bandage on so I can board up the—"

Mike appeared in the doorway, a hammer in his hand, his upper body drenched. "I found a board in the basement and a hammer and some nails, but I can't get the tree out of the way to cover the window."

Bart made to stand, but Haley shouted at him. "You wait until Mom's finished! A little more rain isn't going to hurt the kitchen."

She started to follow Mike out, but Bart's voice stopped her. "Do not try to help him move that branch! I'll be there in a minute."

Haley ignored him and spoke to her mother. "Take your time with him, Mom."

"Relax, Bart." Adeline's voice floated out to Haley as she walked out of the bathroom. "She's been hardheaded since she was a little girl. You can't expect to change her."

"I don't want to change her," Haley heard Bart say. "I'd just like her to survive long enough for me to understand her."

"Is that important to you?"

There was a moment's pause. Haley stopped halfway across the kitchen, straining to hear his answer against the howling of the storm.

"Yes, God help me," he said finally. "It is."

Haley felt a weird little glow of happiness. She didn't want to, but she did.

CHAPTER SIX

BART RUSHED into the kitchen the moment Adeline freed him, and found Haley and Mike pulling on a rope they'd tied around the branch. They'd also placed a blanket under the branch to help move it without scarring the floor.

Haley, the rope over her shoulder as though she were some old bargeman, grinned at him. Mike ran to the sink to support the thick end of the branch as it fell off the rim of the counter and onto the blanket.

"Well done," he praised, wanting to shout at her for straining her small body like that but deciding that praise might confuse her. And keeping her off balance seemed to be the only way to keep her open to his seduction.

Because seduction was what he had in mind.

She stopped pulling, to stare at him in surprise. He ignored her. He snatched up a kitchen stool and took the board Mike had found in his other arm. Mike followed him with hammer and nails. They had the board up in a few minutes.

The roar of the storm was quieted once again, and he handed Mike the broom to sweep up glass, while Adeline went for her mop and bucket.

"Okay, Xena," he said, taking the rope from Haley and tugging the branch toward the back door. "You push, and we'll get this outside. I'll cut it up for firewood as soon as the storm's over." He smiled at her. "Or would you prefer to do that yourself?"

"That's one skill she doesn't have," Adeline revealed, returning with the mop. "The last time she tried to chop wood she made sandals out of her hiking boots."

He couldn't help but ask Haley in concern, "What happened to your toes?"

She smiled sheepishly. "They curled up instinctively, so I still have them all. But it took me an hour to straighten them out again. You're welcome to chop the wood."

"I appreciate that. "

He hauled the branch outside and down the back porch steps, insisting that she stay inside under cover. Mike handed Haley the broom and hurried to help him. Rain beat on them as they dragged the branch against the wind into a corner of the yard.

Adeline brought towels to the service porch and left Bart and Mike to dry off while she continued to clean up.

"You're a good man in a crisis," Bart told Mike. "Thanks for the help."

"Everybody else thinks I'm a dork." Mike buffed at his hair until it stood up in peaks. "My mom, my brother…"

"You have a brother?" Bart had never heard mention of him

"Not anymore. He and Bonnie ran away last year, before we moved here."

"Bonnie?"

"My sister."

"You miss them?"

Mike shrugged. "Not really. They were from another dad and they never liked me."

Haley appeared with two short-sleeved sweatshirts of Bart's. "I didn't pry into your things," she said, giving one to Bart and one to Mike. "These were right on top of your case. You don't mind lending one to Mike?"

"Of course not."

They pulled on the shirts and went to help Adeline, Bart speculating on Mike's remarkable resilience.

By early evening the storm had quieted, and the seven o'clock news on the radio said that the hurricane was moving away.

"I should go home," Mike said reluctantly.

They all sat around the kitchen table by candlelight, eating cheese and crackers and fruit.

"My mom doesn't like me around when she has... clients, but she gets mad if I don't show up once in a while." He smiled, though his thin shoulders sagged. "I know it's weird, but this hurricane was fun for me. Thanks for bringing me with you."

Haley patted his hand. "Mike," she said without preamble. "Would you like to live here with my mom and me?"

He appeared astonished for a moment, then he smiled widely. But he frowned again almost immediately.

"Thanks. But my mom wouldn't let me."

"I might be able to make her let you," Haley said. "If I could, would you want to?"

He didn't seem able to focus on the positives in her suggestion. "Before my grandma died, *she* wanted to take me, but Mom wouldn't let her." He looked Haley in the eye, clearly adjusted to the hard facts. "She'd lose the welfare money she gets for me."

Haley's mouth firmed, but she simply patted Mike's hand again. "But would you want to if I could work it out?"

"More than anything," he finally replied.

"All right, then. The power's out on the streetlights, too, so it wouldn't be very safe if we tried to take you home. Why don't I call the police on my cell phone and tell them where you are. Maybe an officer will drive by to let her know. You mind sleeping on the sofa?''

He appeared delighted. ''No, that'd be cool.''

Haley phoned the police department as she'd promised, and Brody agreed to send an officer to tell Mike's mother where he was. Haley was not surprised to learn that the woman hadn't even been in touch with the police to check on Mike's whereabouts.

Haley and her mother and Bart and Mike played several more games of rummy by candlelight, then went to bed just before ten. Adeline brought a pillow and blankets and a flashlight down for Mike.

''You won't be frightened here by yourself?'' she asked.

He seemed surprised by the question. ''No, ma'am. I'll be fine.''

Bart imagined that to a boy who sometimes wasn't even allowed home, darkness was the least of his worries.

Bart had showered, thanks to a gas water heater that was still functioning despite the power outage, and was climbing into jogging shorts and a T-shirt, when he heard a knock on his bedroom door.

He opened it to find Haley standing there, and he knew a moment of anticipation. Maybe she had come to suggest the very thing that had been on his mind since he'd heard her ask Mike if he wanted to live with her.

Bart had decided at that moment that he was in love.

''Can we talk?'' she asked, walking past him into the room without waiting for an answer.

He pushed the door closed behind her, thinking that in this instance, he loved a woman of action. She, too, wore shorts against the sticky heat, and a V-neck T-shirt in pale pink. It made her look delicate, an image he suspected she'd hate.

''Sure.'' He pointed her to his bed and sat down beside

her, leaving a small space between them. "What's on your mind?"

"Is there any way I can get custody of Mike," she asked, "without dragging him through court?"

Completely demoralized by the nature of her question when he'd so hoped for something else entirely, he shifted mental gears to concentrate. "I don't think so, unless you can get his mother to agree. And that doesn't sound likely if he's right about the money thing."

She groaned and let her body slam backward onto the mattress. "I can't believe that nothing can be done about her and the way she treats that kid! I'll bet the mayor's one of her clients and that's why she's never investigated."

He let his eyes trace her body, the small bosom rising, the ribs jutting above her flat stomach. When he got to her firm thighs, he had to look away.

"We could build a case," he said, forcing his professional mind to the fore, "but it would take time. You'd have to document everything, find witnesses, then probably torture Mike as it's all played out in court."

She groaned again, sat up and faced him earnestly. "That's exactly what I don't want to do. But his life just can't go on this way. There must be an answer."

He had a thought. "There might be," he said, feeling the tug of her pleading gaze, the energy from her body as she leaned toward him. He leaned toward her, lust lively in him. "I'll need a day or two, though."

"Take three, but find a solution for me. I'd be very grateful."

"You're sure you can deal with having me around that long?" he taunted gently.

He expected a smile, and was a little surprised when she studied him seriously. "I don't understand you," she said frankly, frustratedly.

"Is that important?" he asked.

"Isn't that usually the way things work?" she questioned in reply.

"If two people intend to have a relationship, it is." He felt an electricity between them, like lightning about to strike. "Is that what you had in mind?"

She opened her mouth as though she would have denied it, then closed it again, suddenly resigned. "It seems to have happened without my cooperation."

Well. Progress. He tried not to look shocked.

"They say admitting a problem exists—" he laughed lightly "—is the first step in dealing with it."

"You saved my life today," she said gravely, ignoring his attempt to lighten the mood for her. "After I'd done everything possible to discourage you. After I'd been rude to you. That's what I don't understand."

"You probably would if you thought about it. There are men who are cowards, but there are men who try to be heroic for the women they care about."

She sat up a little straighter and pointed her finger at the air between them. "That's it right there," she said, her brow furrowed. "Why would you care? I mean, I know you promised Hank you'd get me out of jail, but you've gone far and above that promise."

"Several reasons." He caught the hand with which she gestured and brought it to his lips, surprising her, satisfying his desperate need to touch her. "You're a beautiful and very interesting woman, for one thing. You're intelligent, involved, caring. But what gets to me the most…" He had to pause a moment, emotion that surprised him clogging his throat.

"I had a warm and wonderful home," he said after a moment. "And I lost everything in a heartbeat. With your brother's help, I dragged myself out of a long, dark year-

and-a-half and back to life again, but with no purpose that I could see. Then here you are, trying to help this poor, forlorn kid and provide him with a home, even when your own life has been plagued with pretty scary stuff. It's hard not to fall in love with someone so willing to give to a child.''

Her eyes were wide with surprise. ''It's been just a little more than twenty-four hours.''

''But a pretty intense twenty-four hours. Time doesn't matter, anyway, once the light goes on.''

STRANGELY, SHE KNEW precisely what he meant about the light. Last night when he'd insisted on taking her home, the light had gone on for her. The good things inside her were brighter, and the dark things revealed for what they were. For the first time in five years she wanted to change them, fix them. She wanted to be able to trust, maybe even to lean.

But something still prevented her. Old habits. Old fears rusted in place.

She felt a rush of emotion, a fear of losing the moment because she couldn't make a move.

''Don't panic,'' he said, apparently reading her mind. He kissed her knuckles again and freed her hand. ''You just gave me a few days. You'll come to terms with it by then.''

She wished she could be as confident.

He got to his feet, caught her hand and pulled her to hers. Then he walked her to the door, opened it and gently pushed her through. ''Meanwhile, you'd better get out of here before I do something that forces you to prove that you've earned that brown belt.''

She ran to her room, worried that if he did do something, she'd forget she had any self-defense skills at all.

CHAPTER SEVEN

HALEY AWOKE the following morning, after a mere two hours' sleep, to find power restored. She showered quickly, pulled on her favorite stone-colored shorts and a yellow T-shirt and hurried downstairs, determined to have a quick cup of coffee and set out in search of damage photos.

Haley was halted by a telephone call from Deb, who said she was already at the office, working on the layouts.

"You going out for pictures this morning?"

"Yes. I was just on my way."

"Okay. You can take your time getting in. I've got everything handled here."

"You're a peach, Deb. Thanks."

Haley's momentum was halted again by a small crowd in the kitchen. Adeline, Mike and Jackie Bourgeois, a city councilwoman and Haley's good friend, were gathered around the table, eating waffles. Bart waved from across the kitchen where he leaned against the wall, talking on the telephone. His smile was warm but knowing, perhaps because of their conversation the night before.

She smiled back, unable to deny that he was now important to her. She'd spent most of the night awake and worrying about that.

Mike and her mother were finishing up, but Jackie seemed to have just started.

Adeline pushed away from the table, taking her empty plate and Mike's. "I'll drive Mike home, Haley," she said.

"I've got quite a few errands to run, and I know you're eager to get to work. Your waffle's in the oven."

Mike stood, too, giving her a shy wave. "Thanks for everything," he said.

"Sure," she replied. "Just be on time for work tomorrow. We have some subscription address changes."

He started for the door, where her mother waited, then hesitated and turned. "You're really going to try…" He stopped, apparently unwilling to be specific in front of Jackie.

"I will."

He nodded. "Okay. I'll see you tomorrow."

Haley went to retrieve her waffle, then sat across the table from Jackie. Her friend was a small redhead, far too youthful-looking to be the mother of two little girls. She'd had a stormy marriage to a local boy, and two months ago, after a reconciliation, her husband had died in the arms of a cocktail waitress while on a business trip to New York.

Though Jackie had been horrified and humiliated, she had held her head up, continued to work and done her best to shield her children from the scandal. Haley admired her strength and her ability to remain gentle and kind in adversity—a skill Haley had never quite mastered.

Jackie indicated the boarded window. "I understand you had a flying foreign visitor during the storm."

Haley rolled her eyes. "Was quite a day. You sustain any damage?" Jackie and her daughters lived in a very old house in town.

"No, everything's fine at home. Well, sort of."

Before Haley could ask what that meant, Jackie leaned toward her, her voice lowered to a whisper. "Who's that on the phone?"

"My lawyer," Haley replied.

"I heard some out-of-towner got you out of jail, but where did he...?"

"Hank sent him. It's a long story." Haley glanced up, happy to see Bart still engrossed in his telephone conversation. "What's up? What are you doing here at this hour?"

Jackie leaned even closer, lowered her voice even more. "I came to tell you that I went to my office at City Hall early this morning to see if everything was okay, and found a couple of windows broken at basement level. The archives storage room was soaked. Guess what I saw."

"Flooding?" Haley asked practically.

Jackie patted her hand. "Good try," she said quietly. "The mayor was removing something from a storage box way in the back."

Haley felt her reporter's instincts twitching. "What was it?"

"I don't know. I was afraid to get too close for fear he'd see me. But he was working quickly and kept looking around. He put it in a plastic trash bag."

"An incriminating document, or something?"

"Maybe. But it was obviously something he'd been hiding and was forced to move. I followed him upstairs. He took the bag into his office. You want to meet me there at one o'clock? He has a damage assessment meeting at the police station at that time."

Excitement built in Haley. This might be her opportunity to finally find out what the mayor was up to. But if she and Jackie didn't proceed carefully, they'd be in more trouble than they could ever make for him.

"We can't rummage through his stuff," she said.

Jackie smiled smugly. "I know that. But the damage protocol is kept in his file cabinet. As a councilwoman, I'm entitled to access to it."

"Won't the mayor have that with him at the meeting?"

"Yes, but there are several copies. That'll at least get us into his office."

Haley grinned at her friend, who was usually scrupulously honest. "You little dickens. You *do* have criminal tendencies."

She pretended to stretch casually. "It comes from my highwayman ancestor."

Jackie's great-great-great-grandfather, Thomas Fortin, had helped found Maple Hill after running from the law and hiding out in Jackie's soon-to-be great-great-great-grandmother's barn.

"If we're going to embark upon skullduggery," Haley said, pointing to Jackie's untouched waffle, "you'd better eat something."

Jackie made a forlorn face and pushed the plate away. "Thanks, but I can't. Your mom insisted, but I… Oh, jeez! Excuse me!"

Jackie ran to the bathroom but was back in a moment, dabbing her mouth with a washcloth. "Sorry," she said, resuming her chair. She looked positively green.

"Flu?" Haley asked in concern. "Food poisoning?"

Jackie shook her head and said with a resigned bob of her head, "Baby."

Haley fell against the back of her chair. "Oh, Jackie."

She nodded, drawing a breath, folding the washcloth and putting it to her cheek. "Well, you know, Ricky and I were trying to rebuild our marriage. At least, I thought we were. Is it possible for the living to haunt the dead? I'd really like to hurt him a little."

Haley leaned across the table to cover Jackie's hands with hers. "I'd say I'm sorry, but I know you, and this is going to be the luckiest child on earth, second only to Erica and Rachel. It must be terrifying to be widowed with two children and find yourself pregnant. I'll do everything I can to help.''

Jackie squeezed her hands. "I'm sure you will, and I appreciate that. I just keep wondering if I'm ever going to feel I have my life together, as though I'm on the right track. I started over after Hank left, I started over three or four times with Ricky, and here I am again.''

"Your life's always been together,'' Haley said. "It's the clueless men you were involved with who didn't appreciate you. My brother included.''

Jackie made a face and got to her feet. "Need to go. I have an early meeting. See you at one o'clock.''

"In your office?''

"Right. Then we have some hope of knowing when the mayor leaves his office.'' She smiled thinly. "Does this make you feel like one of Charlie's Angels?''

Haley laughed at that. "I think we're more like Lucy and Ethel.'' She walked Jackie to the door and waved her off.

She was heading back to the table, when Bart hung up the phone and studied a piece of paper on which he'd been taking notes. He came toward her with a smile of satisfaction.

"You might not have to put up with me for three days, after all,'' he said, waving his note. "I may have the problem solved.''

Curiosity warred with panic. Did that mean he wanted to leave? That he intended to leave? What would she do, she demanded of herself, when he was gone? He'd brought blinding sunlight into a hurricane.

"What do you mean?'' she whispered.

"Mike's mother,'' he replied, taking his empty cup from the table and refilling it from the coffeepot. "I think I know how you can get custody of Mike.''

She blinked in astonishment. "How?"

"I did a little sleuthing." He carried his cup to the table, then pulled out her chair for her. "Sit. I'll explain while you eat."

"I'll sit, but I can't eat until you tell me."

He put the note down and folded his arms on the table, looking very self-satisfied. "Annette McGee is collecting welfare on three children."

"Three? But there's only Mike."

He shook his head. "Mike told me yesterday afternoon while we were hauling the branch out back. His elder brother and sister ran away last year before they moved to Maple Hill. They used to give him a lot of grief, so he doesn't talk about them much. I checked, and his mother hasn't even reported them missing."

"God!"

"I know. I'll send the names of the other two to the runaway team at Children's Services to see if they can find them. We could take her to court with all this, or the police can hit her with it and see if she caves. Either way, the court's bound to find another home for Mike, and since you're already looking out for him and are a respected member of the community, there's every reason it should be you. And I don't think any of this has to be messy for Mike."

Haley threw her arms around Bart, forgetting in her excitement that she had issues with him. She'd been worried about Mike for so long that her relief at finding a solution was overwhelming.

"Bart, I *love* you for this!" she exclaimed, tightening her grip on him, feeling his arms come around her.

And that was when she realized her words weren't just a figure of speech. He was everything that had died for her the night Paul had run off and left her to the mercy of their attackers—a sense of security, of comfort, of faith in the world she lived in.

She was aware of clinging to Bart, as if holding on against his joke about leaving. At least, she hoped it was a joke.

She pushed against his chest and looked up at him, feeling as though they were tethered, like climbers on a cliff face and if she fell, they would both go.

"Maybe…not just for this," she whispered, the old terror and her balancing defenses sloughing away. She felt like someone new. Not different, exactly, just better.

He cupped her head in his hands, his eyes turbulent. "I love you, too. For all kinds of reasons. But I'd rather not discuss them now. I'd rather just…"

KISS HER. That was all he had on his mind. To taste her lips, to draw her back into his arms and feel the beaded tips of her breasts against his chest, the fabric that separated his flesh from hers frustrating and intolerable.

He suddenly had a fistful of the hem of her shirt and pushed it up. She tore it off over her head and wrapped her arms around him again, the vital warmth contrarily making him remember what she'd been through.

He tried to draw a breath, to slow the pace of this suddenly intimate communication.

"Haley…" he began, but she covered his mouth with her lips and was reaching under his shirt to explore his back.

His nerve endings shuddered under her touch. "Haley," he began again. "We…"

But she'd looped her arm in his and was leading him toward the stairs. "I want to make love to you right now," she said, leaning her head against his upper arm. "What do you want?"

His answer was to lift her off her feet and carry her upstairs. She pointed to her room. He edged through the doorway and put her down beside a double bed dappled with sunlight now that the storm had cleared the air. No boards covered the open window up here, and the smell of honeysuckle wafted in.

They shed their clothes and wrapped themselves around each other in the middle of the unmade bed. It smelled of her cologne and her shampoo.

He thought about how much he'd missed real intimacy, as they explored each other, fingertips tracing, learning. He hadn't made love to a woman since Marianne died. Not that he'd chosen to be celibate, but lovemaking was so entwined in his consciousness with shared dreams, kept promises. With Marianne, it had offered a richness he'd been sure no one else could duplicate.

Until now.

It wasn't that he compared Haley with his wife, but that she filled his being in the same way—a way that meant life was right. That he was right.

He rose over her and entered her tenderly, doing his best to explain that to her without words.

PAUL HAD BEEN Haley's first lover, and since him there'd been no one she could trust with all the love she had to give, no one who could banish the darkness that filled her.

But Bart had made the darkness disappear. He was the kind of man her mother had taught her to wait for, the kind of man many women believed no longer existed. He was a strong protector and a tender lover, a man who could excite her and cherish her at the same time.

And he did both now as his tender ministrations and his bold possession made her forget everything but the moment. Fulfillment racked her until she was helpless and gasping in his arms.

The instant she was coherent again, she knelt astride him and returned his generous lovemaking with her fingertips and her lips, until he, too, seemed to lose all reason. They finally collapsed together, spent and very happy.

CHAPTER EIGHT

IT WAS ALMOST NOON when Haley finally stirred, reluctantly lifting herself with a forearm on Bart's chest. "You are the worst thing that has ever happened to my work schedule," she complained with a yawn. "I've got to get to the office."

"I'll come with you," he said, running a hand gently up and down her arm. "We scouting damage pictures?"

She looked away, guilt surfacing in her as she leaned down to plant a kiss on his chest in order to avoid his eyes. "You stay home and relax."

She pushed herself to a sitting position and turned her back to him as she reached for her robe at the foot of the bed. "Deb called me on my cell phone before I even woke up this morning, and told me she got lots of good stuff." Lie number one. "I have a couple of meetings to cover." Lie number two. "Then I'll be typing boring stuff for the rest of the afternoon." Major lie—but she could just imagine how he'd react to news of what she was really doing this afternoon.

While usually desirable, a strong protector could put a serious crimp in a reporter's ability to do her duty.

"Are you moving to Florida?" he asked lazily, "or am I coming to Maple Hill? Or maybe we'll have to locate somewhere neutral. What's in the middle? North Carolina?"

Pleasantly surprised, she turned to look at him. "You won't be able to live without me, either?"

"Not a chance." He beckoned seductively. "Come back to bed."

She almost weakened, then shook her head firmly. "I've *got* to get some work done. You stay there while I take a shower."

THE BED LOST its appeal with Haley gone, so Bart swung his legs to the floor and pulled on his clothes. He was tying his shoes, when the telephone rang. He picked up the receiver, unaware that in the quest to be at the ready for news, Haley had a bathside phone. He heard her pick up and was about to hang up, when he caught a woman's voice whisper urgently.

"Haley, our caper in the mayor's office is postponed thirty minutes."

Apparently unaware that he was on the line, the woman continued. "His meeting's delayed, and we have to make sure he's out of the building before we try to find that trash bag."

Bart's blood pressure went up twenty points.

"All right," Haley replied. "Stay calm, Jackie. We don't want to blow this."

"I am calm. I'm just a little...not, you know?"

"That makes no sense."

"Well, this is my first spy job. Show a little understanding."

Spy job? Bart bit down on his lip to silence an oath.

"As soon as I find out what's in the trash bag. I'll be in your office about one-twenty. He'll probably have to leave by then to get to his meeting."

"Okay—one-twenty. I'm calm."

"Good. Goodbye."

Bart heard the click of a broken connection, slammed down the phone he held and marched to the bathroom doorway. Haley, in her shorts and a black lace bra, stood at the sink, brushing her hair. She turned to him in surprise, the brush held in midair.

"Caper?" he asked tightly, leaning a shoulder against the door frame. "Spy job? Mayor's office? What the hell's going on, Haley?"

She squared her shoulders—an almost comical gesture given her attire. "My job is going on, Bart," she said, clearly annoyed with his question. "It has nothing to do with you."

"I want to know what you're doing."

"I'm getting something on the mayor. I think," she added. "Jackie saw him removing a trash bag with something in it from one of the flooded storage rooms in City Hall. He seemed anxious about it and put it in his office."

"You can't invade his privacy without a—"

"Warrant. Would I be a newspaper publisher for two-and-a-half years and not know that? Jackie's worked it out so that she has an excuse to go into the office. We'll just see if we can spot the trash bag."

That all sounded so vague that his concern was growing by the moment. "You should call the police." He tried to remain calm, but her stubbornness was making it difficult.

"There isn't time." She pulled her shirt on over her head and began to brush her hair again. "Will Hamilton, an old boyfriend of mine, is one of two officers on day shift. We have a fifty-fifty chance of getting him. The way he's been acting, I'm not sure whose side he's on. And if I don't check this out now, the trash bag could be gone tomorrow and I'll have lost my chance to put the mayor away."

She attempted to walk past Bart into the bedroom, but

he stood deliberately in her way. "You're not doing this," he said.

She drew a breath and said with forced patience, "It's my job, Bart."

His temper snapped. "Your job is not to flirt with danger at every turn. I realize you do it just to prove to yourself that you're not the coward your fiancé was. Well, we're all convinced of that, so back off and let someone who knows what he's doing handle it."

Those words destroyed her beautiful morning. How dared he psychoanalyze her? How dared he— Her brain froze for an instant. God. *Was* that what she was doing?

She put a hand to his chest and pushed, needing him out of her way. This was no time to dissect her own behavior.

She got past him, but she was aware it was because he had let her.

"Don't think," she said, turning back to him, "that making love to me empowers you to prevent me from doing anything I want to do." She took a step closer so that she could look right into his face. "Because it doesn't."

He leaned over her. "I'm entitled," he insisted, "to have peace of mind, knowing that you won't terrify me every day by risking your life when there are—"

"Loving me," she interrupted him, "doesn't mean you can make my life serve yours."

He studied her for a moment. She guessed he was deciding whether he should use whatever was next in his argument arsenal. She braced herself.

"What?" she demanded pugnaciously. "Say it!"

"All right," he said quietly, pacing away from her toward the window, then veering to come halfway back her. "I think you *want* a man who's willing to tell you what to do."

That startled her. She never expected such bald chauvinism from him. "I can't believe you said that!" she gasped.

He took two more steps toward her, his expression scolding. "You know that's not what I mean. You don't want a man to push you around, and you don't need one to feel complete. I mean that you've been chasing men away from you since the night your fiancé chickened out on you because none of them was as strong as you've made yourself. You need proof that the man in your life is stronger and tougher than you are, so that nothing like that night ever happens to you again. I *am*."

Had he scraped fingernails down the front of her, she could not have felt more hurt or—and this was surprising—more revealed. He understood that she wasn't really tough at all. That while she had the skills to be strong, and her body could protect her from most threats now, inside she still felt alone and abandoned. She stood motionless as his words penetrated her awareness. Until that moment, she herself hadn't understood it.

At a loss for a reply and feeling defensive, she fell back on her old standby. "I can take care of myself!"

"Yes, I'm sure you can," he agreed. "But it's my theory that God made man first to clear the road, kill the spiders, check under the bed. If you don't want that kind of man in your life, don't look at me with those longing eyes."

She couldn't deny that she did, and she didn't seem able to admit it, either. So she sidestepped the issue. "Get out of my way. I'm going."

"Not without me you're not."

He reminded her of Hank at his brotherly bullying best.

"Bart, get a grip!" she shouted at him. "I don't have time to argue."

"Fine," he said, going to the door. "Then, let's just go."

She assumed a challenging stance. "Have you forgotten that I'm a brown belt?"

He pulled the door open. "No. But I did forget to tell you that I'm a black belt. Fourth degree."

She closed her eyes for a moment, trying to think of an alternative to murder.

"You're not more stubborn than I am."

"I'm still here, aren't I?"

"A hurricane kept you."

He grinned and opened the door a little wider. "I think of you more as a tornado. You coming?"

"We'll settle this later," she said, marching past him.

She heard his voice behind her as he followed her down the stairs. "It's already settled."

SHE SHOULD HAVE stuck to her belief that men weren't worth the trouble, Haley decided as her truck bumped along Lake Road on the way to town. She'd trusted one, made love with him, and now he thought...

"You don't control my life now, you know!" she said, punctuating her declaration with a glower in his direction.

"I just want to control your self-destructive tendencies," he said, relaxed in the passenger seat, his body moving easily as the truck jostled him.

"I'm not self-destructive," she argued. "And we've just been over this. My job requires—"

"Haley, I'm a lawyer." He cut her off with a scornful tone. "Don't lie to me."

"I don't lie!"

"Oh? And what was that when you told me you had a meeting, then were going to spend the morning typing— when all day you had plans to meet Jackie for this 'caper'?"

Busted. "That was...subterfuge," she said weakly.

"Is that what they call 'lying' in the spy game?"

She sighed. "It was more expedient than trying to explain to you, given your conviction that I'm helpless."

"I don't consider you helpless," he corrected. "Just vulnerable. Despite your brown belt."

"I wasn't going to do anything *really* dumb."

"There are no degrees of dumb. A move is either smart or dumb. That's all there is. And confronting the mayor alone would be dumb."

She slapped the steering wheel in exasperation. "The mayor is going to be out of the office!"

"You've never heard of things not being what they seem? Or not going according to plan? What if he comes back early? What if he leaves someone to watch the office?"

She turned off Lake Road and onto the far end of Main Street. "Then, we'll be fine, won't we," she said dryly. "Because Jackie and I will have a lawyer with us. If it all goes bad, you can object or cross-examine or something."

"Now you're being smart," he scolded.

"Imagine that. A minute ago you called me dumb."

"I said what you were about to *do* was dumb."

"Same thing."

"No, subtle difference."

"Are you going to challenge everything I say and do?" she demanded hotly.

"Yes," he replied, not hesitating even for a second.

CHAPTER NINE

CITY HALL, a federal mansion that had once belonged to an ancestor of Jackie's husband, was white, with black shutters and a large brass eagle over the double front doors. It was situated on one edge of the town square.

Inside, various officials scurried around in the wake of all the local problems the hurricane had created.

"Where's Jackie's office?" Bart asked Haley quietly.

She pointed to the large central staircase that led to a railed gallery on the second floor. "In a corner to the left under the stairs," she replied softly. "The mayor's office is on the second floor, right at the top."

And then, as though hearing his name had cued him, Mayor Waltham burst through the double doors, headed for the stairs. He noticed Haley and Bart.

"Well—" he said, coming toward them, his expression unusually congenial.

He had to be up to something.

"What brings you and your attorney to City Hall, Haley?"

For an instant, she couldn't think of a reply he would believe.

"Haley," he said, as though her silence grieved him. "There are no hard feelings, are there? Has your home sustained hurricane damage? Is there anything I can do?"

"No hard feelings," she fibbed, playing for time. "No hurricane damage..." And then it struck her. She entwined her fingers with Bart's and held their hands up for the mayor to see. "We're just here for a marriage license."

Bart blinked at her once, then smiled at the mayor. "Yeah. Marriage license. Stormy relationship. Stormy times. Seemed appropriate."

"Well, congratulations!" The mayor shook their hands, then led the way to a counter under a sign that read Marriage Licenses.

"Melanie," he said to the little blonde looking eager to serve them, "please give these two your full attention." He backed away with a smile. "You'll have to excuse me. I have a meeting in ten minutes." And he hurried for the stairs.

The moment he was out of sight, Haley turned to Bart, who grinned expectantly, apparently willing to wait for whatever would happen next.

Haley smiled a little nervously at Melanie, who was filling in the date on a form. "Actually, Melanie," she said, "I think maybe we'll have lunch first."

"Lunch can wait, darling," Bart said, tugging her back as she tried to draw him away. "Let's do it now."

"I'm hungry, darling," she answered a little forcefully. "Let's do it *after* lunch."

"But it was your idea, love." Amusement brightened the depths of his gray-blue eyes.

She smiled again for Melanie's benefit, when she really wanted to punch him. "And it'll be even better after lunch. Excuse us, Melanie."

Bart allowed her to pull him away.

"What do you think you're doing?" she demanded in a whisper, as they rounded the corner into the main hallway. They stood against the wall, making certain the mayor had topped the stairs and was out of sight. "You're supposed to be working *with* me!"

"Really. I thought you didn't need me."

"I don't, but if you insist on coming, the least you can do is cooperate!"

"I was willing to get a marriage license."

"Bart…" She was going to kill him in a minute—gleefully.

"All right, all right. Let's go. The mayor's not around." He caught her hand. "Take us to Jackie's office."

Haley led the way hurriedly across the foyer to a door with a sign that read: Councilwoman Jacqueline Bourgeois.

The door opened the moment they reached it, and Jackie hauled them inside, then closed it hurriedly. "Where have you *been?*" she demanded of Haley. "You're late!"

Haley pointed to Bart without hesitation. "It's all *his* fault. He didn't think I should come alone."

Jackie rolled her eyes. "Men. Like anything could hurt us more than they do." Then, as though she'd complimented Bart's gender rather than insulted it, she offered him her hand. "Hi. Jackie Bourgeois. I saw you at Haley's this morning, but you were on the phone the entire time."

"Hello." He shook her hand, feeling its fragility, noting that she looked pale and tired. "I apologize for whatever it was that one of my comrades did to you. I assure you, though, it wasn't with my approval."

She shook her head and smiled. She was really quite pretty. "No, *I* apologize. I'm not feeling one hundred percent today, but that's no excuse to take it out on you."

"Do go ahead," Haley urged her. "He's been picking on me all day."

He sent her a smile over Jackie's head. "Not *all* day. And you did try to get us a marriage license."

"What?" Jackie asked, openmouthed.

Haley rolled her eyes. "It was my excuse to the mayor for why we were here—we ran into him in the foyer. Don't pay any attention to Bart.'' She pretended to be frightened. "He thinks he's along to prevent us from getting killed.''

Jackie eyed him suspiciously. "I hope you're good at that.''

"I guess we'll see.'' He went to the door and opened it just a crack. He could see the door to the outside.

He glanced at the clock on Jackie's desk. It was now 1:26. He shooed Haley and Jackie toward the far end of the office. "Stay there,'' he said, "and please keep your voices down.''

As he kept an eye on the door, he listened to the women's conversation.

"He thinks he's an absolute ruler or something,'' Haley groaned.

"He did say 'please.' ''

"Yes, he's very sweet about being a complete tyrant. Who needs it?''

He discerned a sigh. "Some lonely, confused, frightened woman who hasn't had a secure moment in the past five years.''

"Jackie!''

Bart heard heavy footsteps on the stairs, then a woman's voice, "Mr. Mayor! Your wife wants to know if you'll be home for dinner!''

Bart motioned Haley and Jackie to silence.

"Tell her…'' Waltham hesitated. "Tell her I've got Kiwanis tonight.''

"But, Mr. Mayor, isn't that tomor—''

"The Kiwanis *board* meets tonight.''

"Yes, Mr. Mayor.''

Bart caught sight of the short, rotund body as the mayor approached the door that led outside, then watched him pull it open, walk through and disappear.

Bart turned to Jackie. "Was that his secretary? And where's her desk?"

"In the office next to his," Jackie said, dismissing that as a problem with a wave of her hand. "But she's at lunch. That was Melanie, and she works downstairs at the license counter, remember."

"All right!" He pulled the door open and beckoned Haley and Jackie. Before Haley could go through the doorway, he caught he arm. "I'm going first," he said with a firmness he hoped would discourage any argument. "I want both of you to stay behind me. Understood?"

"Yes," Jackie replied.

Haley sighed impatiently. "You give so many orders, I would have to be *comatose* not to understand."

"Is that a yes or a no?"

"It's a yes, okay? I, Haley Barbara Whitcomb, an adult woman of considerable skill and intelligence, promise to stay in your shadow so that you don't freak out unnecessarily!"

Hank would owe him big for this. Really big.

"Good," he replied. "Try to do it with a little less mouth."

He walked out of Jackie's office, making an effort to look like someone on a simple, unhurried mission somewhere on the second floor of City Hall.

At the oak door with the leaded-glass window and the sign that read Mayor John Waltham, Bart looked around to make sure no one was in the hall, then turned the knob. The door was locked.

"This way," Jackie said quietly, leading them to the ladies' room at the end of the hall.

Haley made an impatient sound. "For goodness' sake, Jackie! You should have thought of this bef—"

Jackie glared her into silence. "An old fire escape runs

down the back of the building,'' she said softly, ''from the ladies' room window to the mayor's office.''

Haley subsided penitently. ''Oh.''

Bart hesitated.

Haley stepped ahead of him, penitence quickly over and a smirk now on her lips. ''This time, you'd better follow *us*.'' She walked inside, bent over to check the stalls for feet, and beckoned him in.

Jackie followed, then went to the window over a convenient radiator and pushed it open. Bart lifted her onto the sill. ''Wait for me right there,'' he ordered.

''Yes, Your Worship,'' she replied.

He lifted a giggling Haley onto the sill, then boosted himself up. The crenellated radiator was an unforgettable experience on his kneecaps, before he was out the window.

Haley and Jackie waited as they'd promised, and then he led the way to the mayor's office.

''Fourth window down, I think,'' Jackie said.

He counted windows as his footsteps rang on the metal support. He reached the fourth window, tugged on it, and it opened.

He let himself in, then helped Jackie in. They both reached back to assist Haley.

The office was ornate, with a window seat in the window through which they'd come, and a fireplace. The decor was in a very imperious white and gold. The large desk and appointments looked as though they might be antiques.

''Where would he have put the bag?'' Haley asked, standing in the middle of the room.

Jackie walked toward a series of oak cabinets along one wall. ''The file cabinets?'' she asked, then shook her head. ''No, I think the bag was too large to fit in there. Unless he took the stuff out of the bag and distributed it among the cabinets.''

She pulled one open and looked inside. Then she tried another, then the other two.

"Nothing," she said grimly. "Maybe it's in the cupboard."

Bart folded his arms and studied the large maple cupboard to the left of the door. "I have to tell you, we're on really shaky legal ground here if we rummage through his things. And I'd hate for us to find something on the mayor that we were unable to prosecute him for because of the tainted way in which we got our information."

"We have to do something!" Haley argued.

"I agree," Bart said, as frustrated as she was. "What do you suggest that won't get a case against him thrown out of court?"

"You're the lawyer."

"That's why I'm advocating taking a minute to think. Are you absolutely sure, Jackie, that the damage protocol is something you have a right to look for?"

As it happened, it didn't matter. Suddenly there was the sound of footsteps beyond the door, then a key in the lock.

Bart shoved the women toward a coat closet. He got Jackie inside and Haley halfway in, before the office door opened.

Bart turned his back on the closet door and tried to shut it the rest of the way, as the mayor walked into the office, his attention on a document in his hands. Haley took that opportunity to push her way out of the closet through the small opening, then close the door on Jackie, who was whispering urgently.

He really had to do something about Haley, Bart thought in concern, giving her a look that told her so. She was pale and her eyes were enormous, but she just stared back at him, daring him to try.

FOR A MOMENT, Haley was fascinated by the awkward and potentially dangerous situation in which she and Bart found themselves. A corner of her mind recalled his argument earlier: *Haven't you ever heard of things that aren't what they seem? Things that don't go according to plan?*

He'd been right. The mayor was supposed to be gone for at least an hour, yet here he was with—what were those? plane tickets?—in less than fifteen minutes.

She felt a flutter of excitement along with a cold finger of fear along her spine. Something was about to happen, and she was right in the middle of it.

She'd wanted to hide in the closet, but she'd spent five long, hard years teaching herself to be strong. She'd toughened her body and her attitude. Still, she hadn't had to look danger in the face since *that night*. She had to know if she could do it.

The mayor looked up, an expression of pure surprise on his face. It was followed almost instantly by anger, and then by a chilling resolve.

Talk about looking danger in the face, Haley thought.

She wasn't surprised when he pulled a gun out of his pocket, but she did feel as though her rapidly beating heart would choke her.

"Mayor," Bart said, stepping sideways so that he stood in front of Haley, his back a wall of white cotton between her and Waltham. "Going somewhere?"

"An island paradise," the mayor replied. "You'd be wise not to try to stop me."

Haley tried to move out from behind Bart, but he pushed her back.

"We know about the money." Bart didn't know for certain that the issue was money, but the only other thing that drove men to corruption, besides a woman—and Waltham didn't seem the type—was power, and Bart doubted there was much of that in Maple Hill. "The only person who'll get shelter out of the fund for the homeless is you, isn't it? What'd you do? Cash the check, and now you're absconding with the money? How long do you think you'll have in paradise before the feds come and get you?"

"You're the only ones who know—" the mayor said.

Haley could no longer see Waltham, but she certainly heard the threat in his voice.

"Make it easy on yourselves and don't interfere. The paperwork shows that I've used part of the money for building contracts, with the balance gaining interest until the contracts are paid in full."

"But no one's really been contracted?" Bart guessed.

"Just the driver to take me from the airport in the Seychelles to the hotel." Waltham sighed. "I'd have preferred to wait just a little longer until everything I needed was set up on the other end, but Miss Nose here has become a real problem. Everywhere I turn, she's in my way. I finally just cashed the damn check so that she couldn't chase bank deposits or other incriminating paperwork. But cash is bulky, which makes moving around with it a problem."

"We could mail it to you," she heard Bart say, amusement in his voice.

She wondered how he could be amused at a time like this.

"Funny," the mayor said. He moved to the cupboard, his gun still leveled on Bart. Bart turned with him, staying between Haley and the weapon. "Open the cupboard," Waltham ordered.

Bart complied, and Waltham followed his movements with the gun.

Haley noticed two things simultaneously: first, how safe she'd felt behind Bart's protective shoulders, and how that sense of security extended far beyond this moment. He'd protected her from her own stubbornness by forcing her to do what she had to do to get out of jail; he'd gotten between her and the flying tree limb during the hurricane; and he'd stepped between her and the mayor's gun. He *was* tougher than she was.

But what finally rang true for her, though it was still confusing, was that leaning on him didn't diminish her in any way.

Second, that after all she'd done to teach herself to be strong, she was still afraid. But, she realized with a sudden clarity, she was afraid for Bart, not for herself.

As Bart reached into the cupboard for a large plastic trash bag, Haley noticed that the mayor had his attention riveted on him, probably expecting him to make a suspicious move.

She waited with barely contained impatience, while Bart put the trash bag on the desk.

"Get the duffel under the desk," the mayor directed.

Bart reached in and drew out a large, nylon duffel that would easily hold a lot of cash and could be carried onto a plane and stowed in an overhead compartment without ever arousing suspicion.

Haley waited, the silence deafening.

"Put the money into the duffel," the mayor said.

Haley detected a subtle difference in Bart's easy movements. He was getting ready to make his move. But she didn't want him to take that risk while the gun was on him.

She waited one more moment, until Bart pulled the first handful of money out of the plastic trash bag and the mayor's eyes followed it greedily.

Then she heaved herself at Waltham. Unfortunately, just at that moment Bart chose to pitch the money in the mayor's face and throw a punch at him.

Haley saw large-denomination bills fluttering in front of

her face, then caught Bart's blow on her shoulder. She screamed, the mayor shouted and the three of them went down on the carpet in a tangle of flying, kicking limbs.

On her stomach under several hundred pounds of struggling males, Haley saw that the gun was within reach and slapped her hand on it—

The door was suddenly kicked open, and Officer Will Hamilton walked into the room, weapon drawn.

BART COULDN'T quite believe the Keystone Kops quality of this little adventure. The mayor had struck the floor pretty hard and Bart easily pushed the man off him and onto the carpet. Haley's legs were trapped under his upper back, and he sat up to free her.

He *had* to be in love with a woman who couldn't just let him take the lead but had to second-guess every move so that she could be part of it—or, more to the point, take over.

He would have had Waltham if she hadn't chosen that moment to be heroic. She didn't seem to understand that that was *his* job.

And what was going to happen now? Whose side *was* Hamilton on?

The officer's eyes went over the money that was on the desk and spewed all over the floor, the stunned mayor, and Bart, helping Haley up.

Hamilton kept the gun on Bart and asked, "You all right, John?"

The mayor shook his head, trying to focus.

"Will!" Haley said, apparently surprised to learn that her suspicions about him were well founded.

Bart had a plan, but he had to implement it quickly before Haley became aware of it and the mayor gathered his wits.

He caught Haley's arm and moved toward the door with her, forcing Will to turn, too, if he was to keep them covered.

"Stay away from the door," Hamilton said in a nervous tone, darting a glance from Bart and Haley to Waltham. "John! Let's go, John! Get the bag so we can get out of here!"

"Will, you're not serious!" Haley exclaimed. "Stepping on everybody else in the interest of your career is one thing, but stealing from the homeless…"

He gave her a scornful look. "Grow up, Haley. Life's about taking care of yourself."

"Odd attitude for someone whose job is to protect and to serve."

"Not at all. I've just chosen to protect and serve me." He pointed her toward the desk with the gun. "Put that money in the duffel bag for me."

Haley folded her arms defiantly. "If you're going to steal from your own community, you can do it yourself."

So, Bart thought, she apparently no longer had fear issues. But her courage was coming at the damnedest time.

He pushed her gently toward the desk. "Do as he says," he ordered quietly.

"I will n—" she began, bristling.

Bart gripped her arm, trying to tell her with his eyes that he had a plan that required her cooperation.

She took several reluctant steps toward the desk, seemingly trying to read his mind and worried about what he intended.

He ignored her, satisfied that she was now out of the way. He slowly closed in on Hamilton.

"Hey," Hamilton said, backing away, "I can't miss you at this range. Stop right there."

"Bart…" Haley said anxiously from behind him.

"When did Waltham bring you into it?" Bart asked Hamilton.

"I've been a trusted ally for some time," Hamilton replied. "A few traffic stops unreported. A few gambling raids at Balducci's where he was allowed to get away..."

"A few Children's and Family Services reports that stopped with you?"

All the while they talked, Bart was backing Hamilton toward the closet door.

"The McGee kid can take care of himself," Hamilton said with a shrug. "And the mayor has a thing for his mo—"

With a force that surprised Bart, even though he was waiting for it, the closet door flew open and slammed into Hamilton's head and back. He was thrown forward into Bart's arms, and the gun came flying out of his hand. Hamilton's body crumpled, and Bart eased him to the floor.

Bart turned quickly, on the chance that Waltham was conscious, and was just in time to see Haley bean the mayor with a bowling trophy from his desk. Waltham fell before he'd even gotten to his knees.

"Thank you," Bart said, sending Haley a grin across the office. "Just can't stay out of things, can you?"

"I'd have had him before," she said, coming toward Bart, "if you hadn't thrown money in my face and socked my shoulder."

"If you'd just trusted me to handle it..."

"I didn't want you to get hurt."

She reached him and threw her arms around him. Her body was trembling.

"Are you all right?" he asked in concern, kissing her cheek. "Did this bring up all those bad memories?"

She leaned back in his arms to see him more clearly, her expression free of fear despite her tremors. "Not even remotely. Paul ran. You not only didn't run, but kept getting between me and the gun.''

"Yeah, well, why didn't you just let me?" he asked, smoothing her tumbled hair out of her face. "You kept trying to interfere."

Her dark eyes were soft with love; her bottom lip quivered just a little. "Because I was more afraid for you than I was for me." She swallowed and asked on a whisper, "That's love, isn't it?"

"Big-time," he declared, kissing her gently.

"It makes you bossy and meddlesome."

"Yes."

"So...you're in love with me, too."

"I thought we'd already confirmed that."

She smiled and kissed his chin. "I like hearing it."

So did he. "I love you," he said, holding her gaze, "and I promise I'll tell you every day for the next sixty years."

Her eyes were grave, then amusement sparkled in them. "We'll have to come back for that marriage license."

"Pardon me," Jackie said, suddenly appearing beside them. "I'm delighted that your relationship is now going so well, but how about a little 'Well done with the door, Jackie,' or 'Thanks for the heads-up about the bag of money, Jackie.'"

Bart wrapped an arm around her shoulders and drew her into their circle. "You were wonderful," he praised. "I wasn't sure if you'd realize what I wanted you to do when I backed him up against the closet."

Jackie nodded a little ruefully. "Well, considering I'm the one who called the police from the closet, taking the chance Hamilton was in cahoots with the mayor, and got you two in even more trouble, I figured I'd better try something."

"We did it!" Haley said excitedly, hugging Jackie. "We got the goods on the mayor. We have to celebrate!"

Jackie, wincing, pushed away from them. "I agree, but not at the moment. Right now I have to barf. Excuse me."

As she ran from the office, Officer Brody and another officer Bart didn't recognize appeared to take charge of Hamilton and the mayor. City Hall workers crowded around the door.

"Councilwoman Bourgeois phoned us," Brody explained, appearing puzzled. "Said she was in a closet and that Will Hamilton was about to shoot you."

Bart nudged the inert body with his toe. "We changed his mind."

Brody looked from the unconscious men to Bart and Haley. "You two the Starsky and Hutch of Maple Hill now?"

Haley smiled, leaning into Bart. "I'd rather think of us as William Powell and Myrna Loy."

She'd lost him. "Who?" he asked.

"You know. The *Thin Man* series. Nick and Nora Charles, a couple who solved mysteries while happily married and crazy in love."

That had definite appeal. "Okay, Nick and Nora it is."

HALEY AND BART filed their report at the police station. They were sitting and waiting for permission to leave, just before 6 p.m., when the door opened and Hank Whitcomb walked in.

"Hank!" Haley cried, and ran to him.

He caught her in his arms and held her close. Then he put her aside and frowned at Bart as he walked over.

"I asked you to get her *out* of jail," he chided.

Bart laughed and shook his hand. "I challenge you to keep her from doing anything she wants to do. How come you're here?"

"The shuttle landed safely in Southern California this morning," he said, "and I took the next flight home. I was going to sleep for three days, but Mom told me Haley had called and said you'd be at the police station. Something about the mayor holding you at gunpoint?"

Haley recounted the events of their afternoon.

"Whoa!" Hank sank onto a chair. Bart and Haley resumed their seats. Hank touched Haley's arm. "Are you all right?"

Haley understood that he, too, wondered if the experience had brought up the past. "I'm fine. Bart was there." That would explain the absence of all her fears now, she realized. *Bart was there.*

Hank looked from one to the other with dawning perception. "Oh, no," he said.

"Yeah," Bart confirmed. "I'm sorry. You're going to be looking at my face at every family reunion from now on."

"You're getting married?"

Haley loved the way Bart nodded without hesitation. She felt a glow of happiness that the man who'd lost everything had found something in her with which to rebuild his life.

"As soon as we can manage it," he said.

Hank pretended dismay, but quickly hugged Haley again, then Bart.

"You realize you're starting your married life as parents?" he asked.

Both blinked at him.

"A caseworker from Children's and Family Services brought over that McGee boy who works for you, Haley. Seems his mom's going up the river for a while, and they think he should stay with you. They took him to Mom since no one could find you."

Haley looped her arm in Bart's. "You won't mind that?"

"Of course not," he replied. "I helped you get him, didn't I? So, that's one more reason to celebrate tonight. Hank, can you stay awake long enough to come?"

Hank yawned but nodded. "Sure," he said. "I have no-where to sleep, anyway. Somebody's got my room."

Haley, heart swollen with happiness, leaned her head against Bart's upper arm. "Don't worry. I can solve that problem for you very easily."

Hank glanced from one to the other again, trying to see beyond what was visible. "This happened pretty fast. I mean—two whole days?"

Bart shrugged. "I knew I loved her yesterday."

"The moment the light went on." Haley smiled.

Hank raised an eyebrow. "The light?"

Haley loved the intimate look Bart gave her before he turned to Hank to tell him that it was hard to explain.

BRODY APPEARED and told them that they could leave. They stepped outside into the balmy evening and inhaled the fragrance of the woods surrounding the town, the roses in the square.

Bart remembered his first glimpse of Maple Hill, and how he'd felt that he was driving into an alien environment. He realized now that he could not have been more wrong. In less than forty-eight hours he'd come to feel he would never belong anywhere else.

"I understand Jackie Bourgeois was with you today," Hank said.

"She was." Haley walked between Bart and Hank, link-ing an arm through each of theirs. She explained Jackie's role in the day's adventure. "She left half an hour ago to pick up her kids at the baby-sitter's."

He nodded. "How's she doing since Ricky died?"

Haley sighed. "She'll be all right eventually, I guess.

But she's dealing with a lot. And she just found out she's pregnant—from their last attempt at reconciliation, just before he died.''

He had a grim look of concern on his face, Bart thought.

"Hank and Jackie were high school sweethearts," Haley explained to Bart, who wondered if that look suggested that Hank still had feelings for Jackie.

He got the answer a moment later, when Hank said, "Well, when you see her, tell her I said hello."

"She's meeting us at the Old Post Road Inn tonight." Haley freed her arm. "You can tell her yourself. You driving home with us?"

The grim look on Hank's face deepened.

"Ah…no, thanks. I've got a rental car."

Haley noted his fatigued expression. "Are you okay?"

"He's been up for days," Bart said. "Why don't you start the truck, and I'll walk him to his car."

She studied them suspiciously. "You're not going to plot anything, are you?"

"That's entirely possible."

She pulled his face down for a kiss. "As long as I get the exclusive story."

She hurried off to the truck, and he stared after her a moment, unable to believe she was his and he was hers. Life had taken an astonishingly happy turn in such a short amount of time.

Then he concentrated on Hank's beleaguered expression. "*Are* you okay, Hank?"

"I…uh, I'm thinking about coming home," Hank said.

Bart didn't get it at first. He put a diagnostic hand to his friend's forehead. "You are home."

Hank slapped his hand away. "Jerk. I mean I'm thinking about *moving* back home."

Bart stared at him in astonishment. "You mean…give up NASA?"

"Are you giving up Cocoa Beach?"

Bart had absolutely no hesitation about doing that, which amazed him. "Yeah. I need Haley."

"Yeah." Hank sighed wearily and folded his arms. "Well, I'm getting to the age where I need a life."

Bart understood that.

"I can't think of a better place to be."

Hank nodded, then seemed to come out of whatever was upsetting him. He clapped Bart on the shoulder. "And now that we're going to share a family, it'll be even better."

Temperature Rising
Bobby Hutchinson

Dear Reader,

Sixteen years ago, I sold a business and spent a year writing a story dear to my heart. I sent it off to Harlequin Superromance, and when the call came saying it would be published, I felt humble and grateful and filled with joy. I'd found the work I loved, and a special home for it, so of course when the time came to participate in an anthology celebrating Superromance's 1000th book, I felt honored and thrilled.

I've written many Superromance novels, and whenever one is published, the emotions are as intense and heartfelt as they were with that very first book. In recent years, my stories have been part of a series, EMERGENCY! They take place in and around St. Joseph's Medical Center in Vancouver, British Columbia. *Temperature Rising* is set there, as well, and just as in the longer stories, bodies are healed, hearts are broken and, with love as the antibiotic, mended again.

May this prescription touch your heart and strengthen your belief in the power of romance.

Much love,

Bobby

CHAPTER ONE

TRAUMA SURGEON James Burke methodically soaped and scrubbed his knuckles, wrists and forearms. He was preparing to operate on the man with the perforated appendix, who had just come up from St. Joseph's ER. It was 7 a.m., Monday, and in addition to the emergency surgery, he had a full day of elective procedures. Others might view this as stressful, but it gave James a sense of well-being.

The door behind him opened, and he glanced up to see the nurse from the desk hurrying in. He could tell from her apprehensive expression that he was about to be bumped from an operating room for the fourth time in as many days, and his temper flared before she'd uttered a word.

"I'm sorry, Dr. Burke," she began, "but Dr. Seeley has to handle a ruptured aortic aneurysm. He'll need to use Room Two. And I don't have another room available until the pneumothorax in Four is closed. I checked, and Doc Rundle said she'll be about another forty minutes."

"Forty minutes, hell," Burke snarled. "You know as well as I do Rundle won't finish for at least another hour." He glared at the plump nurse and threw the scrub brush into the sink with such force that it bounced twice. "My guy's appendix is becoming septic. It has to be done *now*." That wasn't entirely true, but he did have an elective gallbladder scheduled before lunch, and this would delay it. "I'm sick and bloody tired of having every surgery put back. Can't you manage things better?"

She lifted her chin and gave him a level look. The red

blotches on her cheeks and neck testified to her controlled anger. "I'm sorry, Doctor, but you're aware how many operating rooms we have. I can't just manufacture more. You can sort this out with Doc Seeley. He'll be here in a minute." She marched out to her desk, her back stiff.

James turned off the water in disgust. There was no point in even broaching the matter with Seeley. He knew that both the other doctor and the anesthesiologist assigned to run the OR for the day would agree that the aorta surgery took precedence over the appendectomy. James knew it, too. It was just that the constant disruption in his OR schedule was making him crazy.

Cursing under his breath, James dried his hands and stalked off down the hall. He shoved open the door to the doctors' lounge, still seething with frustration.

David Chow, one of the senior surgical residents who had scrubbed with James a few days earlier, was slumped on the sagging couch, chewing on a slab of pizza. He took in James's disgruntled face and the green scrubs he wore, swallowed and cleared his throat. "Bumped again, huh? Bummer."

Chow had earned the sharp side of James's tongue the day he'd assisted on the torn gullet. The big, sloppy man was as casual about surgery as he was about his appearance, an attitude that James abhorred and wouldn't tolerate in his OR.

James prided himself, though, on not holding grudges. What happened in the OR stayed there—if, of course, he could ever get into one to do his damn job in the first place.

Chow took a swig from a can of soda and burped. Then he picked up a newspaper and waved it at James. "Did ya see this? The docs in interior B.C. are threatening to go on strike unless the government loosens up the purse strings and starts allotting more funding for rural health care."

James read the article, titled "The rural doctor is in—

trouble, that is." "I sympathize with them, but right here in Vancouver things aren't that much better," he grumbled. "This shortage of operating rooms has reached crisis proportions. The doctors in the ER are complaining they're overworked—short-staffed because two highly qualified ER physicians left for the U.S. last month. The nurses say there aren't enough beds and they haven't had a raise in years. My elective surgical patients bitch at me because of the long waits." He'd discussed the situation with St. Joe's chief operating officer, Melissa Clayton. She'd brought it to the attention of the ministry, but nothing had changed.

"Well, maybe we oughta try a little job action." Chow reached for another slice of pizza. "No percentage in gripin' unless it leads to action, right?" he queried, talking around a mouthful of salami and spilling tomato sauce down the front of his rumpled T-shirt.

James stared at the younger man with grudging respect. Chow was absolutely correct. Why hadn't he thought of it himself? It was past time to take affirmative action. James was a board member of the Canadian Medical Association. Maybe the doctors needed to call a meeting and get tough.

He'd get his secretary on it that very afternoon.

MELISSA CLAYTON had canceled a late-afternoon meeting with the medical advisory committee in order to do something she hated and usually avoided at all costs—shopping for clothes.

The expedition hadn't been her idea. Arlene O'Connor, her personal assistant and trusted friend, had looked at Melissa that morning and rolled her eyes. "It's eighty-seven degrees outside, Vancouver's in the middle of the hottest August on record, and I swear that's a wool dress you're wearing."

"I don't think so." Melissa couldn't admit even to Arlene that she wouldn't know wool unless a sheep had it on.

"It's got short sleeves." It was also prickly and hot; she had to admit that.

"Short sleeves or not, you've gone long past the glowing stage to plain old sweat. That's wool, Boss." Arlene, seven months and nine days pregnant with her first baby, managed to look impeccable in something blue, loose and so fashionable it gave Melissa a headache.

Or maybe it was the heat that was causing her headache. The air-conditioning in her office at St. Joe's had been on the fritz for four days now. It only worked when the repair people came to check it. The moment they left, it thumbed its nose and died again.

The air-conditioning in this fashionable department store, however, was working way too well. It must be under forty degrees, Melissa thought as she shivered her way out of a dress that even she could see made her look like a thirty-six-year-old hooker. It was the only item she'd chosen herself.

"How's that little navy skirt and jacket fitting, Ms. Clayton?" a male voice queried.

"Melissa. Please call me Melissa."

Wearing her black bra and yellow flowered bikinis, she snatched the navy skirt and jacket off their padded hanger as if the personal shopper Arlene had hired was about to burst into the store's luxurious dressing room and chastise her for not wearing coordinated underwear.

"I've got a doctor's appointment today and Lamaze classes tomorrow, which means I can't come and supervise you," Arlene had said. "And there's no way you can be trusted to buy clothes on your own—you're style challenged. So I'm lining you up with a professional wardrobe consultant from The Bay."

Why had it never entered Melissa's head that a man could be a wardrobe consultant? It just showed that she, who prided herself on being an equal-opportunities advocate, still had massive blind spots about who did what work-wise. Wrestling herself into the blue skirt and top, Melissa could only cringe at what a horrifying revelation that was, particularly when six short months earlier, she had been hired to do a job that in the entire history of St. Joseph's Medical Center had traditionally been male.

"I'll have this on in a minute, Barry," she called, as she tried to figure out the complex order of snaps and buttons that kept the top closed.

"No rush—take your time."

She fumbled with fastenings and blew impatiently at the annoying strands of wavy red hair that had slipped out of the clip at the back of her head. At last she stepped out of the change room.

"So what do you think?" She frowned at herself in the three-way mirror. The outfit didn't look too bad. At least the skirt was longer than the dress had been, and not half as tight.

Barry put a finger on her shoulder and turned her around, surveying her from all angles. Melissa found it amazing that he could do so and not make her feel at all self-conscious. He seemed to view both her tall body and her flamboyant coloring as a palette from which to create what he called "a stellar look." The process was as impersonal as her reviewing a budget or determining policy for a department at the hospital.

"Looks *très* chic, but how does it *feel?*" he said after a moment's scrutiny. "Is it comfortable, cool, something you could put on in the morning, sit through three meetings in and then, with a change of accessories—pearls, say, a pair of stilettos—wear to go out to dinner?"

Tall himself, skeletal, dark skinned and elegant, without being intimidating in the least, he reached out and tweaked the shoulder of the jacket into place.

Clearly, Arlene had described Melissa's workdays to

him. Barry had assumed the going-out-to-dinner part all on his own. Melissa didn't correct him. Why admit that dinner was almost always something out of a carton she picked up on the drive home and ate while she scanned reports or jotted notes? The last time she'd been out to dinner was New Year's Eve—a blind date, a nephew of her mother's friend Gladys Perkins.

Even now Melissa shuddered at the memory. Maurice was probably a nice enough man, but he was four inches shorter than she was, he'd talked nonstop about mutual funds and he'd had his pants pulled up so high that his equipment had stood out in bold outline.

"So what do you think?" Barry was waiting, the soul of patience.

She shoved Maurice's less-than-impressive equipment out of her mind and tried to see herself objectively. "I think I like it." She frowned at her reflection, doubt mirrored in her eyes. "Is this skirt still too short?" As the first female chief operating officer, the last thing she wanted to project was sexuality.

"Absolutely not. Just above your knee is very tasteful. Although, with your legs you could certainly wear a micromini if you chose." Barry stood back and surveyed her from top to bottom, head tipped to the side. "That shade of navy is wonderful with your titian hair, and it complements those hazel eyes perfectly."

"Titian? Hazel?" Melissa giggled. "It's okay, Barry. You don't have to be diplomatic here. You can just say red and brown. And even I know that any dark color tones down these freckles. I've had them all since I was a kid. I'm not sensitive anymore."

"But you have *fabulous* skin and hair," he countered with a wide smile. "And don't you know that freckles are in this year? So should we add this ensemble to the affirmatives or the negatives?" He gestured at the outfits she'd already hesitantly agreed to, and the others that they'd mutually rejected.

"I'd say this goes with the affirmatives. If you agree?" How she could be so confident in her work and so totally uncertain about a dumb thing like clothes was something she'd never figured out.

"Absolutely. Good choice, Melissa."

Back in the change room, she wearily shucked off the suit and tossed it to him over the door. Then she slipped into a shirtwaist-style dress in green paisley patterned cotton, the next item he'd suggested. Who would have imagined that trying on clothes could be so exhausting?

But by the time she exited the store an hour-and-a-half later, she had four fat garment bags laden with what her mother called "outfits" and Barry referred to as "ensembles." The bags held color-coordinated dresses and blouses and skirts and suits and lightweight jackets, any of which she could snatch off a hanger and put on without agonizing over whether they were suitable.

So what if her credit card was now close to its upper limit? For the first time in her life, she actually had a wardrobe she felt good about. She staggered through the steamy evening heat to her jaunty little sports car and dumped her purchases on the tan leather seat. They were worth every cent.

She'd told herself the same thing about the car, and she'd been right. She'd bought it from a radiologist at the hospital who was moving to Trinidad, and she loved it. She turned on the air-conditioning and waited impatiently for it to cool the interior, but she was halfway home before that happened. What was it about her and air-conditioning?

She was thankful that her apartment was cool and welcoming. The cleaning service had been in that morning, and the cluttered rooms she'd abandoned as she'd raced out the door to work were now in pristine order. Melissa dumped the garment bags on her bed and was staring into her shiny clean, but nearly empty, refrigerator when the phone rang. Wishing she'd stopped to pick up Chinese, she lifted the receiver and said an absent hello.

"Lissa?"

It was her mother, but Betsy Clayton's normally strong, decisive voice was so faint and quivery that it was barely recognizable.

CHAPTER TWO

"Mom? Mom, what's wrong?" Melissa was alarmed. "You sound terrible."

She usually had lunch with Betsy on Sunday afternoon, but her mother had called yesterday morning and canceled, claiming that she hadn't slept well the night before and needed to have a little nap. Melissa had been relieved that Betsy hadn't suggested she come by later in the day; she'd had a stack of reports to read by Monday morning. Now she felt a stab of guilt for not at least calling last night and checking on her mother.

"I'm sick, Lissa." Betsy drew a shuddering breath. "I've had this awful pain in my stomach all weekend, and I kept thinking it would go away. But it's gotten worse instead of better. Now I'm really sick to my stomach. And dizzy. I'm real dizzy."

"Mom, lie down and stay there. Don't take anything. I'll be right over." Melissa hung up the phone and grabbed her keys and handbag. Her mother prided herself on never being ill, and the odd time she was, she wouldn't admit to anything more severe than a touch of flu or an annoying little cold, even when she sounded as if she had pneumonia. For Betsy to call and say she was sick could only mean that her mother was desperate.

Even exceeding the speed limit, the trip to the Vancouver suburb of Burnaby took twenty-five frantic minutes. Melissa screeched into the driveway of the tiny bungalow where she'd grown up, abandoned the car and raced to the door, which was locked as usual; Betsy worried about intruders.

Melissa swore under her breath as she unearthed her key, and then wrinkled her nose as she stepped inside. The house was like an oven; she'd tried repeatedly to put air-conditioning in for Betsy, but her stubborn mother would have none of it.

"That's how people get sick," Betsy insisted. "Breathing secondhand air." Once the woman had an idea in her head, there was no changing it.

"Mom, it's me," Melissa called. There was no answer. Filled with apprehension, she hurried through the living room and into Betsy's small bedroom off the hallway.

Her mother was slumped across the bed, her long, thin frame curled into a tight ball. That she was lying on top of her cream-colored heirloom bedspread was another disturbing indication of extreme distress. Melissa had never seen Betsy so much as sit on the treasured bedcover.

Melissa crouched beside Betsy and put a hand on her forehead. Her mother had a fever.

"Mom, can you talk? Tell me exactly what's happened, exactly where you hurt."

Betsy made an effort to sit up, but the pain was obviously too intense and she slumped down again. Her face, normally either wreathed in smiles or screwed into a frown of disapproval, was contorted with pain and pasty white. She was perspiring heavily, which was understandable in the heat, but she was also shivering so hard her teeth were chattering.

"I'm sure it's nothing," she gasped. "I've been constipated for a while. I took some of those laxatives Gladys brought over. If my bowels would just move, I'm sure I'd feel better."

Melissa knew that wasn't the solution. Constipation was a symptom. She'd begun her career as a nurse, working in the ER for some years before going back to school to get her master's in health administration. Talking in a soothing tone now despite her alarm, she asked questions as she felt her mother's abdomen and again assessed her temperature.

It was immediately obvious that Betsy needed medical attention—and fast.

The problem would be getting her to agree. Along with her dread of intruders, Betsy had what amounted to a paranoid fear of doctors and hospitals. When Melissa was still a toddler, her mother had lost both her parents and Melissa's father within a six-month period. Their illnesses, in Betsy's opinion, had all been misdiagnosed and mistreated by the family physician. He'd put Melissa's father, Frank, "under the knife" when an ulcer perforated. Frank had never regained consciousness, and Melissa had listened to complaints of professional bungling throughout her growing-up years.

She wondered sometimes if her own attraction to the medical field wasn't some sort of rebellion on her part.

Betsy hadn't been to a doctor since she'd broken her wrist nineteen years ago—a long enough time between doctor's visits, Melissa decided.

"Mom, I'm calling an ambulance. You need to go to Emergency." The closest ER was Burnaby General, but Betsy had no family doctor. Melissa had met all the doctors at St. Joe's, and she wanted someone she knew to care for her mother.

Betsy shook her head.

"Mom, you've got something seriously wrong, and there's no other alternative. You have to be seen by a doctor."

"No, Lissa," Betsy moaned. "I won't go to any hospital. Once they get you in, that's the end of you."

Betsy had responded as Melissa had expected, but the lack of willfulness in her tone showed exactly how sick she really was. Melissa didn't bother arguing. She phoned 911, and within twenty minutes paramedics were gently loading Betsy on a stretcher. She had stopped objecting, which Melissa found almost as terrifying as her mother whimpering.

At St. Joe's, Dr. Greg Brulotte was in charge of the evening shift, for which Melissa was grateful; he was highly proficient. Betsy couldn't be in better hands, but it didn't quell the fear that made Melissa's own hands tremble as she filled out the necessary forms.

She paced the waiting room while her mother was being examined, and her heart hammered when Brulotte came hurrying toward her, his slight limp not slowing him down at all.

"Your mother has a bowel obstruction, Melissa," he said without preamble. "X rays show a sizable mass, which has to be removed. We're taking her up to surgery immediately."

CHAPTER THREE

MELISSA SWALLOWED HARD, assessed the information and then nodded. "Which surgeon?"

"Seeley's on."

Melissa shook her head. She was in a position to pull rank, and she didn't hesitate. She wanted the finest surgeon in the country for her mother, and although she knew Seeley was more than competent, he wasn't her first choice.

"I want James Burke," she stated. She had on file a number of glowing letters of praise from former patients of Burke's. His genius as a surgeon was fast becoming a legend at St. Joe's. That his difficult temperament was as well-known as his surgical skill wasn't even a consideration. Melissa wanted and needed expertise at this moment, not a good bedside manner.

Dr. Brulotte nodded. "Okay, let me try to get hold of him. You can visit your mom meanwhile."

Melissa hurried into the treatment room.

Betsy grabbed her hand and clung to it. "I don't want any operation, Lissa. Please," she begged in a frail voice. "Don't let them put me under the knife. You know what happened to your father."

Seeing her mother so frightened and helpless broke Melissa's heart, but what she had to do was clear. "Mom, that was years ago—another time, another hospital. I know these doctors and nurses. I promise I won't let anything bad happen to you," she said in her most reassuring tone.

"Besides, there's no choice. You have to have this operation."

"Maybe if they just gave me another laxative…"

"Did you tell the doctor you'd already taken some?"

Betsy nodded; her eyes filled with tears. "I want to go home," she said. "*Please,* Lissa, take me home. Please?"

Melissa maintained her composure, but it was difficult. She recognized the depth of her mother's fears, and she wished with all her heart that she could do what Betsy wanted, but she couldn't.

"Mom, I've asked for the best surgeon there is to do your operation. I'll be holding your hand when you go in and I'll be there the moment you come out."

Apprehension made her heart pound. No one knew better than a nurse how many things could go wrong in the OR. But nothing would, Melissa assured herself—not here in the hospital where she was chief operating officer. Not with the best surgeon doing the procedure.

Greg Brulotte came in the door. "We're in luck," he announced. "Dr. Burke was at home. He'll be right over."

"Thank goodness." Melissa's sigh was shaky. "Thanks, Greg."

"No problem." He smiled and touched Betsy's shoulder. "We'll all be sending you good thoughts."

Melissa walked beside the gurney up to the surgical floor, and she kissed her mother as the nurses rolled the gurney into the operating room.

She was talking to Louise, the nurse at the desk, when James Burke stepped off the elevator a few minutes later. Her heart swelled with gratitude and relief as he strode toward her.

"Here comes Lord Burke," Louise said in an undertone. "Ramrod firmly inserted."

Melissa didn't approve of the nurse's words. To her, Burke's erect posture inspired confidence, not ridicule. He was an imposing figure, three inches over six feet, with a well-proportioned, broad-shouldered build.

Melissa had heard the rumors about him—that he was a tyrant in the OR when some hapless resident made a mistake; that he was unforgiving if staff deviated from his strict protocol; that he didn't socialize with his co-workers, was a workaholic, a loner; that half the nurses hated him and the other half fantasized about going to bed with him.

At this moment, though, the only thing that mattered to her was his near-mythical prowess in the operating room, and the fact that he was here for her mother.

"Hello, Melissa." He nodded, but didn't return Melissa's strained smile or acknowledge Louise's polite murmur. Nor did he try to reassure Melissa or ask her anything about Betsy; instead, he walked right past the two women as if they were simply props on a stage where he was the star. Which, of course, he was.

In spite of her gratitude, Melissa found his brusque manner a little irritating. Still, he'd come at her request, and Betsy would have the benefit of his expertise. That really was all that mattered, wasn't it? So he had the manners of a Neanderthal, so what?

For the next two hours, Melissa experienced firsthand the emotions she'd so often witnessed during her days as a nurse when the relatives of a loved one could only wait for an outcome that was never certain.

She felt nauseous; her throat was dry; her heart beat at twice its normal speed. Louise was wonderfully reassuring and affectionate, brewing cups of green tea from her own private stock, taking minutes from her own busy schedule to spend as much time with Melissa as she possibly could. It was at her suggestion that Melissa finally went down to the small chapel and spent twenty minutes fervently praying for her mother's well-being. When she came back,

James Burke was waiting, impatience evident in every line of his elegant body.

"The operation was a complete success," he announced. "We removed a large growth. The preliminary lab report indicated the tumor was benign, which is very good news." Still in his operating room greens, he ran a hand through his silky dark hair, pushing it off his forehead. "Your mother is as yet unconscious, but she'll be awake soon. You can see her if you wish."

"I'm so relieved. I promised Mom I'd be there when she woke up. Oh, Dr. Burke, thank you." Melissa felt her eyes filling with tears. "I can't thank you enough."

She had an insane impulse to grab his hand and press it to her lips. She resisted, but heard herself start to babble, instead. "Mom's my only relative. My dad died when I was a little girl. I'm an only child. I don't know what I'd do if—" She suddenly noticed how uncomfortable Burke looked, and stopped. "I'm very grateful to you for coming so quickly tonight and for doing Mom's surgery," she finished in a more formal mode.

"All in a day's work," he said with a stiff attempt at a smile. "And by some miracle we actually got into an OR immediately," he added testily. "Now, if you'll excuse me, I have a meeting to attend." He hurried off toward the doctors' lounge.

"At ease, troops," Louise said sarcastically. "It wouldn't kill him just once to flip the switch from exalted savior to human being." She snorted. "C'mon, I'll walk you to the Acute Care Unit."

For the next half hour, in the postanesthesia recovery unit, Melissa sat holding Betsy's hand, and true to her promise, she was there when Betsy came around enough to realize the operation was over and everything was fine.

The eastern sky was pink and Betsy had been moved to

a private room on the surgical floor by the time Melissa left the hospital and drove home.

Weary to the depths of her being, she thought about the scant two-and-a-half hours before she was due back at work, and for the first time in years she actually considered taking the morning off. She'd call Arlene at seven; if things on her morning schedule could be canceled or rearranged, she'd crawl into bed and sleep for a few hours.

It was still too early to call, plus she felt shaky and wired instead of sleepy. She washed her face, and realized she hadn't eaten since wolfing down a bagel the previous afternoon, but when she looked in the refrigerator, she decided she wasn't the slightest bit hungry. It was a good thing; the fridge was still as empty as it had been the night before. The light on her answering machine was blinking, but she couldn't face even listening to messages.

Maybe she'd lie down, just for half an hour. She headed into the bedroom and saw the four garment bags she's tossed on her bed the previous evening—it felt as though months had passed since her shopping spree instead of only hours. She unzipped the bags, but when she started to shove her new clothing into her cramped closet she realized that she'd have to discard things to make room. Cleaning closets wasn't any higher on her list of priorities than shopping, but it seemed the perfect mindless occupation right at the moment.

She was in the midst of trying to decide if she'd ever again wear a lime-green shirt she'd bought on sale, when the phone rang.

Her heart thumped. What if Betsy...

"Melissa, it's Arlene. I hope I didn't wake you."

Melissa's heartbeat settled down.

"I called last night. You were out picking up boy toys in clubs again, right?"

Melissa explained about her mother. "She came through

fine. The tumor was benign. She'll be back home within a week. The nurses will make sure of that—because the moment Mom starts feeling better, she'll be an impossible patient.''

Arlene expressed concern. Then she went on. "I thought you should know the doctors had a private meeting last night, and according to my mole, they've decided to take immediate job action over the shortage of ORs and the long hours they put in."

Arlene was married to Frank O'Connor, an ER physician.

"I figured you might like a little warning, instead of walking into St. Joe's this morning and getting the news along with your morning coffee."

"Immediate job action, as in—not today?" Her dreams of spending a morning in bed evaporated.

"You got it. They move fast when they're really pissed off. Sorry to be the bearer of bad tidings, but hey, what're friends for? Gotta run—or walk, rather. This tyrant I'm married to insists I get a half hour of exercise every morning, *out* of bed. See you at eight."

"Arlene, thanks." Melissa hung up the phone and her brain went into overdrive, assessing what had to be done first off. Job action would mean surgeries canceled, beds closed; she'd have to come up with a policy for moving urgent surgical cases to other hospitals. There would be the press to deal with. The Ministry of Health would demand a meeting right away. Her already busy days were about to become frantic.

Coffee. She'd need lots of caffeine to get her through. Melissa set up the automatic coffeemaker and headed for the shower, telling herself there were two definite advantages to this situation.

The first was that working right at St. Joe's, she could pop by and see her mother whenever she had a few moments. The second was that—thanks to Barry—she wouldn't even have to think about what to wear.

Now, if only the technicians could repair the air-conditioning in her office, she might get through this crisis without a coronary.

CHAPTER FOUR

THE STIFLING ATMOSPHERE in her office was the least of Melissa's worries that day. The hours passed in a controlled frenzy. Her handpicked team of consultants made suggestions; she listened to endless concerns from managers, sat in on three conference calls in an effort to transfer patients to other hospitals and managed only two hasty trips up to Betsy's room.

Both times, Betsy insisted she had no pain and was feeling just fine, which seemed highly unlikely just a few hours after surgery. Inevitably, those assurances were followed by a plaintive "When can I go home?"

Melissa told the supervising nurse about her mother's stoic refusal to complain even if she was in agony, and the nurse promised to keep a particular eye on Betsy.

By four in the afternoon, the sleepless night Melissa had spent was taking its toll. But there was no possibility of leaving the hospital. A mound of urgent faxes and messages sat on her desk, and if she didn't deal with them immediately, a mountain would be there by morning and the task would be insurmountable.

For an hour-and-a-half she worked, struggling to stay alert while her body signaled exhaustion. At 5:45, Arlene, who was also working overtime, brought in an egg salad sandwich, a chocolate doughnut and a bottle of iced tea, and plopped them on Melissa's desk.

"If you don't eat something, you'll get sick," she scolded. "I'm gonna go look in on your mom before I leave. If I think she needs you for anything, I'll buzz you on your cell.''

''Thanks.'' Tears choked her, and it was all Melissa could do to keep from crying at her assistant's kindness. Being tired and stressed made her weepy.

The other three secretaries had long since gone home, and the outer office was deserted. As the day ended and evening came, Melissa could sense the old hospital relaxing around her.

She ate the sandwich and drank the sweet tea, but the moment arrived when the last shreds of her energy fled and she knew she couldn't do another thing. She got to her feet, then had to bend over as a wave of dizziness washed through her.

Whew. She shook her head and hung on to the edge of the desk as she slowly straightened. She needed a good eight hours of sleep.

In a weary fog, she made her way up to her mother's room. Betsy was sleeping, and Melissa took her hand and kissed her cheek, but her mother didn't awaken.

''She's doing really well,'' the nurse at the desk assured Melissa. ''She was a bit restless this afternoon. A good sleep is the best thing for her.'' She smiled her reassurance. ''Go home and get some rest. We're keeping a close eye on her for you. We've got your phone number at home if we need you.''

Soothed, Melissa dragged herself out to her car. The intense heat outdoors shocked her. The parking lot seemed to shimmer with it, but at least her personal parking spot was in the shade, under one of the cedar trees that bordered the lot.

The leather seats in her car were almost hot enough for third-degree burns. Sweating, she climbed in, drove home and headed straight for the shower.

Five minutes later, feeling clean and blessedly cool at

last, she staggered from the bathroom straight to her bed. Never had fresh sheets and soft pillows felt so good. She groaned and wriggled deeper into the nest, and between one breath and the next she was asleep.

The phone was ringing. It took her a long time to surface enough to fumble it to her ear and mumble hello.

"Ms. Clayton, it's Rena Johns calling from St. Joe's. I'm the nurse in Surgical Recovery, where your mom is a patient."

Melissa sat up and her heart began to hammer.

"Ms. Clayton, could you come as quickly as possible? Your mother suffered cardiac arrest a few moments ago. The emergency medical team have resuscitated her. Her heart rhythm is stable at the moment, but she hasn't yet regained consciousness."

"C-cardiac arrest? But—but how can that be? Mom's heart is strong. Are you su-sure—" Melissa gulped and then croaked, "Are you sure it's the right patient? My mom is Betsy Clayton…."

But even before the nurse assured her it *was* Betsy Clayton, Melissa knew there was no mistake. Nurses didn't make mistakes like that. She also knew from personal experience that they didn't call in the middle of the night unless it was urgent, unless they thought a patient was dying. All of a sudden she could hardly get her breath.

"How—how long was she…?" If Betsy's heart had stopped briefly, she had a good chance of recovering without side effects. If, however, her heart had stopped for a prolonged period before resuscitation, she would probably have suffered irreversible brain damage.

"We were really lucky. One of the nurses heard something and went in to check. She was there when it happened. We had a team on her in seconds."

Melissa sent a silent *thank-you* heavenward. "I'll be right over."

The bedside clock said 2:33 a.m. It took her shocked brain moments to figure out it was Wednesday morning.

The normally traffic-choked Vancouver streets were nearly deserted at this hour. Melissa's tires squealed as she pulled into the parking lot. This, too, was nearly deserted, although brightly lit. She tore out of the car and ran through the eerie, flickering yellow light toward the hospital.

She'd never realized how long it took to get to St. Joe's from the lot, or how slow the elevators that led to the upper floors were.

Betsy was now in the Coronary Care Unit. Her eyes were partly open, the left more than the right, but it was obvious she wasn't awake or aware. She was hooked to a battery of machines. Melissa threaded her way through them and took Betsy's limp hand in her own.

"Mom? Mom, it's me, Melissa. Can you hear me, Mom?"

No response. Melissa went on speaking, reassuring Betsy that she was going to be fine, that everything was under control, that there was no reason to be alarmed—all the lies that Melissa had tried to console herself with on the way over, with no success.

Rena Johns, a tiny nurse with a long braid of blond hair, reconfirmed that Betsy hadn't regained consciousness after the resuscitation, which Dr. Wong had supervised.

There was no sign of him. He was an intern, Rena explained, and he'd been called away to another emergency. Because of the job action, the hospital was already seriously short of doctors.

Melissa saw compassion in the nurse's dark eyes. "Didn't Dr. Wong order an MRI? A CT scan?" The tests would show if any damage had occurred, and give some indication of how Betsy should be treated.

Rena shook her head. "There was no point in running

tests at this hour—there aren't any doctors around to read the results," she stated.

Melissa was losing control. "Did anyone call Dr. Burke? Mom's his patient."

"Of course we did," Rena soothed. "He's on his way. He'll be here any moment."

For the next ten minutes, Melissa stood beside Betsy's bed, murmuring comforting words, while inside her head a madwoman shrieked that this couldn't be happening, not to her mother. She wouldn't *let* it happen. There had to be something she could do.

But for the life of her, she couldn't think what it might be.

CHAPTER FIVE

MELISSA HEARD James Burke before she saw him. He was talking in a low, intense voice to Rena at the nursing station. Melissa knew he was getting the medical lowdown on Betsy—what drugs had been administered, what procedures had been followed. Having him here taking charge, doing something, was a relief. A little of her anxiety dissipated.

"Melissa—"

She turned toward him. He was wearing jeans and a white T-shirt, and his hair was sleep rumpled. He wasn't looking at her. Instead, he was frowning down at Betsy as he spoke, his expression disapproving, as if his patient wasn't behaving the way he'd ordered and he was not amused.

"If you'll excuse me a moment, I'd like to examine your mother."

Melissa felt like saying that he could do so with her in the room, too, then thought better of it. She swallowed the words and walked over to the nursing station.

Rena poured her a cup of coffee and silently handed it to her. It was strong and hot, and Melissa sipped it, feeling the caffeine jolt her nervous system.

The cup was almost empty by the time Burke joined her.

"Your mother's vital signs are all fairly normal again," he commented. "There was no indication whatsoever of any heart problems, and the operation was successful. I don't understand why this happened."

"Well, success or not, she's unresponsive now," Melissa snapped.

Burke scowled at her. "I'm well aware of that fact. First thing in the morning I'm ordering extensive tests to determine exactly what's going on with her."

"And will you be around to read them? Because with the job action—"

He nodded, impatient as always. "I'll be here, of course. After all, your mother is my patient." He sounded irritated, but Melissa was beginning to realize that for Burke, irritation and impatience were probably the norm.

He said to Rena, "You have my pager number. Call me if there's any change whatsoever in Mrs. Clayton's condition. I want her monitored closely. I'll be in the doctors' lounge for the rest of the night." He turned to Melissa. "I suggest you go home and get some rest, as well. There's nothing to be gained by sitting around here." He headed off down the corridor.

Melissa knew that, logically, he was right. But she also knew she wasn't about to get in her car and drive home, leaving her mother here in CCU. When Betsy woke up, she'd want her daughter at her side. Didn't Burke understand that?

If Betsy woke up. Melissa was too much of a realist, too much of a nurse even after all these years, not to fully understand that her mother might well not come out of this. She shuddered and had to struggle against the urge to burst into tears. Worst of all was the memory of how she'd promised her mother everything would be fine.

"I'm not going home. I need to be here when Mom wakes up," Melissa said to his retreating back.

"Of course you do. Burke has all the people skills of a rock sometimes," Rena, who had been quietly observing the exchange, remarked. "There's an empty room just down the hall. Why don't you try to get some rest. If there's the slightest change in your mom, I'll come and get you.''

"Thanks, that's what I'll do." Melissa realized she wouldn't be able to sleep, but she also realized she needed to be alone, to get her emotions under control and figure out what else she could do to help her mother.

For the remainder of the night, she lay sleepless on the narrow hospital bed, alternately agonizing about Betsy and going over the millions of details she'd have to see to in the morning. Each day the job action continued, the problems she had to contend with would multiply. Why did everything have to happen at once? She'd only been in her position for six months, and those who'd opposed her appointment would be watching gleefully, waiting for her to make some fatal mistake.

Well, they'd better not hold their breath. About her job, at least, she was confident.

At five in the morning she went back to CCU. There'd been no change whatsoever in Betsy's condition.

"I'm going home to shower and change for work. I'll be back by six-thirty at the latest," she told Rena. "If there's any change, call me on my cell."

"Absolutely," Rena assured her.

But Melissa could see by the expression in her eyes that the nurse had no expectations Betsy would wake up while Melissa was gone.

Outside the hospital, the dawn air was blessedly cool, although the clear blue canopy overhead and the coral pink in the east where the sun would soon rise heralded another record-breaking day in Vancouver's uncharacteristic heat wave.

Melissa drove home, showered, yanked another of Barry's ensembles from her closet, pulled it on and raced back to the hospital to begin a day even more frantic than the previous one had been.

FOR THE NEXT forty-eight hours, Melissa all but lived at St. Joe's, dealing with one crisis after the next as the job action escalated. She attended meeting after meeting, none of which accomplished much as far as she could see. She held press conferences to reassure the public that emergency services were still available. She frantically called other hospitals to arrange for procedures that couldn't be postponed.

And through it all, a part of her mind was constantly with Betsy. There'd been no improvement at all in her mother. Burke had done an entire battery of tests, and he'd promised to discuss them with Melissa at noon on Friday.

She was late for their meeting. That morning's appointments, first with the Ministry of Health and then with the financial committee, both went past their allotted times. It was twelve-twenty by the time Melissa made it to the Coronary Care Unit, where Burke was waiting. He was standing, arms folded across his chest, foot tapping impatiently.

"I'm sorry to keep you waiting, Dr. Burke."

He didn't nod or accept her apology, or even indicate that he'd heard her.

Melissa was tired to the bone. She hadn't had a decent meal in days. She was sick with worry about her mother, and she had three more meetings that afternoon before she could even hope to get to the paperwork that almost buried her desk. She still hadn't managed to find suitable placements at other hospitals for four urgent surgical patients, three of whom would have been operated on by this same Dr. Burke, who was acting as if *his* time was of the essence. The patients' relatives were out of their minds with worry, and their frustration and anger had to be dealt with—by Melissa.

It was hard to be sympathetic to the doctor's position when she was confronted hourly with the human misery it created.

And how could a man who looked so blasted attractive be so lacking in people skills?

"This office will do," he said in a stiff tone, ushering Melissa into a small room the nurses used for meetings. He gestured to a chair and she sat down, but he remained standing, which annoyed her further. It was such an obvious way of taking control of the proceedings.

She wasn't about to let him get away with it. She was a veteran of subtle power plays. The thing to do was take control of the conversation. "So what do the test results indicate about Mom's condition, and what do you suggest as treatment, Doctor?" She used her most professional tone.

He cleared his throat and shoved a hank of dark hair away from his forehead.

"I've evaluated your mother carefully," he began without meeting Melissa's gaze. He stared at some point three feet above her head. "As a result of the tests I've done, I've decided to withdraw all medication immediately."

"Oh? Why is that, Doctor?" Melissa frowned and waited, not understanding what he was getting at, although a tiny thread of alarm began to wind itself into a knot inside her.

"In my opinion, your mother has suffered irreversible brain damage."

Melissa heard the words, and her blood seemed to freeze in her veins. She swallowed hard and stared at him in horror, unable to say a word.

"I don't believe your mother is going to recover or improve. I suggest you begin looking at placement in a care home for her. Not immediately, of course. But there are a limited number of openings in the better facilities, and it would be best to get her name on lists."

"A...a care home?" Melissa was aghast. She'd trained herself to deal with emergencies in a controlled and rational manner. As an administrator, she'd attended numerous workshops on anger management. But none of the techniques she'd learned even occurred to her now.

"You're saying—" Rage, red and urgent and violent, began somewhere in her gut and traveled to her brain as if it were a lit fuse linked to nitroglycerine. "You're saying I should put my mother in a *care home?* My mother is only fifty-six."

As she got to her feet, she was dimly aware that he was still talking.

"As I mentioned, there are waiting lists, and getting into the best of these facilities may take some time, as I'm sure you're well aware." His voice was composed, his manner cold, distant and totally impersonal.

"But—I just can't believe—this is my *mother* we're talking about here, Doctor." Melissa's voice was suddenly so loud he jumped. "It hasn't even been a *week* since you operated on her, and you're suggesting placement in a *care home?*"

Her voice was getting even louder, and it felt wonderful. She let all her feelings surface; they spilled out in a gush of invective. "You arrogant, egotistical, insufferable—why, a *veterinarian* would show more compassion for a patient than this. How can you possibly be so certain my mother isn't going to improve? Do you actually believe you're God, Dr. Burke? Because you sure as hell sound as if you do."

His expression didn't change an iota.

"Don't you have a mother of your own? Don't you have some concept of how this feels, to be told that—that—" Melissa tried to go on screaming at him, but instead of words, a mental image of her poor mother, helpless and trapped in a coma, frightened and alone in a place Melissa couldn't go to comfort her, came vividly to mind. A sob caught in her throat. She couldn't hold it back, and neither could she stop the explosion of tears that burst from her. She covered her face with her hands and wept.

He made no attempt to comfort her. He didn't even offer a tissue.

Melissa heard the office door open and shut, and she knew James Burke was gone. She sank onto the chair she'd been sitting in, dropped her head into her hands and gave in to the desperate grief and fear she'd been holding at bay for days.

CHAPTER SIX

JAMES HURRIED PAST the two nurses behind the desk, studiously ignoring their curious stares. He knew they'd probably overheard some of what had gone on just now with Melissa Clayton, because the office they'd been using was directly across the hall from the nursing station and sound carried in a building as old as St. Joe's.

He strode down the hall, around a corner and into an empty room. There, he shut the door behind him and locked it, then leaned back and closed his eyes. He was shaking, and his gut felt as though he'd swallowed a vial of acid. He dug in his pocket and popped an antacid tablet in his mouth.

With painstaking attention to every aspect, he went back over the procedure he'd performed on Betsy Clayton, trying to pinpoint anything that had occurred in the OR that might have precipitated the cardiac arrest.

He'd done so countless times in the past two days, and again he couldn't come up with a thing. The operation had been textbook perfect; the orders he'd given for her postoperative care had been meticulous and detailed.

Whatever had brought on the cardiac arrest and its resulting effects hadn't been his fault, he assured himself. But old feelings of inadequacy, self-doubt and guilt washed over him.

He went to the sink and poured a glass of water, which he drank in one long swallow. Then he stood at the small window and stared sightlessly at the traffic on the side street below, as old memories rolled through his mind.

He'd been a young and arrogant surgical resident, the darling of the head of Surgery because of his prowess with a scalpel. He'd operated on an eight-year-old boy named Paul Renaud, a simple procedure to replace tubes in the boy's ears. The irony of the thing was the procedure was no longer done; it was now recognized that such tubes did no good whatsoever.

He hadn't realized that then, however. Afterward, James gave an order for medication. The child died within the hour from an allergic reaction to the drug. Although there'd been no way of predicting the allergic reaction, James still blamed himself. He'd been so cocksure he'd never for a moment considered the possibility. He hadn't even thought to ask the mother, though it turned out later that she hadn't known any more than he had about the boy's sensitivity to the drug.

Bad as it was, that wasn't the worst part of the disaster. The true nightmare had come when he'd tried to notify Marie Renaud of her son's death.

Mrs. Renaud, blue eyed and young enough to be the boy's sister instead of his mother, either couldn't or wouldn't hear what James was saying to her—that her son had died.

"When can I see Paul? I want to be there when he wakes up."

James had swallowed hard and repeated the fact that the little boy had died.

Marie Renaud had given him a sweet smile and even nodded. "I promised I'd be there when he woke up. Can you take me to him?"

Even now, years later, in a hospital on the other side of the country, James could hear Marie asking repeatedly in her soft, accented English when her son would wake up and when she could see him.

Finally, like a coward, he'd turned and fled. The resulting inquiry had absolved him of blame—the drug he'd ordered was a commonplace one, routinely used after such procedures—but James had spent weeks in hell. He'd come close to quitting not just surgery but medicine. It was a turning point in his career. He'd vowed from that moment on that no detail ever would be overlooked.

He'd become a perfectionist, not just about surgery but about everything regarding the safety and health of his patients. Sure, there were times when a patient died. It was inevitable. He'd learned to distance himself emotionally while he told next of kin the bare facts, as he'd done just now with Melissa.

Betsy Clayton wasn't dead, although she might as well be; she was in a deep coma. In James's experience, such patients rarely woke up.

As chief operating officer, Melissa Clayton was one of the most powerful individuals at St. Joe's. She was a woman he'd noticed, admired and applauded for having the same drive, energy and ambition he had.

And damn it all, he found her vibrant red hair and tall, slender body disturbingly sensual in an understated way that excited and intrigued him; she seemed so totally unaware of her appeal. Every time he was near her his body reacted. He'd thought more than once about asking her out, but he had a long-standing policy of not dating co-workers, and he suspected she did, as well. He'd never heard of her dating anyone from St. Joe's, although he knew she was unattached; the gossip mill was up-to-date on who was available and who wasn't.

He'd dreaded this meeting with Melissa. Yet he'd said only what he believed to be true about Betsy Clayton: that there was no hope now she'd recover; that the extensive tests he'd ordered confirmed that she was in a vegetative coma.

Melissa Clayton had called him arrogant. Insufferable. Had said a veterinarian would show more compassion. But it was her tears that had driven him out of the room, not her accusations. Accusations, he could counter. Tears made him feel impotent and responsible. He saw her face again in his mind's eye—the stunned, incredulous expression in her hazel eyes before the tears had welled up and spilled over.

They had to work together; he was on the physicians' action committee. He'd be seeing her as early as tomorrow morning at a meeting. It was essential that they communicate.

Communicate, hell. He was going to have to apologize to her; there was no way they could work together otherwise. The problem was, he had no idea how to go about it. To him, apologies were like Swahili. He knew that some people could speak the language fluently. He, however, had never learned more than a word or two—just enough to get by.

SOMEHOW, MELISSA made it through the day. She drew on reserves of self-control and competency she'd hardly realized she had, and she delegated everything possible. The one task she had to do herself was a television interview for a local station, explaining the reasons for the job action and the steps St. Joseph's was taking to minimize the effect on the public. It came at the very end of the endless day, and she got through it, but afterward she couldn't remember a single thing she'd said.

She visited Betsy every moment she could squeeze out of her schedule. She took in a radio and tuned it to her mother's favorite station. She talked to her in a bright, cheerful voice, even as tears streamed down her face. She held her hand, stroked her cheek, rubbed her feet and her back. Betsy lay unmoving.

For Melissa, the worst time came in the middle of that night. During the day, she'd been forced to rush from one item on her calendar to the next, and she'd had to concentrate, which kept her from thinking too much or too often about her mother.

She'd been exhausted by the time she got home. There'd been an evening meeting that hadn't ended until nine-thirty, after which she grabbed a burger from a drive-through. Home at last, she filled a tub with hot water, soaked for ten minutes and then collapsed in bed, emotionally and physically exhausted.

She'd fallen asleep in an instant, but at 2 a.m. she was suddenly wide awake, and the first image that popped into her mind was that of James Burke. Every heartless word that hateful man had spoken about Betsy reverberated in her head. The awful thing was that there was no indication his assessment was wrong. Betsy lay unmoving.

In an effort to keep hysterical tears at bay, Melissa planned what to do, aside from playing the radio, to stimulate Betsy. Medical evidence indicated that even patients in deep comas responded to auditory stimulation.

As she racked her brain, the clock crawled from two to three, then to four. She got up and found a tape player to take to her mother's room. Betsy liked old favorites such as "Moon River" and "When You Wish Upon a Star." Melissa vowed she'd hunt down a store in the morning that sold vintage tapes.

She sorted through photos and found the ones of the holiday she and Betsy had taken to Mexico to celebrate Melissa's getting her master's degree. There were pictures of the resort where they'd stayed, the mariachi singer who'd taken a fancy to Betsy. Melissa put them in an envelope.

She'd pin them up in her mother's room and talk to Betsy about them.

When she was exhausted from worrying about Betsy, Melissa turned her thoughts to James Burke. What was she going to do about him? She had a meeting at which he'd be present scheduled for this morning. How could she possibly remain cool and businesslike around him?

She finally fell asleep again at 4:45, and when her alarm went off at six, she could barely force herself out of bed and into the shower.

The day showed signs of being a disaster before it had even properly begun. She'd started her period and her stomach was swollen and crampy. She had a burgeoning zit in the middle of her chin. Her hair needed a trim and a conditioning treatment: it defied all her efforts to contain it in its usual tidy knot at her nape.

She spilled coffee on the first ensemble she put on, and when she clicked on the television to the local station as she ate a bowl of cold cereal, she caught the news clip of her being interviewed the previous afternoon. That took away even the small appetite she had.

She stared at the screen, aghast. Lord, was that really her? She looked downright frowsy and ancient contrasted with the peppy young blonde who'd done the interviewing. The cameraman had filmed head and shoulders, close up. Melissa's makeup was nearly nonexistent, her obstinate hair hung in tired wisps around her face and the camera accented the weary lines around her eyes and mouth. Thank God, she'd sounded better than she looked—she'd actually managed to get across most of the information she'd wanted to convey. But seeing herself was almost painful. She imagined female viewers wondering aloud why she didn't get her hair styled and didn't use some mascara.

Feeling as low as she'd ever felt, Melissa swallowed two aspirin, packed up the photos and the tape player and drove to work, not sure how she was going to struggle through the day. The doctors were picketing in front of the hospital, and when she pulled into the parking lot she found that a battered silver travel trailer was blocking her privileged parking spot.

Amalgamated Plumbers Of Canada proclaimed a banner across the back of the trailer. Honk If You Support The Docs, another hand-lettered sign decreed.

Melissa pulled up in front of the trailer and climbed wearily out of her car. The sun was up, the air already humid. Smells of simmering chili and cinnamon buns permeated the air, reminding her that she'd hardly eaten since Betsy had gotten sick.

A potbellied giant of a man stepped out of the trailer, opened up a collapsible table and began setting up green plastic lawn chairs around it. He was whistling "When The Saints Go Marching In."

Melissa went marching over. "Can I speak to whoever's in charge here, please?" She squinted up at the huge man, realizing she'd left her sunglasses in the car and now her head was aching, as well as her stomach.

"I guess that'd be me, ma'am. Name's Rudy Ransom." He stuck out a massive paw, and she had no choice except to shake it. "What can I do you for?" He grinned at her. He had a silver tooth on the top, just left of center, rosy cheeks, a cherub's face and a full head of curly white hair, all of which made him look a little like Santa Claus without a beard.

Melissa dredged up her most professional demeanor. "This trailer is blocking my personal parking spot, Mr. Ransom. I'd appreciate it if you'd have it moved as soon as possible. I work at St. Joe's and need a place to put my car where I can be assured of its safety. I'd rather not be towed for parking in someone else's spot."

"Sorry about that, ma'am. This is the food trailer for the

picket line. I put 'er here because of the tree. Get's hot as Hades in there, what with the stove goin', never mind the oven. How's about I find you another parking place for a coupla days?''

For a moment, Melissa considered sticking to her rights and insisting that he move the trailer, instead. But the energy that would require could better be used at her job. And her energy was in short supply this morning.

"As long as my car is in a safe place, I guess that'll be okay.''

"Thank you, ma'am." He stuck two fingers in his mouth and gave a piercing whistle that made Melissa wince.

A uniformed security guard came trotting over.

"Lennie, the trailer's blocking this lady's personal parking spot. How about finding her another good one?''

"Sure thing, Rudy.'' The guard smiled at Melissa and jerked a thumb at her car. "This little beauty yours, ma'am?''

She nodded, and Rudy Ransom whistled his approval. "Nice wheels," he said. "1994 BMW, am I right?''

"You got 'er," Lennie confirmed, before Melissa could say a word. "I'll take good care of her for ya," Lennie promised, as Melissa handed over her keys. "I'll bring these back to you in a few minutes, soon as I locate a good spot.''

"Take the load off your feet," Rudy ordered, pointing at a lawn chair. "You got time for a cuppa java. It'll be a few minutes before Lennie gets back." Rudy disappeared inside the trailer, and returned with a steaming mug of coffee and a silver thermos jug.

Melissa hesitated, then sat. She was early, and she needed to find out exactly what the Plumbers' Union was doing here supporting the physicians' job action. The relationship between the two escaped her.

"Had breakfast?" Rudy handed her the mug along with sugar and several containers of cream.

"Yes, thank you." She remembered the television debacle and shuddered.

"Time for a snack, then." Rudy went inside, and was back in a moment with a thick chunk of chocolate brownie on a paper plate and a plastic fork. "Get yourself around that. The wife made it this morning."

Melissa sipped the coffee. It was delicious, strong and fresh. She looked at the brownie, thickly coated in fudge icing, and her mouth watered. Chocolate was the one thing she couldn't resist when she was having her period. A single mouthful of the brownie told her it was easily the best she'd ever tasted. She had another bite, and then a third. She could have sworn it helped her headache.

She swallowed and tried to distract herself. "Do you belong to the Plumbers' Union, Mr. Ransom?"

"Sure do, I'm shop steward for Local 253."

"I see." She frowned at him. "Can you tell me exactly what you're doing here?"

He looked at her as if it was self-evident, but his voice was polite. "Picketing's tiresome business. Lord knows, I've done enough of it in my time. Only thing that makes it bearable is havin' some good hot food ready and waitin' for you when you need a break."

Melissa nodded. "I just don't quite understand why the Plumbers' Union is supporting the doctors."

He raised a fist. "Solidarity," he bellowed, making her jump. "All for one, and one for all." He lowered his arm, refilled her coffee from the thermos and leaned close enough so Melissa could smell brownie on his breath. "Fact is, I owe my life to one of them there doctors," he confided. "Came that close—" he held out two fingers a smidgen apart "—to packin' it in last spring. Pain was somethin' *awful*. The wife called 911. Took four of them ambulance guys to get me on the stretcher.''

Melissa believed it. He probably weighed close to three hundred pounds.

''Got me in Emerg, and damn if my gallbladder wasn't on the verge of bustin' open.'' Rudy's cornflower-blue eyes widened, and he shook his head at the memory. ''Only thing saved me was Dr. Burke. The man's a genius with the knife, let me tell you.''

Melissa nearly choked on her bite of brownie.

Rudy didn't notice. ''Turned on the old telly the other night and there's this stuff about the docs bein' on strike. So I just called up the members of the local, and we figured a little support was in order. Couple of the wives got busy and cooked, and I volunteered to set up the trailer out here. It's the least I can do for the good doc.''

''Does, uh, does Dr. Burke know you're here?'' Melissa looked over at the picket line. She couldn't see Burke. She couldn't imagine him on a picket line, anyway.

Rudy glanced at his watch. ''Should be along any minute now. I called up his answerin' service. They said the doc would be here along about seven-thirty. He rides his bike over.''

Melissa checked her watch. It was twenty past. She snatched up her purse and her briefcase. ''Thanks for the—''

''Hey, there he is now.'' Rudy raised his voice. ''Hey, how d'ya do, Doc. Remember me?''

James Burke looked up and waved. He was locking his bicycle to a bike rack at the back of the lot. He unhooked his helmet and looped it over the handlebars, and then he came striding over.

CHAPTER SEVEN

MELISSA FELT HER HEART begin to hammer. Her hands were trembling. She was still furious with Burke, but damned if she'd let him see how upset she was. Her first reaction had been to run, but she decided to hold her ground. She'd have to face him sooner or later. It might as well be now. Besides, Lennie hadn't yet reappeared with her lousy car keys.

"Hey, Doc Burke, I was just tellin' this lady that if not for you, I'd be pushin' up daisies," Rudy said.

Melissa's skin felt tight and hot, but she stared Burke in the eye. It was gratifying to see that he looked as uncomfortable and ill at ease as she felt. He was wearing black biking shorts and a tight-fitting top that emphasized his lean build. His forehead was covered with sweat and he used the back of his hand to wipe it.

"There're a coupla guys I wanna introduce to ya, Doc, if you gotta minute." Rudy raised his voice. "Hey, Stan. Vern."

Two men on the picket line set down their signs and walked over.

"This here's Doc Burke. He's the guy I told ya about. If you ever need to get anythin' cut out, this is the man to do it." Burke shook their hands, although his discomfort at Rudy's testimonial was evident.

Melissa made a move to leave, but Rudy stopped her with a hand on her arm. "Dunno where my manners are. I didn't even get your name, ma'am."

"It's Melissa. Melissa Clayton," she said.

"How d'ya do, Melissa." Rudy reached out and shook her hand all over again. "You know Dr. Burke, Ms. Clayton?"

"We've met, yes." Melissa eyed him, and James Burke turned an interesting shade of magenta.

"How 'bout a coffee, Doc? And a cinnamon bun." Rudy had the coffee poured and the bun on a plate before Burke could refuse.

"Let me warm that up for you, Melissa." The thermos was poised over her cup, but Melissa shook her head.

"I have to get to work. Thanks for the coffee." She glanced down at the empty plate that had held the sweet. "And the brownie." God, she'd eaten the entire thing. "I need my—" Before she could finish, Lennie appeared like an apparition and handed her the car keys.

She stuffed them in her bag and hurried across the lot to the hospital entrance, but once inside she had to wait for the elevator.

"Melissa." Burke's voice sounded from behind her, but she didn't turn around.

"Melissa, wait just a moment. We need to talk." He came up beside her, and the dratted elevator still wasn't showing any sign of arriving. She debated escaping up the stairs, but part of her knew he was right; they did have to talk. It might as well be now.

"What I said about your mother was clinically correct, but it came out the wrong way, and I apologize." He rattled the words off as if he'd memorized them.

"Your people skills need a lot of improving, Doctor." Her tone was cold and distant. "St. Joe's has courses, you know."

The elevator finally arrived, and she stepped on.

He did, as well. For the first time in recent history, the blasted thing was empty except for them. Melissa punched the third-floor button; she wanted to pop in and see Betsy before going to her office to start the day.

Burke didn't punch any button; obviously, he was going to the same place.

The elevator stayed where it was for what seemed an eternity before it began to move.

"Melissa, I'm sorry." This time he appeared to mean it. "The last thing I intended to do was upset you," he went on. His tone was becoming less certain with each sentence. "I never know what to do when someone cries."

"A handkerchief or a kind word work a heck of a lot better than walking away," she snapped.

"You're probably right." He sounded miserable. "You *are* right," he corrected, when she glared at him. "Will you accept my apology? Please?"

She would, of course. She pretty much had to. She didn't want bad feelings between them; they did work in the same hospital. Still, she let the silence stretch because it wouldn't hurt him to squirm a little.

The elevator stopped. They were at the third floor, but before the doors could open he reached around her and put his finger on the button that kept the doors shut. She was cornered; his head was close to hers, his chest only inches away. She could smell clean sweat underlaid with aftershave. His hair flopped onto his forehead. He gazed into her eyes for a moment. Then his gaze wandered to her mouth and he swore under his breath.

"Damn, you make me want to—"

Instead of finishing the sentence, he bent his head and kissed her.

It was so unexpected that for a moment she couldn't believe it was actually happening. But his lips were warm and tender, and he kissed well. She was enveloped in his scent, woodsy and intimate. The kiss wasn't a long one by any means, and he certainly didn't do anything invasive with his tongue, but her insides were humming when she pulled away.

He looked every bit as startled as she felt. He still had his finger on the button, so the elevator doors stayed closed.

"Exactly what do you think you're doing, Doctor?" She tried for steely and outraged but instead got shrill and uneasy.

"Beats me." He gave his head a bemused shake. Then he frowned at her, and his deep brown eyes went from abstracted to alarmed. "Damn it, Melissa, I hope you know I didn't plan that," he burst out. "Because I didn't. Being close to you makes me—oh, God. *Please* don't think sexual harassment here."

It hadn't crossed her mind until he mentioned it.

"It's—well, s-see—"

He was stuttering. She wondered if anyone aside from his mother had ever heard James Burke stutter. She waited. She managed to raise her eyebrows in what she hoped was a cool, questioning manner, but her face was burning. She cursed her coloring.

"It's just that you're the sexiest—" He stopped short and tried again. "You're a lovely woman. I've always found you attractive. And just for one minute there, I lost my head." His shoulders slumped and he sighed. "I guess now I *really* owe you an apology."

She drew in a shaky breath. "No," she said softly. "You don't." She swallowed and said the first thing that came into her head. "It was a nice kiss. It's also nice to find out that you're human, after all."

Lord. Was *nice* the only word she could think of?

"People might be starting to wonder what's wrong with the elevator, though," she added, when he still didn't make a move.

"Oh. Yeah. Of course." He released the button and the door slid open. No one was waiting, and Melissa was relieved. She felt warm and rumpled, and she knew her cheeks were still flaming. She'd just as soon nobody saw her for a couple of minutes, until she had time to regain her composure. *Had he really said she was sexy?*

"I'm going to see Mom," she said to fill the sudden awkward silence.

He waited until she'd stepped out of the elevator, then followed her. "That's where I'm going, too." He sounded preoccupied.

They walked together down the hallway and turned the corner. No one was at the nursing station, but that was because the entire staff was gathered around Betsy's bed.

Melissa's heart almost stopped. "Oh, my God, what's wrong? Is she—"

"She's the same. There hasn't been any real change in her condition," the nursing supervisor, Lydia, said quickly. "We did have an incident, but it's over now."

"What sort of incident?"

James moved toward his patient to check her pulse and examine her eyes. Betsy was obviously unaware of anything. She lay as limp and unresponsive as ever, but there was an angry red mark on her neck. "Exactly what happened here?"

Melissa saw the concerned looks the nurses exchanged. "Mrs. Clayton somehow fell out of bed," Lydia said. "She became tangled in a sheet, and would have strangled if we hadn't found her immediately."

Melissa was horrified. "But how could that happen? Weren't you watching her?"

The words were out before she could stop them. She didn't want to blame the nurses; she knew from her own nursing career that accidents occurred, and that it was always the nurses who bore the brunt of the blame.

"That's totally unacceptable," James snapped. "Weren't

there signs that she was going to have a seizure? Surely the nursing staff had recognized that something was different.''

But no one had. A nurse had come in, talked to Betsy, turned on the radio, checked the IV, and Betsy had seemed the same.

James did a thorough examination. "The fall doesn't appear to have done any harm," he told Melissa when he was finished. "But there's been no improvement, either."

His voice wasn't exactly warm, but Melissa could see by his expression that he was both concerned and disappointed. Maybe he wasn't as unfeeling as everyone imagined. Maybe he was just incapable of verbalizing emotion. Maybe—

Stop making excuses for him just because he kissed you, she chastised herself.

"Your bedside manner is atrocious," she accused. "You haven't once spoken directly to my mother. You know there's a possibility she can hear you."

Melissa caught the indrawn breaths of the nurses.

To her amazement, he took the criticism well. "You're right, of course. I will from now on. I'm sorry, Melissa," he added. He sounded sincere.

Suddenly, Melissa was sorry, too. Her mother didn't deserve what was happening to her. She bent and kissed Betsy's cheek to hide the tears that gathered in her own eyes.

"Hang in there, Mom," she told her, squeezing her hand. "Things are gonna get better soon, I promise. And don't go trying to get out of bed again by yourself. Call one of the nurses. The button's right here." She put her mother's hand on it and tried not to notice how it toppled away. "I've got to get to work or I'm gonna be late for a meeting, Mom." She scrabbled in her oversize handbag. "I brought in a tape player. I'll get you some tapes later today. And there're pictures here. I want to talk about them with you, but right now I've gotta go. I'll be here to see you again this afternoon.''

Melissa didn't look at James again. She hurried down the hall and into the elevator, but just as the doors were about to close, he stepped in. This time there was a man from the cleaning staff along, which, Melissa told herself, was a big relief.

On the second floor, James got off with her and walked beside her toward the boardroom where the meeting was scheduled. He was quiet until they reached the doorway, and then he said, ''If there was anything I knew that I could do for your mother, I would. I hope you understand that.''

She nodded without looking at him and opened the door. She had to compartmentalize her feelings. She couldn't allow herself to dwell on her mother when there was business to be done, or she'd burst into tears and lose control.

The other members of the committee were waiting.

The meeting was with the Ministry of Health, and it was contentious. The doctors were demanding higher pay, fewer hours, more operating rooms, and James delivered an impassioned defense of their position. The government representative spoke of the sanctity of medicine, the irresponsibility of doctors who would choose job action over mediation, the danger they were imposing on the city and the current emptiness of the coffers that funded medicare.

A representative from the nursing staff registered the nurses' strong opposition to the doctors' demands for more operating rooms; the nurses wanted more beds and more nurses. Arguments were heated, and Melissa's task was to find a path through the mine field, to come up somehow with a compromise that everyone might accept.

She did her best, but nothing was settled by the time the meeting finally ended at a quarter to twelve. As the room emptied, Melissa gathered up the notes she'd made and stuffed them in her briefcase.

"Melissa."

James Burke was at her elbow. She turned, raising an inquiring eyebrow.

"I wonder—that is, would you consider having dinner with me this evening?" His voice was hesitant, and she paused. He was asking her for a date, and she wanted to go.

But then he blew it. "I thought perhaps we could discuss some of the more relevant issues about the job action over a meal."

He didn't want a date. He wanted a sympathetic ear for his platform. She was so disappointed she wanted to haul off and smack him one. "I don't think that's appropriate," she said in a haughty tone. "I don't believe in mixing my personal life and my job."

"Shit." The expletive burst from him. "That came out absolutely the wrong way. I wasn't trying to lobby. I sincerely wanted to share a meal with you. I didn't mean—" He stopped short and pulled in a breath, then grinned.

It took her by surprise. It changed his face entirely. He went from handsome to hunk in a flash of perfect teeth.

"How many times is this I've apologized to you today?"

She tilted her head and pretended to reflect. "Three. Maybe four."

"So can I just delete what I said and start over?"

She shook her head. "I'd like to have dinner," she confessed. "But I have a seven o'clock meeting with a patient's family, I want to spend as much time as possible with my mother and I have to find a store that sells vintage tapes."

"Vintage tapes?"

"For my mom. She loves golden oldies."

"I see." He turned to leave, then turned back. "Would you have time for a coffee with me tomorrow morning, out at Rudy's trailer?"

She considered it. It would mean getting up even earlier than her usual 6 a.m., but she hadn't been sleeping much, anyway.

"Yeah. Yeah, I could manage that. How early is Rudy there?"

"Six-thirty. I asked. He's an early riser."

Melissa nodded. "I'll be there at quarter-to-seven."

He smiled again. "Great. Good. Quarter-to-seven it is."

James Burke wasn't exactly a ray of sunshine. Did she really want to be with him first thing in the morning? Still, there were those wonderful teeth, very white and even.

The better to bite your head off with, my dear. Lord. She needed to get a grip.

She also needed to find a bathroom, and then something to eat. She hurried off in search of both, but her thoughts lingered on Burke. Where had he learned to kiss like that? Had he ever been married? Did he have kids, a family, a mother and father, sisters and brothers?

Doctors weren't employees of the hospital, so there wouldn't be a personnel file on him. And even if there was, it would be unprofessional and unethical of her to read it simply to satisfy her own very personal curiosity.

She'd have to get the information another way.

She'd ask Arlene.

CHAPTER EIGHT

"BURKE JUST TURNED FORTY. He's a Leo. His long-term goal is to be chief of Surgery. He was married once—he was twenty-six or -seven," Arlene related later that afternoon, lowering herself into a chair with a sigh and rubbing a hand absently across her burgeoning belly.

"Lasted eighteen months. She's an eye surgeon in Victoria. Dr. Anita Malpass. She married again, to a GP. She and the doc didn't have kids. The word is they were both more interested in their work than they were in each other. He doesn't date anyone from St. Joe's, although one of the lab techs saw him walking down Granville one night with a blond bimbo in a miniskirt. Great legs and lotsa hair. He was holding her hand. They went into a vegetarian restaurant. This was six or seven months ago now. Nobody knows who or even if he's dating at the moment. Many have offered, but none was chosen. All of that's scuttlebutt. I asked Frank about him, and all he said was that Burke doesn't eat meat, works out on a treadmill and a weight machine, rides his bike to work every day, and that he's a pain in the butt about details. But Frank would trust him with his life in the OR. He likes the guy."

"Thanks, Arlene." Melissa felt like a spymaster being briefed by a mole who'd pumped her own husband for secrets. The bulk of the information came from the underground gossip network at St. Joe's, which was extensive and surprisingly accurate—but because of her position, Melissa was out of the loop. She wondered briefly what was being said about her, but she didn't dare ask. She had enough to worry over.

Arlene heaved herself to her feet. "This kid's got his foot stuck in my ribs. I wish there were some way to get him to move it."

"You've only got four more weeks to go. You sure you don't want to take some time off and just relax?" Melissa dreaded being without her, but she also fretted that Arlene was on her feet too much.

"Not on your life. I'd go snaky at home with nothing to do all day long. Nope, I'm staying right here until my water breaks and the baby crowns. You better get going. You've got that meeting with the department heads in ten minutes." She lumbered out of the office.

Melissa watched her go, wistfully wondering if the day would ever come when she'd be able to complain of a baby having a foot stuck in her ribs. She wondered, as well, if the gossipmongers at St. Joe's knew about Nadim Salem, the Egyptian internist Melissa had married in haste and divorced the same way.

She'd been twenty-three, newly graduated as a nurse. He was an internist at St. Joe's on an exchange program. She'd known him three weeks, married him and had it annulled two weeks later, a result of Nadim's making it plain he expected her to quit her job and devote herself to being his wife. She'd suspected that being someone's wife wasn't a smart career move.

Getting Nadim out of her system had involved taking food in, and she'd gained twenty-seven pounds in the next six months. She'd lost confidence; she'd hated the way she looked; she'd mourned the loss of her first real love. It had taken effort and a great deal of self-discipline to regain her slender figure.

She'd learned from that disaster. She'd vowed never again to let a man disrupt her life, and she never had. Other men had come along, some of whom she'd even thought she loved. Each time, in one form or another, she'd ended up having to choose between them and her career. And her career had always won, hands down. She wondered if it had been the same for James. She guessed it probably had; he was ambitious.

Chief of Surgery, huh? He'd get her vote. He was well qualified for the position.

She glanced at her watch and snatched up the notes Arlene had prepared. She had no time to think of babies with their feet stuck in her ribs. She had no time to think about James Burke and the blonde with the big hair, or whether or not he still took her to the vegetarian restaurant on Granville.

She had work to do, a ton of it, and for the rest of the day she attended to it, but at odd moments she thought about meeting James the next morning and realized she was looking forward to it.

HE WAS ALREADY WAITING when she drove into the lot at 6:45. He was at the food trailer, standing beside Rudy, and wearing biking shorts and a short-sleeve blue golf shirt. His butt definitely rivaled his smile for appeal.

Melissa pulled into the new parking spot Lennie had commandeered for her and walked over to the trailer. She'd put on a sky-blue silk thing with a short-sleeve tailored top and a skirt that ended well above her knees, and she could have sworn that James did a swift survey of her legs as she approached the trailer.

"'Morning, Melissa."

He smiled at her, and she smiled back. It was hard not to smile; the early morning was still cool, the air was fresh and tinged with the smell of the sea, birds were singing in the cedars that shaded the lot and the food smells drifting out the door of the trailer were intoxicating.

"Sit down, you two." Rudy grinned at her. "You look pretty as a picture in that rig," he boomed. "I always had a weakness for red hair. Don't tell the wife I said so, though." He filled two mugs with coffee, and before Melissa could object, he put warm cinnamon buns in front of them.

"Thelma didn't make the buns this mornin'," he confided. "George's wife did. They're not up to Thelma's standards. She uses way more butter, but they're not bad. Try 'em, Melissa. See what you think."

To be polite, Melissa took a small piece off one corner. It seemed to melt away on her tongue in an orgy of yeasty dough and sweet icing and cinnamon. Her taste buds begged for more.

"They're delicious," she told Rudy. She said to James, "Are you on the picket line this morning, Doctor?"

He shook his head. "I'm lucky. I get to hang around the ER in case something comes in that can't be transferred. There was a stabbing yesterday, brought in from skid row, but that was the extent of it."

He sounded so disappointed at the lack of desperate injuries that she had to smile. "I guess not being able to do your job has to be frustrating."

He nodded. "Surgery's my life," he admitted.

Rudy was listening. "C'mon, Doc, I know firsthand how good you are at opening folks up and sewin' em back together, but you gotta have other stuff you like doing just as much. Hell, I like what I do, but plumbing don't come close to being with Thelma, dancing up a storm, holding my new granddaughter. You got kids, Doc?"

"No kids. I'm not married."

"How 'bout you, Melissa?"

She shook her head. "No kids, no husband."

Rudy whistled between his teeth. "You two gotta get with the program," he chastised, leaning toward them.

"Neither one of you is getting any younger, no offense. Careers don't keep you very warm in bed when you get to be my age." He laughed his big, booming laugh.

Melissa noticed the look that James gave Rudy. It was thoughtful, as if his words might have struck a chord.

"You know what the kids say," Rudy went on. "*Getta life.* I can't believe neither of you is married."

"Well, Rudy, the statistics on marriage aren't very reassuring," James said. "About fifty percent of marriages end in divorce these days."

"Doc, if somebody told you there was a fifty-percent chance of savin' somebody's life, would you go for it?"

James had to laugh, and Melissa joined him. Rudy definitely had a point.

"Either of you ever been married?"

"Once," James admitted with a shrug. "We were both doctors, both busy all the time. It didn't work out."

So Arlene's info had been accurate.

He turned to Melissa. "How about you?"

She cleared her throat. "Once. Same as you. To a doctor. Didn't last." To sidestep any more questions about that fiasco, she said, "How long have you and your wife been married, Rudy?"

"It'll be thirty-one years next March," he said. "We had four kids, had some rough times. I took to drinking a little too much for a coupla years there. Thelma had to sort me out good over that." His blue eyes grew somber. "And we lost one of our kids. Little Kenny drowned in the neighbors' pool. He was only three. That was a tough one. Thought for a while the old gal was gonna go off the deep end. But we got through it." He shook his head. "You never get over it. You just get through it. Know what I mean?"

Melissa thought of Betsy. How would she get through, if what James believed was true—that Betsy would never wake up? The dark cloud that haunted her had lifted a little during the past half hour, but now it was back. She refused the offer of more coffee.

"I've got to go. I want to see my mom before work."

"Your mother's in the hospital?" Rudy leaned his beefy forearms on the table. "Whatsa matter with her?"

Melissa glanced at James. He was swirling his coffee around in his cup, not looking at her or at Rudy. As quickly and as diplomatically as possible, with no mention of James, Melissa outlined what had happened to Betsy.

"Hey, that's a real shame. Now, if Doc Burke here had done the operation on her—"

"Actually, I did." James looked crestfallen instead of defensive. He sat back in his chair and shook his head. "I've gone over every detail of the operation and the orders for your mother's postop care, and I can't figure out what I might have done wrong," he said to Melissa. "There must have been something."

"You don't think I blame you for what's happened, do you?" As angry as she'd been at him for his less-than-sympathetic attitude, it had never once crossed her mind that he was responsible.

He shrugged. "I guess I blame myself."

Melissa was astounded. No wonder he'd been so defensive. "James, you did your best. She's had the very best care she could have had. I was a nurse long enough to know that where people's bodies are concerned, there are never any guarantees. Mom must have had a weakness somewhere, something that no one could possibly have predicted."

As she said the words, Melissa recognized the truth in them, and a little of her own guilt eased. She, too, had done her best in a difficult situation.

"Don't fret over it. I'll get Thelma on it," Rudy said.

Melissa and James turned to him, puzzled.

"Thelma's got this group of women from our church.

They pray for people every Tuesday and Thursday morning. What's your mom's name, Melissa?''

"Betsy Clayton."

Rudy dug a pen out of his pocket and wrote it on a napkin. "I'll give this to Thelma soon as I get home. It'll help. You watch and see."

"Thank you, Rudy." Melissa didn't share his confidence in the prayer group, but she was touched by his concern. "Bye, now. Thanks for the coffee." She glanced down at the paper plate. "And the bun." God, she'd eaten the whole thing. *Again.*

"Come by tomorrow mornin'. Thelma's makin' coffee cake." He scrunched his fingers up and brought them to his mouth with a smack. "You don't wanna miss Thelma's coffee cake. Believe you me."

"I'll walk you into the hospital, Melissa. I have patients to check." James fell into step beside her. When they were out of Rudy's earshot, James said, "He's a well-meaning man, very kind, but sometimes a bit misguided."

"About marriage, you mean?"

"Well, yes. Certainly. That, too. Actually, I was thinking more of the prayer group. I think it's unrealistic to build up false hope that way."

"I'm not that naive," Melissa said. "Although now that I'm in this situation with Mom, I can really understand how tempting it is to pin your hopes on an alternative when medicine has failed." Realizing how that sounded, she put a hand on his arm. "I didn't mean—"

"I know. I just wish there were something more I could do."

"Thank you, James. It means a lot to hear you say so."

He smiled. He was smiling more these days, Melissa thought. Maybe job action agreed with him. "I enjoyed our discussion with Rudy," she added. "He's an interesting man. And he's your number-one fan."

James rolled his eyes. "He's impossible. As a postop patient, I told him to stick to a low-cal, low-fat regime. Did you *see* the food in that trailer? Every scrap is high fat, sugar-laden. Almost everything has meat and dairy. It's a dietary disaster area."

"I heard him telling a buddy of his that now that you took out his gallbladder he can eat anything he wants—no more heartburn." Melissa couldn't help teasing James a little. "And Rudy said the other fellow shouldn't worry about what he eats, either. You can whip his gallbladder out easy as anything if it starts giving him trouble. Sure you're not drumming up business, Doctor?" She giggled at the horrified expression on his face. "And despite what they're doing to my gallbladder, I did love the cinnamon rolls."

"Enough to meet me again tomorrow morning?"

"Tomorrow it's coffee cake, remember?"

Why not meet him? It was the only time of the day she could really call her own. She'd actually had fun this morning.

"Okay, James. I'll be there, same time."

"I'll be waiting."

CHAPTER NINE

JAMES PEDALED into the lot at six-thirty, and Melissa drove in on the dot of 6:45. He realized how tense he'd been, waiting for her. She gave him a cheery wave and a smile, and his morning brightened considerably.

Rudy had coffee ready, as well as a plate with a giant chunk of oatmeal coffee cake, raisins bursting from its fat golden sides and nuts thickly studding the sugary crumbs on top.

Just looking at it had made James's mouth water, and even though he knew it was a coronary time bomb, he couldn't resist.

"'Morning, Melissa." She made his mouth water, too. She was wearing a short silky dress the color of chestnuts, and her long, lovely legs were sheathed in silk. Her fiery hair was caught back in its usual knot, but tendrils escaped and curled around her ears. He liked her ears. He liked her hair. He liked her freckles. He especially liked her breasts. In fact, he concluded as she sat down beside him, there wasn't anything about Melissa Clayton he didn't like.

"'Morning, James. Rudy, thanks for the coffee. And your wife's cake looks scrumptious."

Rudy beamed. "I'll pass that along to Thelma. And she said to tell you the prayer group's gonna start working on your mom right away."

"I'm grateful." She sipped her coffee and took a nibble of the cake, then smiled at James. "I can't believe you're up and about at this hour of the morning. How come you're not taking advantage of the time away from the operating room and sleeping late?"

"Too many years of scrubbing for surgery at the crack of dawn. It messes up your circadian rhythms."

"What's those, if you don't mind me asking?" Rudy looked puzzled.

"Oh, circadian rhythms are our biological clocks," James explained. "The natural cycles our bodies go through in a twenty-four-hour period, when we feel like sleeping, eating, that sort of thing." *And having sex.* Melissa's presence triggered that circadian rhythm, all right.

"Oh, like all that stuff about women's clocks telling them it's time to have babies," Rudy said with a nod. "When Thelma and I were young, nobody worried over stuff like that. We expected to get married, have kids. It was the natural way of things. Still is, if you ask me. Only, nowadays you young folks put a lot of fancy names on it and set up more resistance than we did." He laughed, and so did James.

Rudy leaned forward, chin resting on his hands. "You plan on having kids someday, Melissa?"

Rudy certainly had no qualms about asking personal questions. James waited for her answer.

"Not soon, as in this year or next," she said. She blushed a little. "But someday, sure, I'd like to have babies." She turned to James, a hint of challenge in her eyes. "How about you? Think you'll ever want some little Burkes?"

"I'm not sure." Six months ago, he'd have given a firm and definite no. But since his fortieth birthday, his ideas about being single were changing. He'd begun to notice families, in the supermarket, on the beach, surrounding someone's bed at the hospital. And for the first time in his life, he'd begun to feel empty. "I suppose everyone thinks about having a family."

"You come from a big family, Doc?" Rudy rested his huge arms on the counter.

James shook his head. "I was an only child. My mother died when I was fourteen. Dad remarried. He lives in San Diego. He's a researcher for the U.S. Navy." He hadn't seen his father in two years. He'd never gotten along with his stepmother; she was possessive of his father, almost to the point of paranoia, and that possessiveness excluded James.

"How about you, Melissa? You have brothers and sisters?"

She shook her head. "Only child, same as James. But my mom and I have always been really close. Well, apart from a couple of years when I was a rebellious teenager." She gave a small, sad smile. "Mom told me from the time I was little that I could do anything I wanted in life, and that education was the key. My dad died when I was a baby. He had life insurance, and no matter how hard up we were, my mom never touched a penny of it." Her voice wobbled, but she went on. "Mom worked as a clerk in a grocery store to support us, and she always told me the insurance money was for my education." Her eyes filled with tears. "She was so proud when I got this job. I was going to take her to Hawaii at Christmas."

With Melissa's words, the detachment about his patients that James always strove so hard to maintain crumbled entirely. Betsy Clayton went from being the bowel obstruction who happened to be Melissa's mother to a woman who'd had dreams and hopes and plans, a woman who'd sacrificed to give her daughter an opportunity at a better life than she'd had.

"Thelma and me are going to Hawaii in February," Rudy said. "We been saving for a coupla years, and last month Thelma won a bundle at bingo that put us over the top. We got all the brochures, and I got Thelma a CD of Hawaiian music—told her if she learns the hula for me I'll buy her a grass skirt when we get there." He chortled. "I bet you get to Hawaii a lot, huh, Doc?"

"I've never been." James hadn't taken a real holiday for three years. "Most of my time is spent here at St. Joe's."

Rudy was perplexed. "But that's work. So what d'ya do for fun?"

"I guess I see my work as fun." James felt a little defensive. "I enjoy riding my bike to work. And sometimes I ride with a group on Sunday mornings, out toward Squamish."

Rudy nodded and waited, and when James didn't continue, he said in an incredulous tone, "That's it—a bike ride now and again?"

"Well, I like to fly-fish," James added. He hadn't done any fishing since early spring, though, and then only for a long weekend. He hadn't really thought about it much, but now he realized that surgery had eaten up his life. He had no close friends, no pets, and his social life at the moment consisted of an occasional movie or a few glasses of beer at the local pub on a Sunday afternoon.

Even his sex life had ended six weeks ago when Heidi Menzies, whom he'd met in the swimming pool just after she'd moved into his building, broke off the relationship they'd had for five months. She was moving to Las Vegas in the hope of becoming a showgirl, she'd told him, and she had a word of advice for him before she left. He needed to take a long, hard look at his priorities. Any guy who'd choose to hang around the ER just in case there might be a surgical emergency rather than go to a club with her— well, a guy like that had some *major* issues he ought to deal with.

He'd brushed her words aside at the time, reminding himself that it wasn't Heidi's brain that had attracted him in the first place. But these past few days, with job action making it impossible for him to immerse himself in his usual routine of surgeries, her words had come back to haunt him. If his work was factored out of his life's equation, there wasn't one hell of a lot left, was there.

James turned to Melissa. "How about you? What d'ya do for fun?"

"Fun? Gosh, I don't know—"

She shrugged, and it was reassuring to James to see the confusion in her expression.

"I've been so busy these past few years, going to school and working at the same time, I guess I haven't given too much thought to fun."

"What did you guys used to like to do, when you were kids?" Rudy wasn't letting either of them off the hook.

She pursed her mouth, thinking. She had a lush, full mouth, made for kissing, James noted.

"Roller-skate. And dance, I loved to dance."

"There ya go." Rudy sounded triumphant. "Why don't the two of you go dancin'? It would do you both good. You need to get out more."

James shook his head. "I don't dance." It was one activity he hadn't been able to master right away, so he'd stopped trying years earlier.

Luckily, Melissa was also shaking her head. "I don't have time enough these days to breathe, never mind go dancing." She glanced at her watch and let out a squawk of horror. "My God, I've gotta run. Thanks, Rudy." She flashed a smile at James. "See you later, Doc."

James watched her hurry off, long legs making the flippy little chestnut skirt swing, red hair gleaming like brass in the morning sunlight.

"She's one good-lookin' woman," Rudy said with an appreciative sigh. "How old is she, anyway—thirty, thirty-one, maybe?"

"Thirty-six." James had made it his business to find out.

Rudy whistled. "She'd better get cracking with the babies. Her clock is on fast-forward," Rudy said. "You got a lady friend, Doc?"

Although it wasn't any of Rudy's business, James shook his head. "Nope, not at the moment."

"Then, why don't you ask Melissa out? Sounds to me like she could use some R and R. Sounds like all she does is work, work, work. That can't be healthy, right? In fact, you ask me, both of you are on the wrong track there. It's kinda pathetic."

Pathetic? Who did Rudy think he was, calling two professional people who took their work seriously "pathetic"?

"I did ask her to dinner," James snapped. "She turned me down."

"So you got rejected. It happens to the best of us." Rudy gave him a disparaging look. "So ask her again, Doc."

James's temper flared. He didn't appreciate being given advice. Didn't Rudy know that meeting Melissa here at 6:45 in the bloody morning wasn't exactly an accident? It had been an inspired move on his part, James felt. And he wasn't exactly a charity case when it came to dating. Rudy needed to mind his own business.

A few days ago, James might have told him so. Now, though, he had to admit he'd grown fond of Rudy, in spite of the endless personal questions and the banal advice on life in general. He didn't want to hurt him, so he swallowed his irritation.

"Maybe I'll do that. See you later, Rudy." James headed for St. Joe's. He was a doctor, a surgeon—responsible and hardworking, and a benefit to society, he reminded himself.

He certainly wasn't pathetic. But as he showered and changed into the fresh pants and the newly laundered golf shirt he kept in his locker, Rudy's words troubled him, and they were still with him when he arrived at Betsy's bedside.

"Any change?" He couldn't remember the nurse's name, although he'd seen her often enough. "No more incidents that involve my patient falling out of bed, I hope."

"No on both counts, Dr. Burke."

He waited until she moved away, and then James leaned close to his patient.

"You can wake up whenever you choose, you know,

Betsy,'' he told her, feeling like an idiot as he did so. He was aware the nurses advised relatives to speak to comatose patients in this manner, but he'd never done it himself, and it felt strange. He glanced around, but there was no one to hear him.

"You have a beautiful daughter who cares about you. She's very upset because you're not getting well," he said in a stern tone.

Maybe stern wasn't the way to go. The lack of any response was strangely freeing, and in a softer tone, he added, "I like your daughter very much, Betsy. And I feel responsible for what's happened to you, which really complicates the situation between Melissa and me. So it would be much better all around if you just *woke up*.'' He looked down at her, for the first time recognizing in Betsy's features faint echoes of her daughter's beauty. "I brought you some tapes I had lying around.'' He fumbled in his medical bag. He'd actually searched them out in one of the second-hand bookstores he frequented. He slid one into the portable player by the bed and turned it on.

"You Are My Sunshine" began playing, and like an idiot James watched for a response. None came, naturally, which annoyed him.

"Damn it all, why don't you just quit this nonsense, Betsy? We need you awake,'' he said forcefully. "Melissa does, and I sure as hell do, too, if I'm gonna get anywhere with her.''

A sound behind him made him turn. The nurse he'd spoken to was standing there, an expression of utter amazement on her freckled face. Why the hell did nurses wear shoes that allowed them to sneak up like that?

James's face burned, and he beat a hasty retreat into the corridor.

CHAPTER TEN

THREE DAYS PASSED for Melissa in a frenzy of activity. Every moment of every day was crammed. Meetings were the worst; she met with the ministry in an effort to come to some agreement about the conflict. She met with the press, and because the strike was attracting province-wide attention, there were swarms of radio and television stations vying for interviews. She met with the union heads of the various departments; they were worried about nonunion people moving in on their jobs. She spent endless hours on the phone trying to get patients to other facilities, and their families often insisted on speaking directly to her, concerned about the care their loved ones were receiving.

Every time she could steal a few moments, she raced upstairs to be with Betsy. And every time she entered her mother's room, she prayed silently and hard that there would be some change, some little thing that would be cause for hope.

There was nothing. Betsy remained in stable condition but unresponsive, and with each day that passed, Melissa's hopes grew fainter and her spirits sank.

The only bright spot was meeting James. Each morning as she pulled into the parking lot, he was there, waving at her from the front of Rudy's trailer. Seeing him, finding out more about him, became something to look forward to, something that took her mind off both her mother and her work for just a while.

They talked about everything, and sometimes about noth-

ing at all. He told her and Rudy about a boy who'd died
from a medication he'd prescribed, and how it had almost
ended his career as a doctor. She found herself able to talk
about her marriage to Nadim and how it had affected her.
Rudy acted like a catalyst, asking the bold questions that
neither Melissa nor James dared put to each other.

She learned that he liked eating fish and chips from a
certain vendor in Stanley Park, that morning was his favorite time of day, that he collected old medical journals
and loved prowling through dusty bookshops.

She heard herself confiding that she'd always wanted to
learn to ride horses, she broke out in hives from shellfish
and she liked watching *Oprah*. That confession brought a
lump to her throat; Betsy had always taped the shows for
her.

On the afternoon of the tenth day of the physicians' job
action, Melissa was sitting through yet another meeting,
when her pager sounded. Glancing at the number, she saw
that it was Arlene. Melissa excused herself and hurried
down the hallway to a phone.

"It's your mom," Arlene said, and Melissa's heart gave
a lurch. "The nurses called down a few moments ago.
She's become very restless. She's moving around and she
seems agitated."

Heart racing, Melissa hurried up to her mother's room.
Two nurses were with her. Betsy was tossing and turning.
She was also mumbling, although the sounds made no
sense.

"We've called Dr. Burke. He'll be along any moment."
The nurse met Melissa's troubled glance. Neither of them
needed to verbalize that this change in Betsy's condition
could be one of two things: either she was improving, or
she was exhibiting signs of brain damage.

Melissa tried to be optimistic, but Betsy had now been
in a coma for more than a week. Brain damage was the

most probable diagnosis, and when James arrived, he reluctantly admitted that he, too, thought Betsy was exhibiting classic signs of trauma to the brain.

He took Melissa into the same little office in which he'd spoken to her after her mother's operation. The difference this time was that his words were gentle, his tone regretful, and when Melissa nodded and then felt her chin wobble, he reached out and drew her into his arms.

"I'm sorry," he murmured, holding her against his chest. "I hope this diagnosis is wrong."

She hoped so, too. Very much. Being in his arms was comforting, but it wasn't soothing. Even through this new worry about her mother, she was aware of his warmth, of the now-familiar smell of his aftershave, of the strength of his lean body against her softness and the surge of desire it brought. She allowed herself extra seconds before she drew away. She liked his arms around her.

He let her go, but she could feel his reluctance. Attraction, sexual attraction, was humming between them like white noise, but this wasn't the time or the place to indulge it, and they were both aware of that. She had to get back to the meeting, and then she had two other urgent appointments this afternoon.

"I wish I could just sit with her for a while." She was torn between obligation and love.

"I will. I'll page you if anything significant occurs," he promised.

"Oh, James, thank you." She felt overwhelmed.

"My pleasure." His grin was wry. "It's not as if I have much else to do."

"Maybe this thing will end soon, and you can get back to the OR."

"I hope so. I'm at loose ends not working." His dark eyes met hers. "Although I'll miss our mornings together at Rudy's."

"Me, too." Melissa smiled at him, thinking how attractive he was. He'd become a good friend, and she was grateful for that. She was far too busy to get involved with anyone, and so was he. Ironically, when he went back to work, her own schedule would ease, which reinforced the fact that they were totally incompatible when it came to timing.

They were totally incompatible when it came to romance. It was ridiculous to contemplate anything other than friendship.

She certainly wasn't responsible for the wild sex they shared in the dreams she'd been having about him nearly every night. She knew the difference between fantasy and reality, and she'd never allow one to influence the other. She prided herself on being a realist.

SHE WAS IN THE MIDST of one of those dreams at four the following morning, when the phone rang. In the dream, she was in her office and James was there with her, and neither of them was wearing clothing. For some reason there was a convenient examining table with a pillow.

Melissa needed a few seconds to figure out that the ringing wasn't just an unwelcome interruption in her office fantasy. She finally sat up and dragged the receiver to her ear.

"It's Angela from Four West," the nurse said, and Melissa's stomach contracted with dread. Her fingers clenched the phone, and she bent over, hugging her knees, forming a defensive ball against what could only be disaster.

"It's your mom, Melissa. She woke up a few minutes ago and asked us for a cup of tea. She seems absolutely normal. Of course, we won't know for sure until Dr. Burke confirms it, but I'd be willing to bet there's no brain damage. She's complaining of being hungry and accusing us of trying to starve her to death, and she asked for you right away. We're all so thrilled. We knew you'd want to know right away.''

For a moment, Melissa couldn't even speak. She had to swallow hard to get past the huge lump in her throat. ''Oh, my God. Oh, that's such good news. Please tell her that I'll be right there.''

''I certainly will.'' Angela laughed. ''And I think we'd better get her a cup of tea and some toast before she lodges a formal complaint.''

Melissa hung up, hands trembling, heart so full of gratitude that her chest felt as if it would burst. She shrieked, ''Yes!'' and jumped out of bed. She showered quickly, pulled on jeans and a top, and raced for the car.

The nurses were changing shifts when she arrived, and they all grinned and gave thumbs-up signs to her as she rushed into her mother's room.

''Mom?'' The tears Melissa had been holding back began to pour down her cheeks when she put her arms around Betsy, who was sitting propped against a stack of pillows, faded blue eyes open, expression alert. ''Oh, my God, Mom, it's so good to have you back.''

''The nurses say I had some trouble waking up,'' Betsy said in a voice barely above a whisper. ''Last I remember was not feeling too good after that darn operation.''

Melissa sniffled and wiped her eyes on the sheet. ''You're fine now, Mom. You're soon going to be absolutely healthy again.''

''That I am.'' There was determination and conviction in Betsy's tone. ''I'll feel lots better soon as I get home. When can I go home, Lissa?''

''You'll have to ask Dr. Burke.''

''Ask me what?''

Melissa hadn't heard him come into the room. She turned and gave him a wide, tremulous smile. He, too, had obviously thrown on the first clothes at hand—a pair of worn jeans and a blue T-shirt. His hair was mussed and damp. He looked vital and alive and unbearably sexy. Melissa blushed. How could she be thinking of sex, with her mother right here, barely back from death's door?

"Hello there, Mrs. Clayton." He was staring at Betsy with a dumbfounded expression on his face. "It's, um, it's wonderful to see you so well."

"So when can I go home?" Betsy was already back to being her single-minded self.

"Let's check you over, and then I can give you an educated guess."

He did a routine but intensive examination, and Melissa waited, hoping against hope that he'd find nothing wrong.

He didn't. He straightened and shook his head, and his smile was wide and jubilant. "I'd like to run a few more tests, but basically, I think you're well on the way to recovery, Mrs. Clayton."

Betsy nodded as if that was a foregone conclusion. "So you can take this awful thing out—" she gestured at her IV "—and I can go home today."

"Well, I'd say in a few days, as long as you have someone there with you until you're stronger."

Melissa envisioned her killer schedule, and tried to figure out how she could bend it. "I could probably—" she began, but Betsy shook her head.

"You've got too much to do as it is," she said in a trembly but firm tone. "Gladys will come and stay with me. She'll be glad to get away from that daughter of hers for a few weeks. You call her for me, Lissa."

"I will. She'll be glad to hear that you're awake. She's been so worried she's phoned every day," Melissa said.

"Prob'ly scared I won't make it to Reno for Christmas like we planned," Betsy said. "Gladys really likes the slots," she explained to James. "Me, I'm more for poker."

"I didn't know you were going to Reno with Gladys."

Melissa had been going to surprise Betsy with tickets to Hawaii.

Betsy grinned, a hint of mischief in her eyes. "A person's gotta have some secrets."

James laughed, and Melissa had to giggle. Her mother was definitely better if her contrary nature had returned full force.

Betsy yawned, patting her mouth and settled back on the pillows. "I think I need a little nap," she said. "Hard to get a minute's peace in this place."

Melissa straightened the sheets, and her mother was already snoring lightly when she and James walked out of the room.

"There's no chance she'll drop back into coma?" Melissa knew her worried question wasn't fair. James wasn't God, after all.

He shook his head. "She seems perfectly fine. I think your mom is over the crisis and, as I said, well on her way to recovery."

Melissa felt like throwing herself into his arms for a massive hug, but there were staff everywhere. She settled for a swirling little solitary dance down the hall and back. "It's a miracle, James," she crowed. "Oh, I'm so happy I just don't know what to do."

"How about a coffee at Rudy's to celebrate?"

Melissa looked up at the clock behind the nursing station. It wasn't even seven.

"I can't wait to tell Rudy. He's going to be thrilled." They made their way out to the parking lot. The sun was already coming up, and the morning air was sweet. Rudy was in his lawn chair beside the trailer, one massive leg crossed over the other. The moment he spotted them coming, he leaped up and disappeared inside. By the time they sat down he'd reappeared with two mugs of coffee and a plateful of sugared doughnuts.

"The wife didn't bake this morning, so I bought these from that Greek fella on Broadway. He makes the best doughnuts in town," Rudy announced. "I wondered where you'd both got to. I saw your car over there," he said to Melissa as he lowered himself into his lawn chair.

With a lilt in her voice and much joy in her heart, Melissa told him about Betsy.

Rudy shot to his feet and threw both fists high in the air. "Hallelujah," he shouted, attracting the attention of people hurrying to work along the sidewalk.

"I knew Thelma's prayer group'd come through for your mama," he crowed. "Wait'll Thelma hears this. She's gonna be beside herself." He sat down again, held his coffee cup high and insisted they both take a doughnut. "To Mrs. Clayton's continued good health," he toasted.

Melissa echoed his words, as did James, and took a nibble of the doughnut. Rudy was right. It was one of the best she'd ever tasted.

"Well, this settles it," Rudy announced, talking through a huge mouthful of doughnut. "No way around it. You two gotta come to the church social Friday night."

"Oh, I don't think I could—" Melissa began, but Rudy held up a hand, palm out, and leaned forward until his face was only inches from hers.

"You—got—no—choice," he drawled. "Miracle happens. You *gotta* come along and rejoice, both of you."

"When you put it that way, we'll just have to do as you say," James told him. "Don't you think so, Melissa?"

It was a chance to have an honest-to-goodness date with James. What could she do but agree?

CHAPTER ELEVEN

MELISSA AGONIZED over what to wear, but when James led her through the open door and into the East Side Community Hall that Friday night at seven, she realized that she could have put on almost any item in her closet, apart from her bathing suit, and felt comfortable. The simple blue cotton sundress she'd chosen was fine.

"Hey, Doc, Melissa—over here." Rudy's booming voice carried over the earsplitting buzz of conversation, the lively music coming from four musicians on a dais at the end of the room and the shrieks of half a dozen little kids playing hide-and-seek under the snowy tablecloths.

Melissa clutched James's hand, and he led the way through groups of people standing and sitting, talking and laughing, eating and drinking. They passed an elderly woman in a wheelchair, a young mother breast-feeding her infant, a group of rowdy teenagers.

Rudy and a dramatically beautiful tiny woman were guarding two chairs at a round table.

"Melissa Clayton, meet Thelma, my better half." Rudy's face was flushed with excitement and pride. "Doc, you remember Thelma from when you took out my gallbladder."

"Indeed I do. How are you, Thelma?"

"Nice to see you again, Dr. Burke." Thelma's smile was breathtaking, reflected as it was in her dark eyes. She reached out with both hands, took Melissa's and held them for a moment. "I'm so pleased to meet you at last, and isn't it wonderful about your mother?"

Melissa was still trying to get used to the fact that this dainty woman was Rudy's wife. "Thank you more than I can say for praying for her," she managed to blurt out.

"We just present our case," Thelma said with a shrug. "What happens after that has nothing to do with us." She swept a graceful hand toward the buffet table. "Let's go and get something to eat, and then we can visit. I want you to meet the other women in the prayer group."

Bracketed by Rudy and Thelma, Melissa and James made their way to the buffet. Accustomed by now to the lavish, high-calorie dishes in Rudy's trailer each morning, Melissa wasn't surprised by the array of mouthwatering food. She tried to select wisely, but with Rudy urging her to try this and that and Thelma indicating which dishes she herself had prepared, it seemed rude not to load up her plate with a little of everything. She noticed that James abandoned his vegetarian, low-calorie rules. His plate was heaped just as hers was as they started back to the table, and he rolled his eyes and shrugged helplessly when he saw her examining his choices.

"Seeley's good at gallbladders," he murmured to her.

Rudy was greeting friends. "There's Dougie. Hey, Dougie, meet the doc and Melissa. This here's my friend Dougie Murdoch. He's a Sheetrock salesman."

Dougie introduced his wife and four children, his mother-in-law, and his aunt. Thelma introduced Maisie and Jean, members of her prayer group. They introduced husbands and cousins and grandmothers, until Melissa's head was spinning.

"Enough socializing," Thelma finally ordered. "The food's getting cold."

They sat down at their table, and Melissa realized how

hungry she was. She'd had a tuna sandwich at lunchtime and nothing since.

"Everything tastes fabulous," she told Thelma, and it did. It might have had something to do with pounds of butter and sugar and gallons of cream, Melissa mused as she ate her way through more food than she usually consumed in a week.

The thing that Rudy and Thelma had in common was their gregarious, inclusive personalities, Melissa soon realized. They were people magnets. As soon as they were finished eating, friends pulled up chairs and slid tables together, with Rudy and Thelma at the center of it all. The laughter and good-natured teasing flowed, underlaid by honest affection. She and James were introduced over and over again as smiling faces joined the ever-widening circle—Melissa soon gave up even trying to remember names.

It was getting warmer by the minute in the hall, and she'd had too many glasses of fruit punch. Melissa excused herself and headed for the bathroom. She was dabbing cold water on her neck and cheeks, when Thelma came in.

"Whew, it's boiling out there. Longest stretch of hot weather I ever remember in Vancouver, and I grew up here, so that's a lot of years," Thelma remarked, wetting a tissue and wiping her forehead.

"How did you and Rudy meet?" Melissa had been wondering about it all evening.

"We were both working at the fish-packing plant in Steveston for the summer. I was seventeen. He was twenty-two. He was going to apprentice with a plumber in the fall, and I needed money to go to college. There was a party and I asked him to go with me." Her smile was tender. "We've been together ever since."

"Did you get to college?"

"Oh, sure." Thelma wiped off eye shadow and reapplied it. "I did business admin. It's been a real help with the plumbing business.'' She outlined her lips with a lip pencil and filled them in with lipstick. ''Rudy says you're the boss of the whole show over at St. Joe's, first woman ever to hold the job. That's what the doc told him. Good for you. It thrills me to meet women who won't take no for an answer.''

''Thanks, but I think that's an exaggeration.'' Melissa laughed and explained what she did. Thelma listened and asked several pertinent questions about the physicians' job action and what effect it had on Melissa's work.

''The doc's lucky he found you,'' she said at last. ''He's way more easygoing than he was when he operated on Rudy. Whew!'' She rolled her eyes at the memory. ''He was a pretty uptight guy. Now he's out there joking and laughing with the best of them. You're really good for him, Melissa.''

''Oh, but—but we're not a couple, not really,'' Melissa stammered. ''This is the first time I've actually been out with him.''

''Rudy said the doc's not too swift on the uptake when it comes to romance. But the way he looks at you, he'll catch on. Don't you worry. Rudy was like that when I met him. Figured he couldn't ask me out because I was going to college and he was a plumber. The doc probably has his own hang-ups. Men get the darnedest ideas in their heads.'' Thelma patted her shining cap of short dark hair. ''We'll put you both on our prayer list. We'll just ask God to give the doc a little shove in the right direction.''

Melissa was flustered. Obviously Thelma had the wrong idea about her relationship with James. ''But you don't understand,'' she tried to explain. ''Neither of us is looking for a long-lasting relationship. We're just—'' She remembered that kiss and her cheeks flamed. ''We're just friends,'' she insisted. ''He operated on my mom, and because of that and the job action, we've spent some time talking, but there's nothing—'' She was babbling, and she shut up.

Thelma tipped her head back and laughed. ''Honey, the electricity between the two of you is strong enough to blow all the transformers in town. You just relax and let the prayer group work on him a little.'' She winked and tucked a strand of Melissa's hair behind her ear. ''C'mon out and dance with him. The band's really warming up. Dancing is a great aphrodisiac.''

''I don't think James knows how to dance.'' Melissa remembered his saying so.

Thelma waved a hand dismissively. ''He'll learn fast enough. Rudy and I'll teach him.''

Couples were dipping and swaying to a sedate waltz, and Rudy took Thelma in his arms and whirled her away, as light on his feet as a ballerina in spite of his bulk.

James smiled at Melissa, but he looked uncomfortable. She sat down beside him and sipped at the fresh glass of punch he'd brought her.

''I know you like to dance. I'm sorry I'm challenged in that—'' Rudy interrupted whatever James was about to say. He swept up to the table and pulled James to his feet.

''Dance with Thelma,'' he ordered. ''She taught me to tango. She can easy show you how to waltz.'' Rudy bowed low before Melissa, his face scarlet with exertion, his eyes alight with pleasure. ''Madam, may I have the honor?''

Before she had a chance to respond, Rudy was swooping her expertly across the dance floor. In a hearty baritone, he sang the words to the tune the band was playing, so there was no need for conversation. He was so confident that Melissa didn't have to do anything except float along in his massive arms. He was an extraordinary dancer, innovative and smooth, totally dedicated to the fun of it all. Every now and then, without missing a beat or a lyric, he would pull an immense white handkerchief out, mop his brow and grin at Melissa.

They floated through three songs. The next set was a series of polkas, and when it finished and another set of waltzes began, they passed Thelma and James, and Rudy smoothly switched partners.

"Watch your toes," James warned Melissa with a grin. He drew her close against his body, and although he wasn't as accomplished as Rudy, she loved the delicious sensation of being in his arms, being held close.

"There's no need to protect my toes," she assured him after a moment. "If you really didn't know how to dance before, you must be a quick study."

"Thelma's a great teacher. She even got me through the polka. I should have had someone like her tutor me in high school."

"You probably just didn't practice enough," Melissa suggested.

"We'll just have to keep doing this then, until I get good at it. Grit your teeth and persevere, woman."

They twirled and gyrated and laughed their way through some variation of the polka, and when the music changed to a romantic ballad, James pulled her close again. His cheek rested on her hair. The music was slow and haunting, and their bodies moved in unison. Someone had dimmed the lights and opened all the doors, and the fresh evening air poured in.

Melissa tipped her head up to smile at James, and caught her breath. His eyes on hers were hot, and he bent his head and brushed his lips across hers, the lightest and most tantalizing of kisses. He lifted the fingers curled in his own and did the same with her knuckles—fire flickered, then caught low in her belly.

She could feel her pulse thrumming, and anticipation ran through her. It had been so long since she'd been in a man's arms, so long since she'd been with someone with whom she wanted to make love.

It was clear to her that that was what she wanted, what she was determined to have. The hand resting on his neck slipped into his hair—soft, thick, sensual hair. She relished the texture of it, traced the shape of his skull with her fingers, and he shuddered.

The hand on her back tightened, drew her closer. She laid her head on his shoulder. She could feel his heart hammering. She could also feel his erection. To know that he wanted her at least as much as she wanted him gave her a delicious female sense of power and pleasure.

"You're driving me crazy, Melissa," he murmured into her ear.

"It's mutual."

"Let's get out of here."

They located Rudy and Thelma. Melissa saw the look that passed between them as she and James thanked them, and she caught Thelma's tiny wink.

It seemed there were dozens of new friends to say goodnight to before they reached the door of the hall, but finally, they were outside.

The moon had just risen, a full moon, fat and golden above the city. James had Melissa's hand, and he led her over to his car, but instead of opening the door, he turned her roughly into his arms.

Their lips met, and this time there was nothing tentative or gentle about the kiss. Melissa surrendered to it, trembling, and felt an echoing tremble in James.

The sound of laughter and voices interrupted them, and they drew apart.

"We need somewhere private," James said, his voice hoarse.

This was the moment of decision, and Melissa made it. "Your place or mine?"

The clichéd line made them both laugh a little.

"Which one's closer?" He held the car door open, and she slid in.

"Mine, I think."

"Are you okay with that?"

"With you coming to my apartment?" Skitters of excitement and nervousness ran through her, and she deliberately chose to misunderstand, to give herself time to consider if she *was* okay with it. "Depends on how fussy you are. You didn't come into the bedroom when you picked me up, but the bed's not made and there're clothes on the chair."

He was behind the wheel now, pulling the car smoothly into traffic.

"I don't care if the whole damn place is condemned by the health department." He reached across the console and took her hand, then placed it deliberately on his thigh and covered it with his own. She could feel the hard, corded muscles, the heat of his skin against her palm. "I want to hear you say you're ready to make love with me."

She admired his honesty and met it with her own. "I wouldn't have invited you home if I wasn't." But the forthright words dulled a little of the romantic shine for her. She wanted to be swept away. "Sounds like a business agreement," she said with a touch of irritation in her voice.

"Why is it I always say the wrong thing when I'm with you?" At the next light, he reached across, pulled her into his embrace and kissed her with all the fervor she needed to reassure her that business had nothing to do with what was happening between them.

When they reached the door to her apartment, Melissa had another attack of nerves. What was she doing? How would she feel in the morning, when she had to face him across a boardroom table? She fumbled in her bag for her key, frantically trying to formulate the words to tell him she'd changed her mind.

Her fingers closed around the key, just as his arms closed around her from behind. His lips found a vulnerable spot just behind her ear, and his tongue trailed a path down her neck.

Her breath caught and she unlocked the door.

CHAPTER TWELVE

JAMES MEANT to go slow. He intended to take them up, notch by careful notch, controlling the heat as long as possible. He managed to hold on to that resolve just until the door shut behind them.

Melissa reached past him for a light switch, her breast grazing his arm. He captured her hand before she could flick the switch on, using her wrist to pull her near, and he heard her quick intake of breath as he drew her tight against him. She'd left a light on in the kitchen, and he could see her eyes, huge and dark.

"We don't need any more light." His mouth closed over hers, and she moaned low in her throat. Her body pressed against him, soft, yielding, pelvis already moving, and he lost all thought of control. "I need you naked."

"You, too." Her husky voice was an invitation.

His fingers found the long zipper at the back of her dress. He felt her step out of her shoes as she tugged at his jacket. He stripped it off, and she loosened his tie, fumbled a little with the buttons on his shirt. They undid, and she slid her hands inside the shirt, warm, greedy hands against his bare skin. Her gasp of pleasure sent a bolt of desire through him, and he was kissing her again—deep, devouring kisses that she returned.

She drew away long enough to murmur, "Hurry. Please, James, hurry." Her voice echoed his own desperation.

"I am, sweet. I am." He stripped her dress off, unhooked the lacy bra and cupped one heated breast, then the other, in his palm, learning their delicate shape, bringing the nipples to full erection with his thumb.

She gave a muffled cry, and it almost drove him over the edge. He'd planned to pick her up and carry her down the hall to the bedroom, but there was no time. They slid, instead, to the carpet.

Her hands unfastened his belt. His pants caught on his shoes, and he kicked them off and stripped off trousers and underwear in one tangled heap. He rummaged in his pants pocket for the foil-sealed packet he'd optimistically placed there.

She wasn't wearing stockings. Her skin was hot and silky, her panties a scrap of satin low on her hips. With shaking hands, he hooked his thumbs under the elastic and slipped them down long, smooth legs.

He took her breast in his mouth, touched her with his fingers. She was wild and hot and wet. She cried out, and all thought but one left him.

He would die if he didn't take her now.

Her hips reared, inviting, and he had just enough sense left to open the condom and roll it into place before he slid inside her in one long, urgent thrust, then paused, desperate to hold on until she could join him.

But she moved, and moved again, and he felt her start to shatter beneath him an instant before he abandoned himself to the swirling ecstasy.

Melissa lay still, letting the rippling aftershocks shiver through her. The carpet wasn't half as soft under her naked back as it felt to bare feet. His weight wasn't fully on her; he'd twisted slightly, resting an elbow on the floor, but still his long, muscular body was heavy. She could feel his heart still hammering, feel his breathing gradually slowing down.

"I guess it didn't matter that the bed wasn't made," she said. "But I should have vacuumed this rug."

He gave a soft laugh.

"As soon as I get my breath back, we'll move," he promised.

"Where to next?" She felt euphoric, and more than a little giddy. "There's the kitchen table, the couch, the countertop—maybe the washer and dryer?" What had happened between them was too powerful to think about just yet. She needed foolishness to bridge the time between then and now.

"Ever considered the bed?"

"Oh, well, if you insist." She made her tone haughty. "Not very creative of you, though."

He propped himself up on his elbows and trailed a kiss across her shoulder. "So it's creativity you want? Well, I'll have to see what I can improvise. It'll take practice." He moved against her, aroused again.

"Ah, persistence, I like that in a man. And maybe the bed's not a bad idea, after all."

He got up and held out a hand, helping her to her feet. They stepped over the scattered clothing, and she led him down the hall. They passed the bathroom and caught sight of themselves, naked and flushed, in the large mirror over the sink.

"Think we should have a portrait done, for over the fireplace?"

"Christmas cards," Melissa decided. "For everyone at St. Joe's."

They were laughing when they reached the bedroom. Melissa switched on a bedside lamp, and James surveyed the room.

"You were just trying to discourage me. The bed's made and there's not a scrap of clothing anywhere."

"That's only because my cleaning service came today. I was describing the way it normally looks," she told him. "So you wouldn't get such a shock the next time."

Oops. Melissa felt her face get hot. That hadn't been a

smart thing to say. She didn't want him to think she was building an entire relationship on a one-night stand— Was that what this was, a one-night stand?

He grabbed her and tumbled her onto the bed. "Try and keep me away," he growled, lowering his head and biting her chin.

"Now, about that creative stuff…"

CHAPTER THIRTEEN

MELISSA AWOKE Saturday morning in his arms. It was early—the gray light coming through the shades told her the sun wasn't up—and it was still cool in the bedroom; she'd opened the windows wide.

He was snoring softly each time he exhaled. She liked that he snored—it made him seem vulnerable. It was an intimate thing to know about him.

She felt blissful and wickedly lazy. She lay without moving, savoring the pleasure of his heavy arm across her midriff, the feel of his warm body against her side, the delicious, musky odor of his skin and their lovemaking.

He was sprawled on his stomach, head turned toward her, and she turned a little and studied his face.

Well-defined cheekbones, bold nose, firm chin. He was going to need a shave soon; dark stubble dotted his cheeks, making him look dangerous and appealing.

Melissa knew how that stubble felt; the skin on her face and other parts of her body tingled a little from it. She was going to have a rash on her belly, she thought with smug pleasure.

He'd awakened her twice in the night, with kisses and caresses and soft words. They'd made love, they'd talked about the social, they'd laughed.

Melissa thought of Rudy and Thelma, wondered if that was how every night was for them—a dark, delicious time filled with mutual sharing and passion and laughter, and then blissful sleep wrapped in each other's arms. Was this envy she was feeling, envy for a married couple? It surprised and disturbed her, and she forced the feeling away.

She'd get up in a minute, shower, make coffee. What did he like for breakfast? Apart from the sweets at Rudy's trailer, the only meal they'd eaten together was the one last night at the social. He was vegetarian. What did vegetarians eat for breakfast? She had no eggs, and she was pretty certain there was no bread, either.

They could go out. Or maybe, she thought with a sinking feeling, he'd wake up and she'd see reserve in his eyes, hear reluctance in his voice. The closeness of the night would be gone, and he'd want only to hurry away. It had happened to her once, in a long-ago relationship, that morning-after desperate need for escape, the sense of being trapped, the realization that what had happened was a huge mistake. She had a vivid recollection of having to sit through breakfast, when all she'd wanted was to leave.

Well, she had too much pride to let that happen again. She slid out of bed, careful not to wake him, and ducked into the shower.

When she was done, a glance into the bedroom told her he was still asleep. Silent as a cat burglar, she donned shorts and a cropped top, pulled her hair back into a clip and found her trainers in the hall cupboard. She hadn't had them on for weeks. Running was going to kill her, but it was an easier death than rejection. She was bending over, lacing them up, when his arms closed around her from behind and one hand patted her bottom in an affectionate greeting.

"Are you running away from me?" His voice was husky from sleep. He turned her toward him and hugged her tight against his nakedness.

"No. Of course not." She felt herself blush at the lie. "I just thought maybe you'd like to be by yourself for a while." She looked into his eyes and waited to see if he'd tell the truth.

"I absolutely wouldn't." He frowned down at her. "Why would I want to be alone when I could be with you?" The denial was immediate and sincere.

Her heart soared and her grin matched his.

"I do understand if you need to work out, though. I'll survive while you're gone, but only if you show me how your coffee machine works."

"I don't have to run right now. I don't even want to." She kicked off her shoes. "I'll make us coffee."

"Great." His relief was obvious. "I'll take a fast shower."

"There're disposable razors in the drawer."

There was, as well, a package of waffles in the freezer. She stuck them in the oven to thaw, and found a jar of homemade raspberry jam her mother had given her and a tin of peaches.

Inspired, Melissa unearthed a yellow tablecloth and two napkins. She set the table, then dialed St. Joe's and learned that her mother had slept peacefully and was now enjoying her breakfast.

The sun shone outside the kitchen window, the smell of fresh coffee filled the air, the shower stopped running—and the sound of James whistling off-key brought a smile.

Being able to relax was so rare. She poured herself coffee and sipped it, leaning against the kitchen counter. Memories of the night floated through her head. Could it be that good again between them, or was it just beginner's luck? Where did they go from here? How long would it last?

If her track record was any indication, two weeks was about the limit.

James came in, silky hair damp, eyes alive with pleasure as he looked at her, then at the sunny table. He was so appealing that he took her breath away.

She handed him a mug of coffee and he kissed her, a

nuzzling, grateful kiss. She pressed her lips into his neck before she stepped back, inhaling the clean scent of him.

He was wearing the pants to his suit. The tails of his shirt were hanging out. His feet were bare. He'd rolled the shirtsleeves up his forearms.

"I'll have to stash some clothes over here. Putting on a dress shirt first thing in the morning feels weird."

Her heart skipped a beat. "Are we?"

He swallowed coffee and squinted at her. "Are we what?"

Asking took courage, but she had to know. She forced her voice to sound offhand. "Going to make a habit of this."

He set the cup down and folded her into his arms. His voice was casual, although his heartbeat wasn't. She could feel it against her cheek.

"I'm game if you are."

She was. Oh, she was.

THEY SPENT THE WEEKEND walking on the beach, swimming in the ocean, exploring antique stores along Main Street. She found two plates and a large creamer in the old rose pattern that matched her mother's china. Melissa bought them for Betsy. He found an antique toy horse, a pinto complete with miniature bridle and saddle. He gave it to Melissa, with a little card that read "Until the real thing comes along." He signed it "Love, James."

He took her comment about creativity to heart. Saturday and Sunday nights were explosive and tender and funny and blissful.

On Monday morning, she drove him to work. Rudy didn't comment when they came walking over, but Melissa knew he'd noticed. She caught the congratulatory wink he gave James as he served them coffee and currant scones, and instead of being outraged at such blatant male posturing, she was amused.

Rudy said, "Wasn't that some party?"

Friday seemed a lifetime ago to Melissa. Since then her life had changed direction. She bit into the currant scone and relished every buttery bite.

They rehashed the party and laughed with Rudy. When they walked off toward the hospital together, he burst into a noisy chorus of "Everything's Coming Up Roses," and Melissa laughed so hard that James had to hold her up.

The day proved Rudy was right.

That very morning, the ministry came through with a viable offer, and after an emergency meeting, the physicians agreed to the government's terms. By afternoon the strike was over.

Before the day ended, James was back in the operating room, doing a hysterectomy, and Melissa was able to take two hours off and drive Betsy home.

Betsy talked about James the whole way. She'd fallen under his spell. "If only your poor father could have had a doctor like him, he'd still be here today," she declared. "He's in love with you, Lissa. He all but told me so. He's a fine man. Don't you chew him up and spit him out like you've done with all the others."

Melissa gaped at her mother, indignant. "I've never done any such thing. And when did James tell you—"

Betsy paid no attention. "You have your career. Now it's time you thought about a husband and a family. I'm not getting any younger, you know, and I'd like a grandchild to spoil before I lose all my marbles. I get good and fed up with Gladys bragging all the time about her grandkids."

Melissa was shocked. Betsy had never even hinted at this before. Maybe her having been close to death had brought this on, Melissa thought after she'd gotten her mother settled in Gladys's care and was heading back to St. Joe's.

Had James actually told Betsy he loved her?

Betsy had said he all but had, whatever that meant.

Melissa hadn't dared put a name on what she felt for James.

She probed at it now, like poking a tongue at a new filling.

It didn't hurt at all when she realized she'd fallen in love.

CHAPTER FOURTEEN

MELISSA SAVORED the sensation during the days that followed, although she didn't see much of James; he was either in the OR or at his office with patients. They did spend the nights together, and that was more than enough.

That they were both busy was good; Melissa had tons of work to catch up on, and to know that James was as overwhelmed as she was was comforting.

The afternoon finally arrived when she was finished at five. Filled with excitement, she called James to invite him for a walk in the park. They could stop at his favorite vendor and have fish and chips, and there was that little place on Denman that made homemade ice cream.

The front desk patched the call through to the OR. Melissa could hear soft music playing, voices in the background, the metallic *click* of instruments.

"Sorry, Melissa, I just can't make it." He sounded apologetic but cheerful. "I'm in the middle of reaming out a prostate, and then I promised the cardiac resident I'd scrub with him on an angioplasty. Can I have a rain check till tomorrow?"

Of course he could. Who understood better than Melissa the pressures that work could impose? She went home and cleaned out her closets.

A spectacular four-car crash the following afternoon brought a contrite phone call from James. He was up to his elbows in punctured lungs and compound fractures. He'd be at St. Joe's until the early hours, and looking at his schedule, the next couple of days were going to be frantic. He'd best sleep at his own apartment rather than wake her in the middle of the night. He apologized and, voice pitched low, told her what he intended to do to her when they were next together.

Melissa appreciated his creativity and his thoughtfulness. She had her hair trimmed, her legs waxed, her nails manicured. She even went for a massage, to a woman Arlene recommended. But instead of feeling relaxed, she came out anxious, and the feeling intensified as the long spell of hot weather broke and Vancouver weather returned to normal. The skies opened and raindrops bounced on sidewalks. Umbrellas bloomed like flowers.

Melissa went to visit Betsy, but Gladys had moved in on a semipermanent basis, and Melissa had grown weary of the friendly bickering between the two older women.

On Thursday evening James called and asked her formally for a date on Friday. He'd cleared his calendar; they'd go somewhere elegant. But Melissa thought it over and decided she wanted something different. The weather was cool enough to light the fireplace. Maybe a quiet, passionate evening alone with him would banish this heaviness she couldn't seem to shake.

"I've never cooked for you, have I?"

"I didn't know you could."

She didn't know if she still could, either, it had been so long. "You don't know half my talents. Come over at six. I'll impress and amaze you."

She canceled an afternoon meeting with the patient advocate and raced through Granville Market, buying Caspian Sea caviar and fresh West Coast salmon, imported Peruvian wine, tiny red potatoes, pistachio nuts, blueberries, crusty bread rolls.

At home, groceries unloaded, she flipped through cookbooks and made zucchini bisque with curry and cream, beet and jicama salad, and a lemon tart topped with blueberries and roasted pistachio nuts. Feeling like a heroine, she scrubbed the potatoes and put them on to steam, turned the oven on for the salmon and laid the table, using the crocheted cloth and linen napkins her mother had given her. She lit the fireplace and glanced at the clock.

There was just time for a quick shower. She washed her hair and left it down to curl around her shoulders, as she pulled on her only set of matching black underwear and an emerald-green rayon dress cut too low in the bosom to wear to the office. She hadn't worn the dress for a while, and it felt snug around her hips. It must have shrunk last time she'd had it dry-cleaned.

But she couldn't worry about that now, because the buzzer sounded, and then she was in James's arms. He brought her coral-colored lilies and white wine and a small box of the best chocolates in the city. She had to put the flowers on a side table so they wouldn't get crushed as he hugged her. His kiss sent her heart soaring, and she had to restrain his hands or she'd get distracted and dinner would be ruined.

"You are so beautiful in that dress."

"Thanks." She flushed with pleasure and reluctantly broke away when he kissed her again. "Take your raincoat off, and come and open the wine. I'll serve the soup and put the flowers in a bowl."

They were a breathtaking centerpiece, and when she tasted the soup, even *she* thought it was delicious.

"I can't believe you made this. It's the best I've ever eaten." He spooned up the bisque, finished his bowl and asked for another.

"Flatterer." But she felt pleased with herself. Cooking for him tonight had been a good idea. The rain sleeted against the windows, the fireplace gave off a warm glow, the soft music she'd chosen created a relaxed ambience.

And they had time to talk, to catch up on the things they hadn't had a chance to share.

"Rudy called the office. He and Thelma want us to come to dinner a week from tomorrow."

"Arlene had pains in her back all afternoon. I told her to go home, but she wouldn't listen. Maybe the baby'll arrive this weekend. I can't wait to see what her little one looks like."

He followed Melissa into the kitchen when the timer for the salmon sounded. She arranged the fish on a serving platter and surrounded it with snow peas and the steamed tiny red potatoes, while he made appreciative comments.

He wasn't much help, but she loved having him there.

And then his pager went off. He didn't have to tell her it was St. Joe's. A kind of numbness overtook her as he dialed the phone, identified himself, listened for a few moments and said in a brisk tone, "I'll be right there." He hung up and turned to Melissa with an apologetic look.

"I'm so sorry about dinner, love. There's been a shoot-out between two motorcycle gangs. They need me in the OR." He was already at the door, shrugging into his raincoat. "I'll call as soon as I get a chance."

He kissed her, but it seemed to her an absent kiss. His mind was already at the hospital.

The door closed behind him, and Melissa felt like kicking it. She wanted to scream and throw herself on the floor and have the kind of tantrum she'd enjoyed when she was three. Instead, she ripped open the chocolates James had brought and viciously bit into one. The first led to a second and then a third, but she still felt empty inside.

The feeling of anxiety that had plagued her the past week returned full force. Maybe she ought to go to bed and read.

She turned off the gas fireplace and the lights, leaving the dishes and the food where they were, and put on an old pair of flannel pajamas. Steeling herself, she stepped on the bathroom scales. She'd avoided weighing herself, knowing she'd probably gained a pound or two thanks to the food she'd eaten at Rudy's trailer.

She gasped in horror as the needle swept up and up. She'd gained *nine pounds.* How could that be? She should have lost weight. She'd lost her heart, hadn't she? Surely a heart weighed something. She crept into her bedroom. The stuffed toy horse James had given her was sitting on her dresser, along with the card. *Until the real thing comes along,* he'd written. She'd been deluding herself into believing James was the real thing.

It was time to take a look at facts she'd been avoiding the way she'd avoided the scales. She got a piece of paper and a pen.

James was a workaholic; surgery would always come first with him.

If the choice was between her career and his, he'd expect his to take precedence.

She'd been assuming they had a relationship. He'd never once told her he cared about her.

Sooner or later, she was going to gain twenty pounds and tell him it was over.

It might as well be now; she only had eleven more pounds to go.

The telephone rang, and she snatched it up, knowing it was James. She would read him her list and end the relationship right now. That way she could start a rigorous diet in the morning.

"Melissa?" The voice was male, but it wasn't James's. This guy sounded on the verge of hysteria, voice trembling, tears threatening.

"Melissa, it's Frank O'Connor, Arlene's husband? We just had a baby girl. She's so beautiful. Arlene's fine. She was such a trooper. Labor's a bitch, isn't it? She says to come over right away and see the baby before our daughter starts to age."

CHAPTER FIFTEEN

JAMES FINISHED STAPLING the ends of the bowel. He'd had to excise an entire segment of it. The bullet had entered the patient's belly and ricocheted off a rib into the small intestine.

"This young man's lucky to be alive," James remarked. "He's also lucky he won't have a colostomy bag for the rest of his life. Another inch and that bullet would have ripped into the large intestine."

The tension had eased in the OR when it became obvious nothing was going to go wrong. Mozart was playing, and the circulating nurse and the scrub tech were talking about a dress one of them had bought on sale.

James turned to the intern. "You want to try your hand at closing, Dr. Gatz?"

The young woman's eyes dilated behind her mask, and her voice shook a little.

"Yes, please, Dr. Burke."

A strained silence fell, and James caught the apprehensive look two orderlies exchanged as Gatz dropped two needle holders in a row. James knew they expected him to explode, to chastise the intern, to launch into an impassioned lecture about competency and standards and bungling ineptitude. A short time ago that's just what he would have done.

Tonight, however, the gaffes didn't seem important. He waited patiently until Gatz had found her rhythm and gained a measure of confidence. Then he quietly made several suggestions, and complimented her when the job was done.

Instrument, sponge and needle count completed, James thanked his team and headed out to tell the young man's distraught father that his son would live. He smiled into the older man's dark eyes and put a hand on his shoulder, and when the man burst into tears, James offered tissues and a sympathetic ear.

In the surgeons' locker room, he shucked off his scrubs and stepped into the shower, trying to figure out what was wrong with him.

The operation had been a success, but his usual elation just wasn't there. He kept seeing Melissa's lovely face, and the disappointment in her hazel eyes when the call had come from St. Joe's.

Something Rudy had said popped into his mind and lodged there.

Plumbing don't come close to being with Thelma.

The moment at hand was mind-boggling and life-changing, but once he got it straight, James knew that he was on the right track. Surgery didn't come close to being with Melissa. He wanted more, and less.

More time with Melissa, less time operating.

More open space, less restriction.

More impulsiveness, less caution.

Less single life. More—he had to take a deep breath, because the idea made him dizzy. More—*marriage?* It was a big concept. He breathed it in, tried it on for size, and after a few moments of getting used to it, he knew marriage sounded exactly right.

Elated, he turned off the water and stepped out of the shower, just as the door to the locker room flew open and Frank O'Connor burst in. He had a box of cigars under his arm and a frenzied look in his eye. He didn't seem to notice that James was buck naked.

"We just had a baby," he crowed, digging out a cigar from the box and shoving it at James. "Seven-ten, first Apgar nine-and-a-half. She's got my ears."

"Poor kid," James said with a grin, sticking the cigar behind his own ear. "Never mind, the plastics people can do wonders these days." He wound a towel around himself and then clapped O'Connor on the shoulder. "Congratulations. I'm happy for you, and more than a little jealous."

"Drop down to Maternity and have a look at her, why don't you. Melissa's there with Arlene. I'm gonna have to get back to the ER. Brulotte's covering for me, but we're shorthanded tonight. I hear they've hired two new ER docs from England. Wish they'd get here so I could have a few days off." He gave James a resounding slap on his bare shoulder and hurried out the door.

Melissa is here, at St. Joe's. Suddenly, everything seemed to be falling into place. James hurried over to his locker and pulled on his clothes. He needed to talk to her, right now, while the whole thing was clear in his head.

CHAPTER SIXTEEN

"SHE'S AN ANGEL." Melissa cradled the baby, letting the tears slide down her cheeks. "I'm just so ha-happy for you." She was. She just couldn't stop crying.

"Here—" Arlene handed her a tissue. "Before you drown her."

"Thanks." Melissa gave the baby to her mother and headed into the bathroom to wash her face. "Sorry, Arlene," she called through the door.

"This isn't just sympathy over my agonizing labor, right?" Arlene yelled from the bed.

Melissa pictured her propped on pillows, wearing a scarlet satin robe from Victoria's Secret. Her hair was brushed, her makeup intact, her pretty face serene. It was hard to believe she'd just given birth.

"What's wrong? I'll bet it's—"

Melissa heard Arlene's voice change.

"Hi there, James. We were just talking about you. Melissa's in the bathroom. She'll be right out. Here, want to hold the baby?"

Horrified, Melissa heard James making admiring noises.

What the *hell* was he doing here? She did *not* want to see him—not now.

She didn't want him to see her, either. A glance in the mirror made her shudder. Her eyes were swollen and her hair was a disaster. Her freckles stood out in sharp relief. She'd pulled on an old yellow sweatsuit, and the color made her look as if she had malaria. Her purse, with her lipstick and comb, was out there beside Arlene's bed.

But she couldn't hide in the bathroom for the rest of the night.

She drew in a deep breath and tried to gather the tattered shreds of her dignity.

"Hello, James." She tried for a smile and missed by a mile. "Isn't she something?"

He was holding the baby, but he wasn't looking at the infant. He was staring at Melissa—and she must look even worse than she'd imagined, because his expression was peculiar.

"Could I talk to you for a moment?" He shoved the baby into Arlene's arms and headed for the door. When Melissa didn't immediately follow, he turned. "Please? I need to talk to you in private, Melissa." There was humble entreaty in his tone.

"Go, go." Arlene shooed her. "You can tell me afterward what he says," she stage-whispered with a wicked grin.

The corridor outside Arlene's room was bustling with fathers and grandmothers and staff. James took Melissa's hand and dragged her along, peering into rooms until he finally found an empty one. He held the door and used a hand on her back to all but shove her inside.

"For heaven's sake, James." Exasperated, she put her hands on her hips and glared at him. "First you ruin a dinner I labored over, and now you drag me away from the baby. This just proves that nothing will ever work between us." She scowled at him. "You're totally inconsiderate and selfish." She hadn't planned on dumping him tonight; she'd planned to be calm and dressed in one of Barry's ensembles when she did it. A loose one, considering what she weighed. But what the heck, she might as well get this over with now.

He looked contrite. "I'm sorry about the dinner. I should have arranged for someone else to take my calls tonight. I will next time. I promise."

He reached out for her, and Melissa backed up. She could get through this, but only if she didn't let him touch her. Why hadn't she brought her list to the hospital?

"There isn't going to be a next time, James. I don't want to see you anymore." She tried to draw a deep breath, but it felt as if there was a rock stuck in her rib cage.

"Don't be ridiculous."

He was annoyed now; she could see by the way his eyes narrowed and his jaw tightened.

"*I've* decided we should get married. Not right now, but after we've been together a few months. After we know each other better. Although, we do know each other pretty well already."

"Married?" She was stunned and aghast. And when it fully hit her, she was also furious. "How dare you tell me such a thing, instead of asking, the way any decent, civilized man would do? And I won't marry you, so don't bother asking. You don't need a wife, James. Your work is your wife. There's no room for a real live woman."

"I can change that. I *will* change it. Surgery isn't that important to me anymore."

He moved toward her again, and she took refuge behind the bed and stared at him in disbelief. "And when did that miracle occur?"

"Tonight. I realized tonight what's important to me. *You* are, Melissa. Please give me a chance to prove it to you."

This was getting scary. She racked her brain for the items on her list and remembered a big one. "I have a demanding career of my own, and you'd expect me to make all the concessions. Well, I won't."

"I won't expect any such thing." He sounded outraged.

"I respect and admire your career path. I'll do everything I can to support you."

He sounded so sincere that she believed him, but there was still something elemental missing, and it hurt her heart. "There's more to marriage than support, James. I don't want just support. When—" The damn tears were threatening again. She sniffed and her voice wobbled. "When the real thing comes along, I want a man who doesn't make a proposal sound like a business contract. I want a man who—" She sniffed again, and the rest came out in a wail. "I want a man who *loves* me. The way that I love him."

Damn. She hadn't meant to add that last bit.

He looked dumbstruck. "But that's what I'm telling you. I do love you, Melissa. I love everything about you. Why do you think I'm talking about marriage here?"

He strode around the bed and took her in his arms. "I'm so relieved you feel the same way."

It felt so good to be held. But there was still something she needed to know. "Did you tell my mother that?"

"Tell her what?"

He smelled of hospital soap. He was stroking her hair. "That you loved me. She said you all but told her."

He sounded a little embarrassed. "I might have mentioned it, when she was in the coma. You told me to talk to her, so I did."

That changed things. He'd been willing to compromise for her once. He could probably do it again. It would just take practice.

"Do you want me to get down on my knees, Melissa?" His arms were tight around her, and the nine pounds didn't matter. She felt slender and fragile in his embrace. "Because I will, if that's what you want."

"Not here. Not now. Not in the maternity ward." Not wearing this horrible yellow tracksuit.

"Okay. Just tell me when and where." He tipped her

chin up and kissed her hard and deep and long. "But make it soon, okay?"

The sense of power was delicious. The kiss was, as well, but there was a lot of planning to do. A proposal of marriage called for a "stellar look." And then there was the wedding gown to think about.

She hated the prospect, but she was going to have to pay Barry another visit.

*Harlequin truly does
make any time special. . . .
This year we are celebrating
weddings in style!*

A
Walk
Down
the Aisle

WEDDING CELEBRATION

To help us celebrate, we want you to tell us how wearing the Harlequin wedding gown will make your wedding day special. As the grand prize, Harlequin will offer one lucky bride the chance to **"Walk Down the Aisle"** in the Harlequin wedding gown!

There's more...

For her honeymoon, she and her groom will spend five nights at the **Hyatt Regency Maui.** As part of this five-night honeymoon at the hotel renowned for its romantic attractions, the couple will enjoy a candlelit dinner for two in Swan Court, a sunset sail on the hotel's catamaran, and duet spa treatments.

A HYATT RESORT AND SPA

Maui • Molokai • Lanai

To enter, please write, in, 250 words or less, how wearing the Harlequin wedding gown will make your wedding day special. The entry will be judged based on its emotionally compelling nature, its originality and creativity, and its sincerity. This contest is open to Canadian and U.S. residents only and to those who are 18 years of age and older. There is no purchase necessary to enter. Void where prohibited. See further contest rules attached. Please send your entry to:

Walk Down the Aisle Contest

In Canada	In U.S.A.
P.O. Box 637	P.O. Box 9076
Fort Erie, Ontario	3010 Walden Ave.
L2A 5X3	Buffalo, NY 14269-9076

You can also enter by visiting www.eHarlequin.com
Win the Harlequin wedding gown and the vacation of a lifetime!
The deadline for entries is October 1, 2001.

HARLEQUIN®
Makes any time special ®

PHWDACONT1

HARLEQUIN WALK DOWN THE AISLE TO MAUI CONTEST 1197
OFFICIAL RULES
NO PURCHASE NECESSARY TO ENTER

1. To enter, follow directions published in the offer to which you are responding. Contest begins April 2, 2001, and ends on October 1, 2001. Method of entry may vary. Mailed entries must be postmarked by October 1, 2001, and received by October 8, 2001.

2. Contest entry may be, at times, presented via the Internet, but will be restricted solely to residents of certain geographic areas that are disclosed on the Web site. To enter via the Internet, if permissible, access the Harlequin Web site (www.eHarlequin.com) and follow the directions displayed online. Online entries must be received by 11:59 p.m. E.S.T. on October 1, 2001.

   In lieu of submitting an entry online, enter by mail by hand-printing (or typing) on an 8½" x 11" plain piece of paper, your name, address (including zip code), Contest number/name and in 250 words or fewer, why winning a Harlequin wedding dress would make your wedding day special. Mail via first-class mail to: Harlequin Walk Down the Aisle Contest 1197, (in the U.S.) P.O. Box 9076, 3010 Walden Avenue, Buffalo, NY 14269-9076, (in Canada) P.O. Box 637, Fort Erie, Ontario L2A 5X3, Canada.

   Limit one entry per person, household address and e-mail address. Online and/or mailed entries received from persons residing in geographic areas in which Internet entry is not permissible will be disqualified.

3. Contests will be judged by a panel of members of the Harlequin editorial, marketing and public relations staff based on the following criteria:

   • Originality and Creativity—50%
   • Emotionally Compelling—25%
   • Sincerity—25%

   In the event of a tie, duplicate prizes will be awarded. Decisions of the judges are final.

4. All entries become the property of Torstar Corp. and will not be returned. No responsibility is assumed for lost, late, illegible, incomplete, inaccurate, nondelivered or misdirected mail or misdirected e-mail, for technical, hardware or software failures of any kind, lost or unavailable network connections, or failed, incomplete, garbled or delayed computer transmission or any human error which may occur in the receipt or processing of the entries in this Contest.

5. Contest open only to residents of the U.S. (except Puerto Rico) and Canada, who are 18 years of age or older, and is void wherever prohibited by law; all applicable laws and regulations apply. Any litigation within the Province of Quebec respecting the conduct or organization of a publicity contest may be submitted to the Régie des alcools, des courses et des jeux for a ruling. Any litigation respecting the awarding of a prize may be submitted to the Régie des alcools, des courses et des jeux only for the purpose of helping the parties reach a settlement. Employees and immediate family members of Torstar Corp. and D. L. Blair, Inc., their affiliates, subsidiaries and all other agencies, entities and persons connected with the use, marketing or conduct of this Contest are not eligible to enter. Taxes on prizes are the sole responsibility of winners. Acceptance of any prize offered constitutes permission to use winner's name, photograph or other likeness for the purposes of advertising, trade and promotion on behalf of Torstar Corp., its affiliates and subsidiaries without further compensation to the winner, unless prohibited by law.

6. Winners will be determined no later than November 15, 2001, and will be notified by mail. Winners will be required to sign and return an Affidavit of Eligibility form within 15 days after winner notification. Noncompliance within that time period may result in disqualification and an alternative winner may be selected. Winners of trip must execute a Release of Liability prior to ticketing and must possess required travel documents (e.g. passport, photo ID) where applicable. Trip must be completed by November 2002. No substitution of prize permitted by winner. Torstar Corp. and D. L. Blair, Inc., their parents, affiliates and subsidiaries are not responsible for errors in printing or electronic presentation of Contest, entries and/or game pieces. In the event of printing or other errors which may result in unintended prize values or duplication of prizes, all affected game pieces or entries shall be null and void. If for any reason the Internet portion of the Contest is not capable of running as planned, including infection by computer virus, bugs, tampering, unauthorized intervention, fraud, technical failures, or any other causes beyond the control of Torstar Corp. which corrupt or affect the administration, secrecy, fairness, integrity or proper conduct of the Contest, Torstar Corp. reserves the right, at its sole discretion, to disqualify any individual who tampers with the entry process and to cancel, terminate, modify or suspend the Contest or the Internet portion thereof. In the event of a dispute regarding an online entry, the entry will be deemed submitted by the authorized holder of the e-mail account submitted at the time of entry. Authorized account holder is defined as the natural person who is assigned to an e-mail address by an Internet access provider, online service provider or other organization that is responsible for arranging e-mail accounts for the domain associated with the submitted e-mail address. **Purchase or acceptance of a product offer does not improve your chances of winning.**

7. Prizes: (1) Grand Prize—A Harlequin wedding dress (approximate retail value: $3,500) and a 5-night/6-day honeymoon trip to Maui, HI, including round-trip air transportation provided by Maui Visitors Bureau from Los Angeles International Airport (winner is responsible for transportation to and from Los Angeles International Airport) and a Harlequin Romance Package, including hotel accomodations (double occupancy) at the Hyatt Regency Maui Resort and Spa, dinner for (2) two at Swan Court, a sunset sail on Kiele V and a spa treatment for the winner (approximate retail value: $4,000); (5) Five runner-up prizes of a $1000 gift certificate to selected retail outlets to be determined by Sponsor (retail value $1000 ea.). Prizes consist of only those items listed as part of the prize. Limit one prize per person. All prizes are valued in U.S. currency.

8. For a list of winners (available after December 17, 2001) send a self-addressed, stamped envelope to: Harlequin Walk Down the Aisle Contest 1197 Winners, P.O. Box 4200 Blair, NE 68009-4200 or you may access the www.eHarlequin.com Web site through January 15, 2002.

Contest sponsored by Torstar Corp., P.O. Box 9042, Buffalo, NY 14269-9042, U.S.A.

PHWDACONT2